DANGER CLUB

VOLUME TWO: REBIRTH

STORY
LANDRY Q. WALKER ·
ART
ERIC JONES ·
COLOR
RUSTY DRAKE

LETTERS AND LOGOS
RICHARD STARKINGS AND COMICRAFT'S
JIMMY BETANCOURT

EDITOR
BRANWYN BIGGLESTONE

PRODUCER
JAVIER JOSE DIAZ

PR DIRECTOR
ROBERT ELY

ADDITIONAL COLORS
PANNEL VAUGHN
GARRY BLACK
JOHN ADAMS

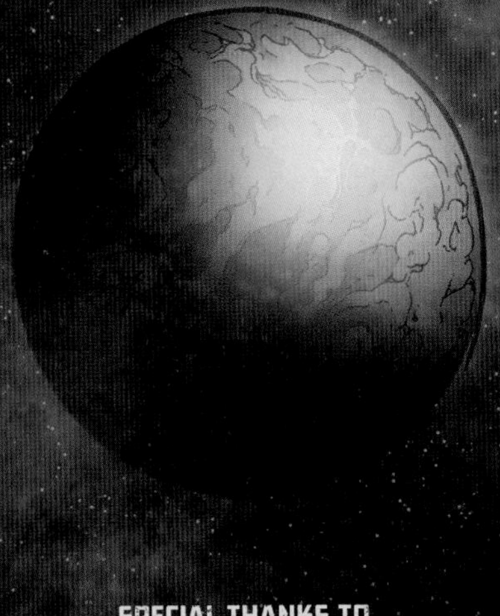

SPECIAL THANKS TO
BELINDA ADAMS · ERIN SAUL · BONNIE DRAKE

TO THOSE WE'VE LOST.

DANGER CLUB, VOLUME 2

First Printing. June 2015. Published by Image Comics, Inc.

Office of publication: 2001 Center Street, 6th Floor, Berkeley, CA 94704.

For international rights, contact: foreignlicensing@imagecomics.com

ISBN: 978-1-63215-367-8

IMAGE COMICS, INC.
Robert Kirkman – Chief Operating Officer
Erik Larsen – Chief Financial Officer
Todd McFarlane – President
Marc Silvestri – Chief Executive Officer
Jim Valentino – Vice-President

Eric Stephenson – Publisher
Corey Murphy – Director of Sales
Jeremy Sullivan – Director of Digital Sales
Kat Salazar – Director of PR & Marketing
Emily Miller – Director of Operations
Branwyn Bigglestone – Senior Accounts Manager
Drew Gill – Art Director
Jonathan Chan – Production Manager
Meredith Wallace – Print Manager
Randy Okamura – Marketing Production Designer
David Brothers – Content Manager
Addison Duke – Production Artist
Vincent Kukua – Production Artist
Sasha Head – Production Artist
Tricia Ramos – Production Artist
Emilio Bautista – Sales Assistant
Jessica Ambriz – Administrative Assistant
IMAGECOMICS.COM

CHAPTER FIVE : SKYBASE ONE

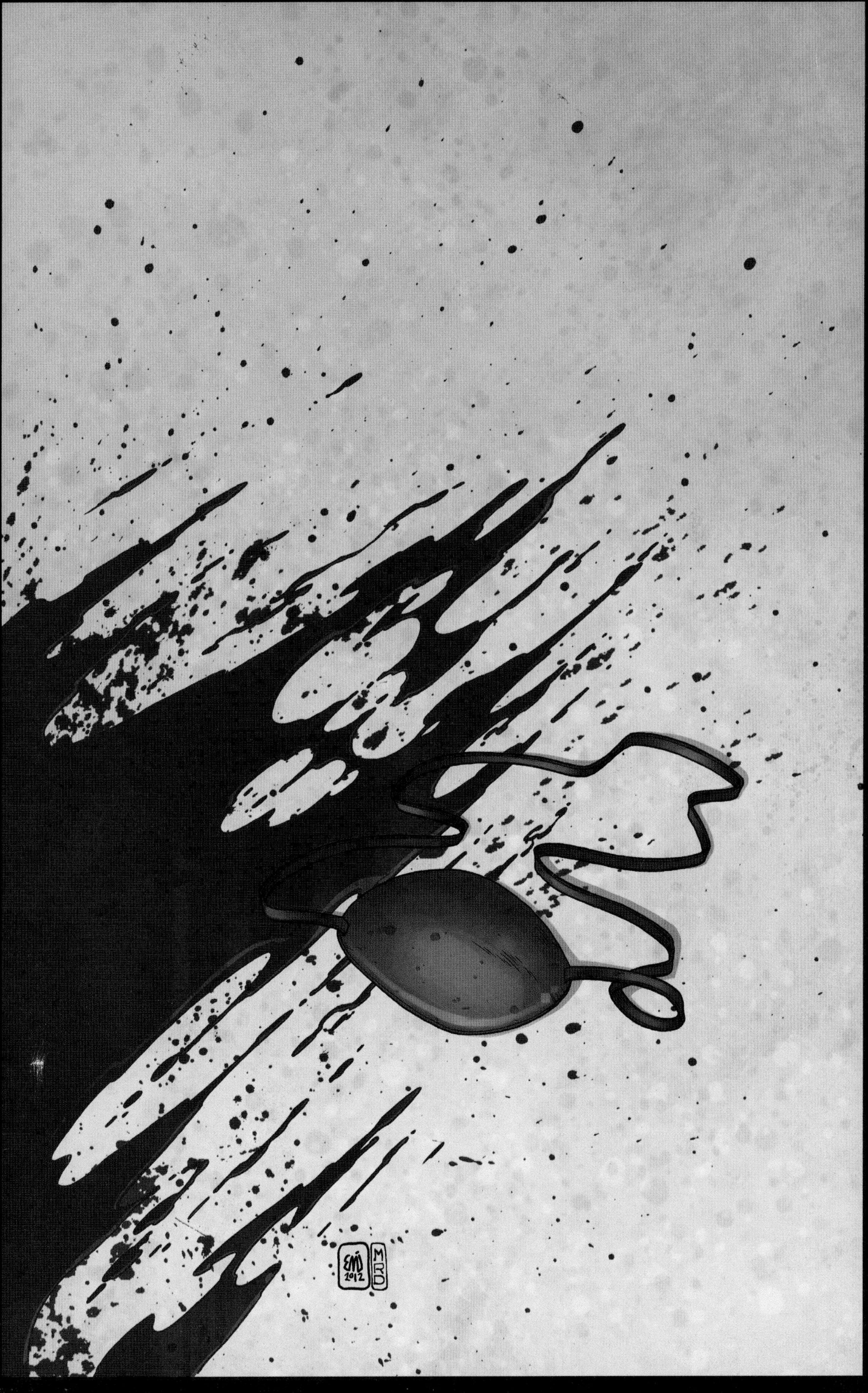

There were no heroes. Not anymore.

Only us.

One by one we would fall to the darkness
that had descended upon our world.

It was the end of everything.

And there was nothing we could do to stop it...

...Except pray.

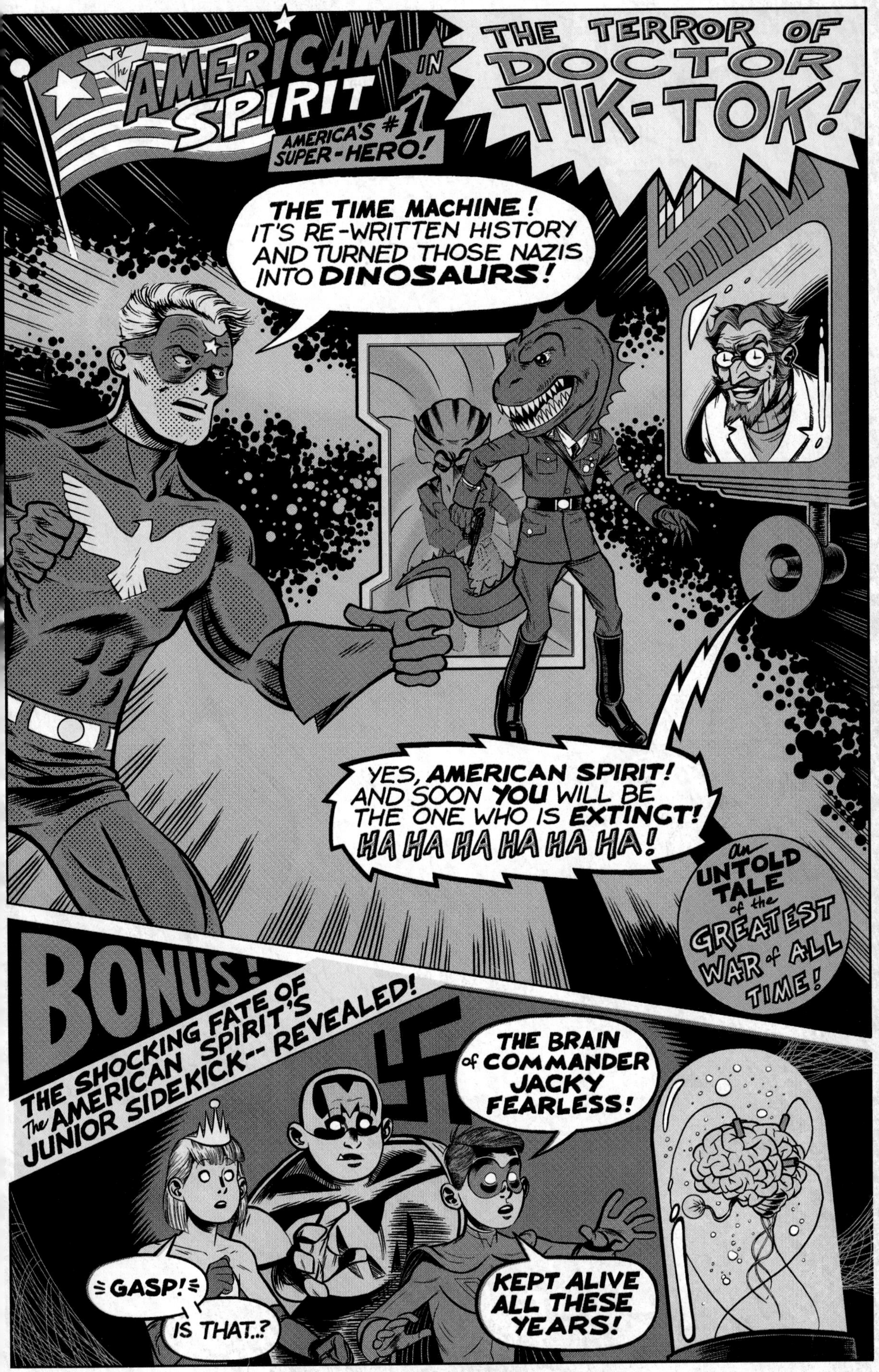
The AMERICAN SPIRIT
AMERICA'S #1 SUPER-HERO!
IN
THE TERROR OF DOCTOR TIK-TOK!
THE TIME MACHINE! IT'S RE-WRITTEN HISTORY AND TURNED THOSE NAZIS INTO DINOSAURS!
YES, AMERICAN SPIRIT! AND SOON YOU WILL BE THE ONE WHO IS EXTINCT! HA HA HA HA HA HA!
an UNTOLD TALE of the GREATEST WAR of ALL TIME!
BONUS!
THE SHOCKING FATE OF The AMERICAN SPIRIT'S JUNIOR SIDEKICK-- REVEALED!
THE BRAIN of COMMANDER JACKY FEARLESS!
GASP!
IS THAT..?
KEPT ALIVE ALL THESE YEARS!

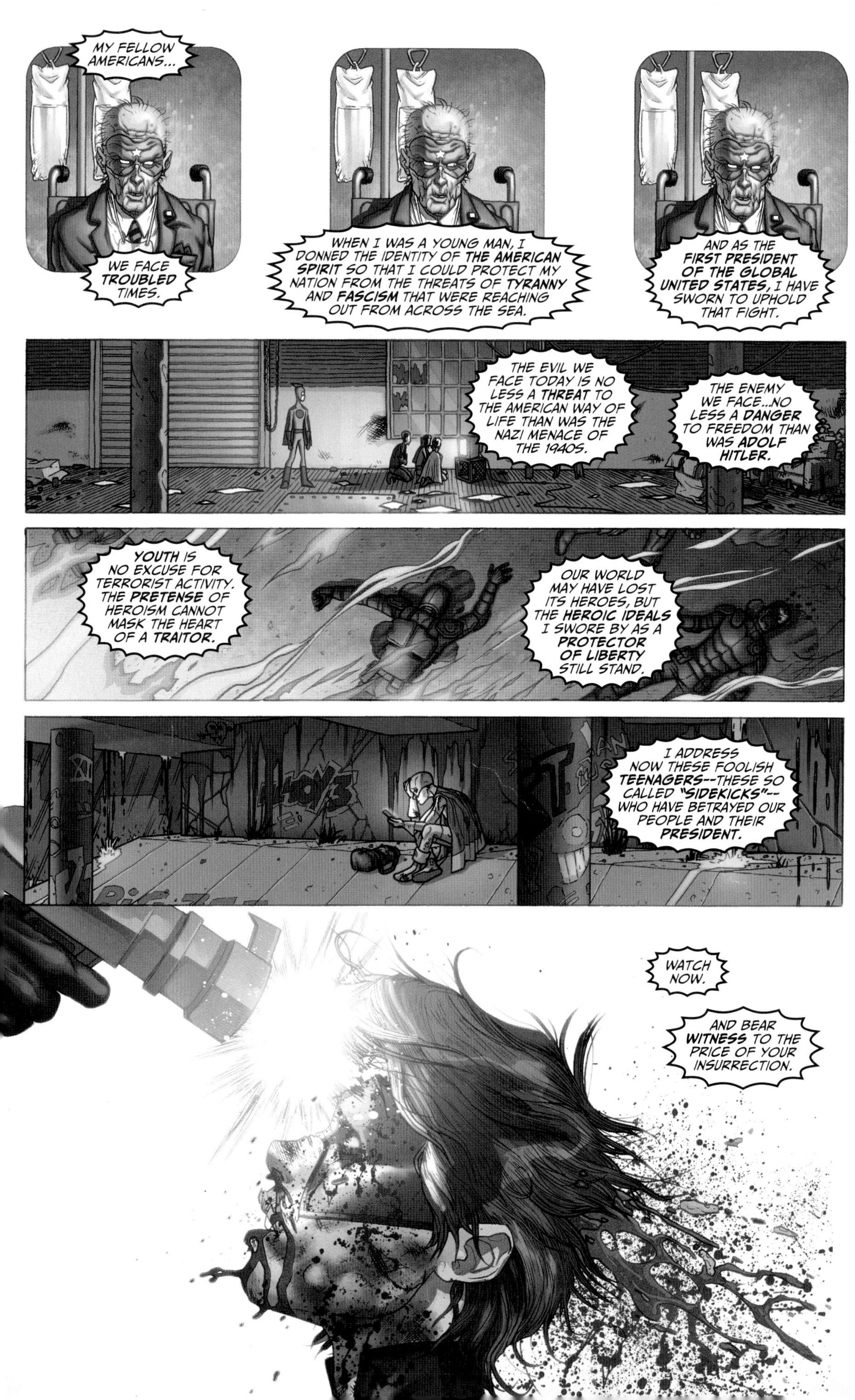
MY FELLOW AMERICANS...
WE FACE TROUBLED TIMES.
WHEN I WAS A YOUNG MAN, I DONNED THE IDENTITY OF THE AMERICAN SPIRIT SO THAT I COULD PROTECT MY NATION FROM THE THREATS OF TYRANNY AND FASCISM THAT WERE REACHING OUT FROM ACROSS THE SEA.
AND AS THE FIRST PRESIDENT OF THE GLOBAL UNITED STATES, I HAVE SWORN TO UPHOLD THAT FIGHT.
THE EVIL WE FACE TODAY IS NO LESS A THREAT TO THE AMERICAN WAY OF LIFE THAN WAS THE NAZI MENACE OF THE 1940S.
THE ENEMY WE FACE...NO LESS A DANGER TO FREEDOM THAN WAS ADOLF HITLER.
YOUTH IS NO EXCUSE FOR TERRORIST ACTIVITY. THE PRETENSE OF HEROISM CANNOT MASK THE HEART OF A TRAITOR.
OUR WORLD MAY HAVE LOST ITS HEROES, BUT THE HEROIC IDEALS I SWORE BY AS A PROTECTOR OF LIBERTY STILL STAND.
I ADDRESS NOW THESE FOOLISH TEENAGERS--THESE SO CALLED "SIDEKICKS"--WHO HAVE BETRAYED OUR PEOPLE AND THEIR PRESIDENT.
WATCH NOW.
AND BEAR WITNESS TO THE PRICE OF YOUR INSURRECTION.

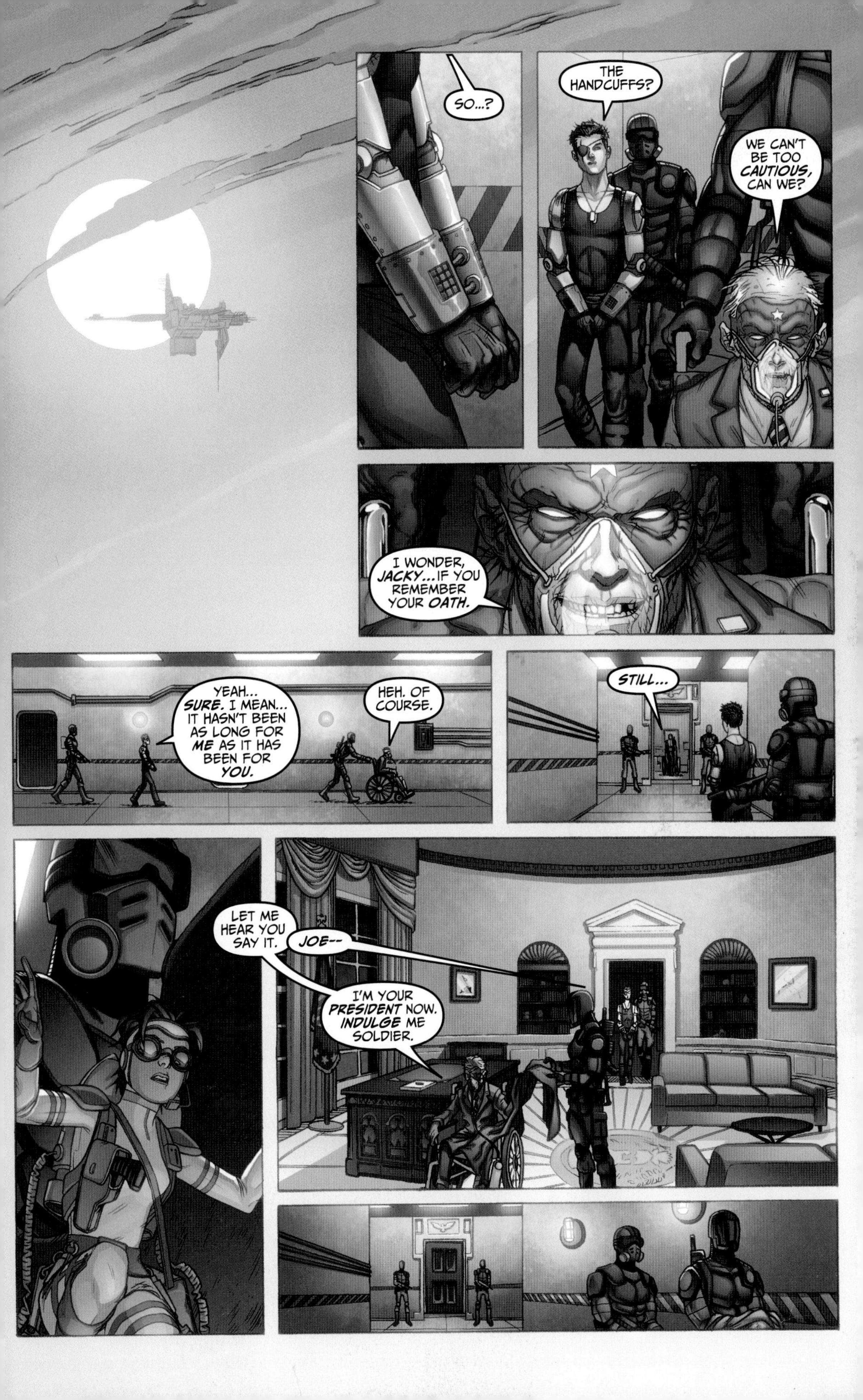
SO...?
THE HANDCUFFS?
WE CAN'T BE TOO CAUTIOUS, CAN WE?
I WONDER, JACKY...IF YOU REMEMBER YOUR OATH.
YEAH... SURE. I MEAN... IT HASN'T BEEN AS LONG FOR ME AS IT HAS BEEN FOR YOU.
HEH. OF COURSE.
STILL...
LET ME HEAR YOU SAY IT.
JOE--
I'M YOUR PRESIDENT NOW. INDULGE ME SOLDIER.

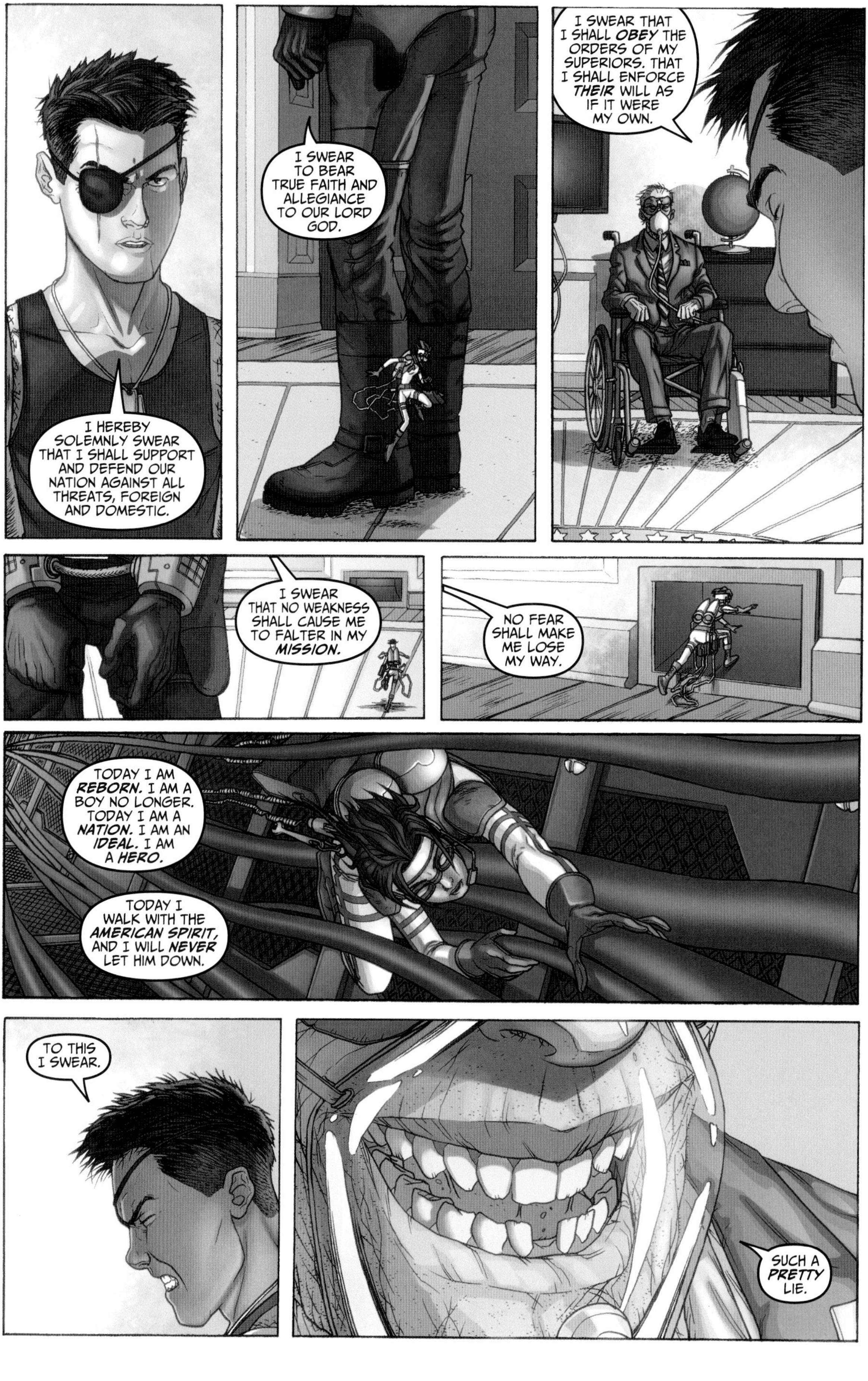
I HEREBY SOLEMNLY SWEAR THAT I SHALL SUPPORT AND DEFEND OUR NATION AGAINST ALL THREATS, FOREIGN AND DOMESTIC.
I SWEAR TO BEAR TRUE FAITH AND ALLEGIANCE TO OUR LORD GOD.
I SWEAR THAT I SHALL OBEY THE ORDERS OF MY SUPERIORS. THAT I SHALL ENFORCE THEIR WILL AS IF IT WERE MY OWN.
I SWEAR THAT NO WEAKNESS SHALL CAUSE ME TO FALTER IN MY MISSION.
NO FEAR SHALL MAKE ME LOSE MY WAY.
TODAY I AM REBORN. I AM A BOY NO LONGER. TODAY I AM A NATION. I AM AN IDEAL. I AM A HERO.
TODAY I WALK WITH THE AMERICAN SPIRIT, AND I WILL NEVER LET HIM DOWN.
TO THIS I SWEAR.
SUCH A PRETTY LIE.

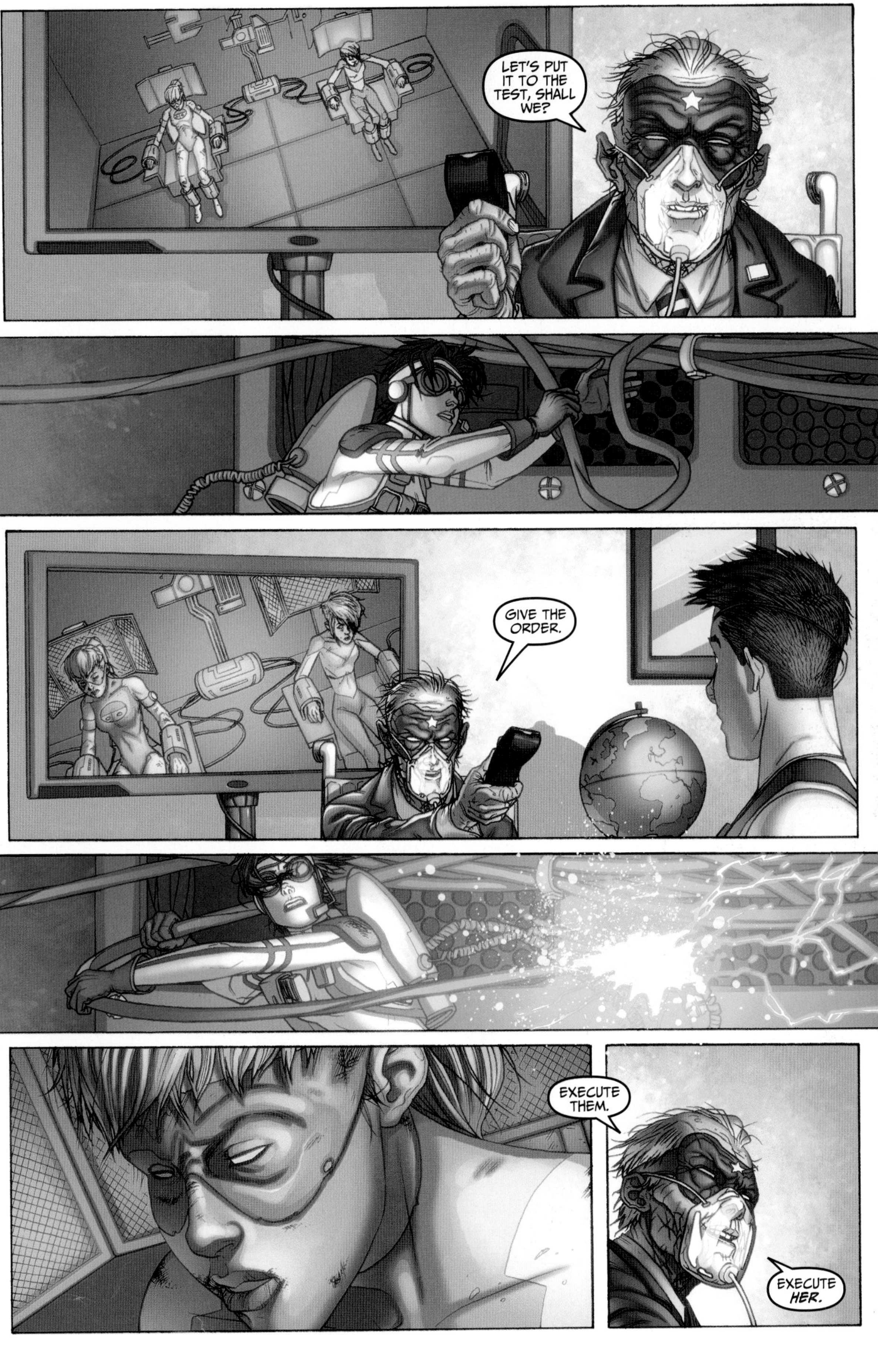
LET'S PUT IT TO THE TEST, SHALL WE?
GIVE THE ORDER.
EXECUTE THEM.
EXECUTE HER.

JOE, COME ON...

JACK *"FEARLESS"*.

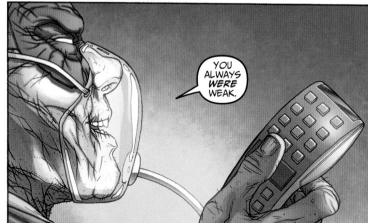

YOU ALWAYS *WERE* WEAK.

NO!

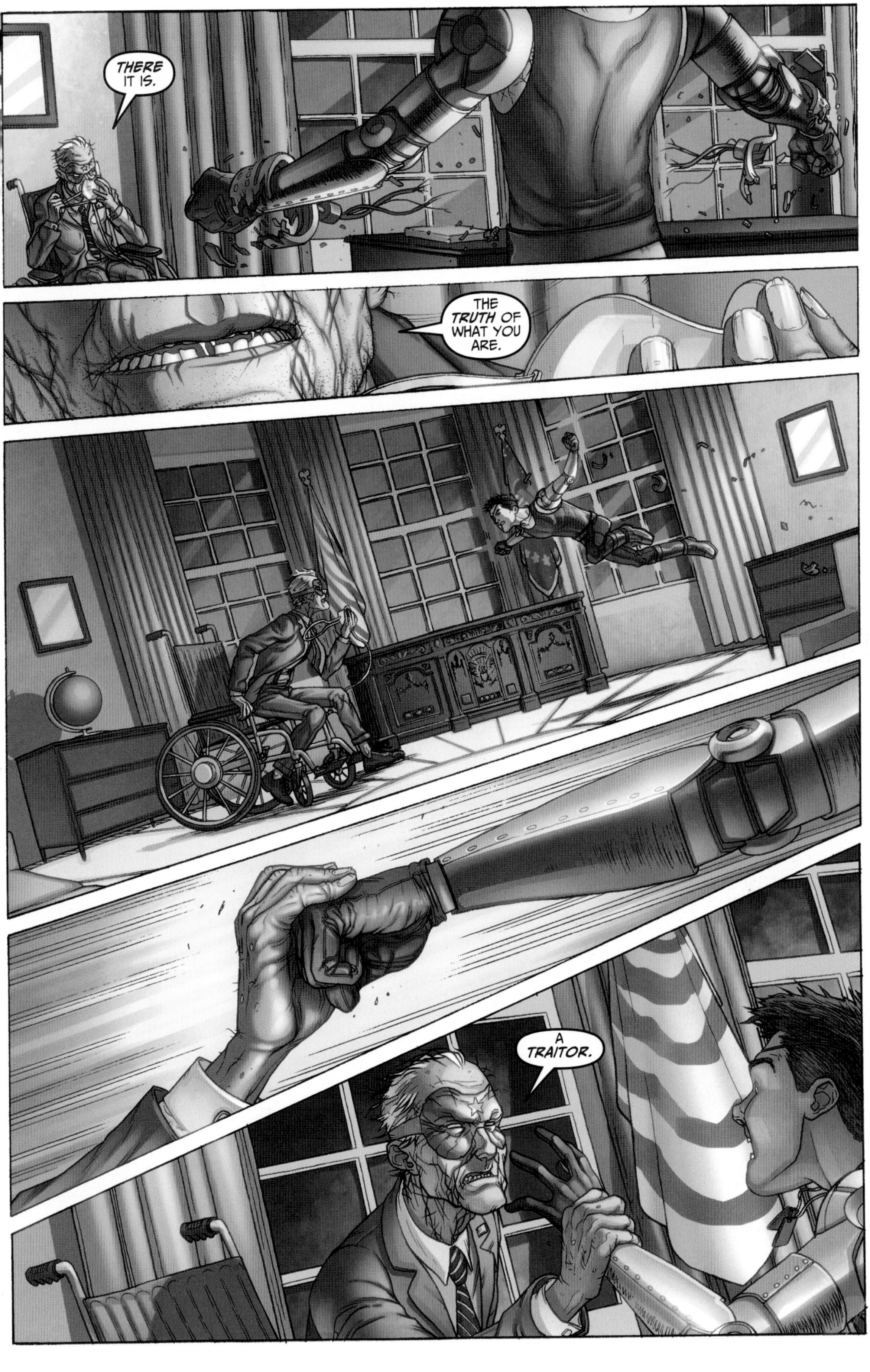
THERE IT IS.
THE TRUTH OF WHAT YOU ARE.
A TRAITOR.

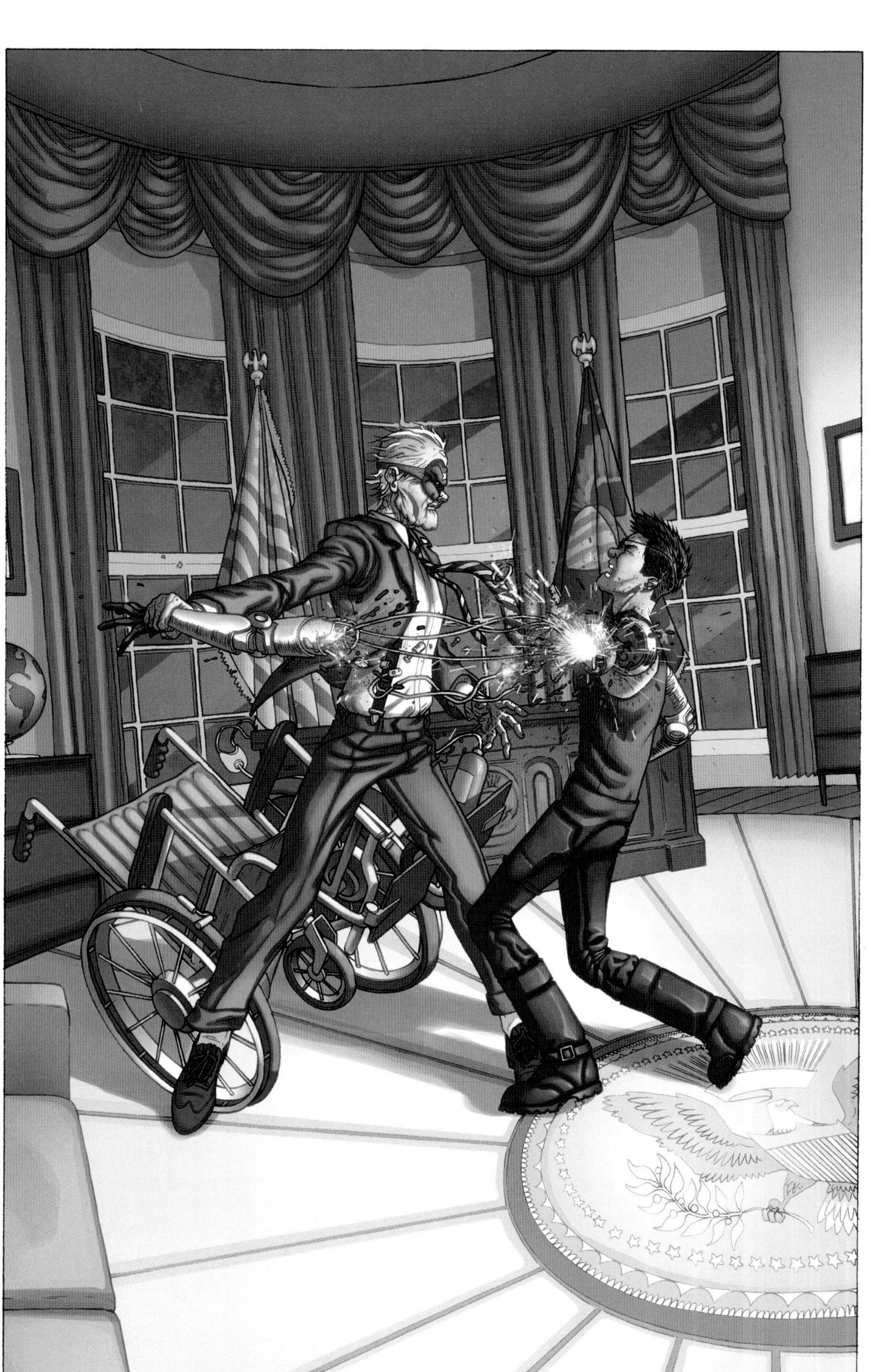

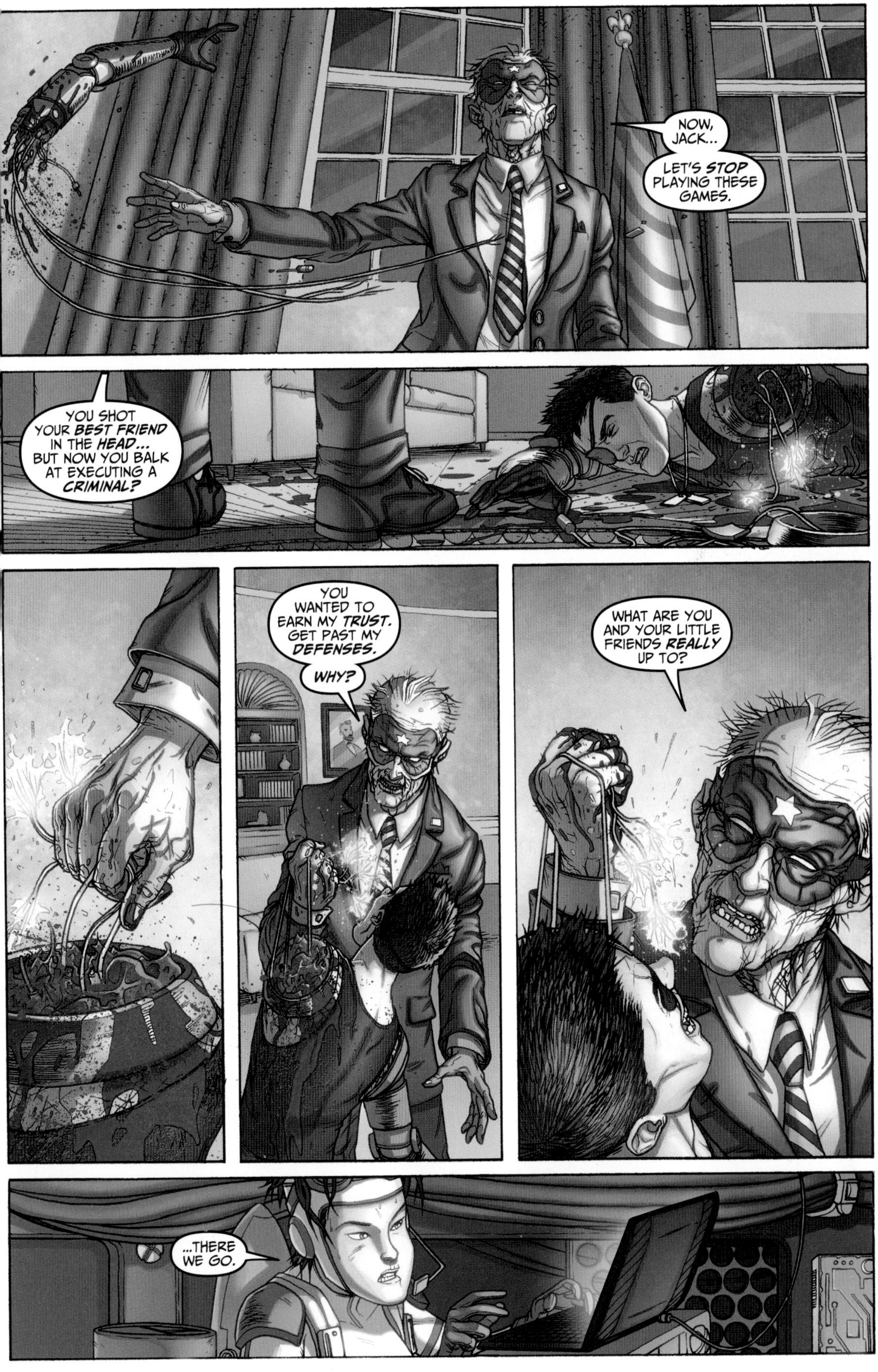
NOW, JACK...
LET'S *STOP* PLAYING THESE GAMES.
YOU SHOT YOUR ***BEST FRIEND*** IN THE ***HEAD...*** BUT NOW YOU BALK AT EXECUTING A ***CRIMINAL?***
YOU WANTED TO EARN MY *TRUST*. GET PAST MY *DEFENSES*.
WHY?
WHAT ARE YOU AND YOUR LITTLE FRIENDS *REALLY* UP TO?
...THERE WE GO.

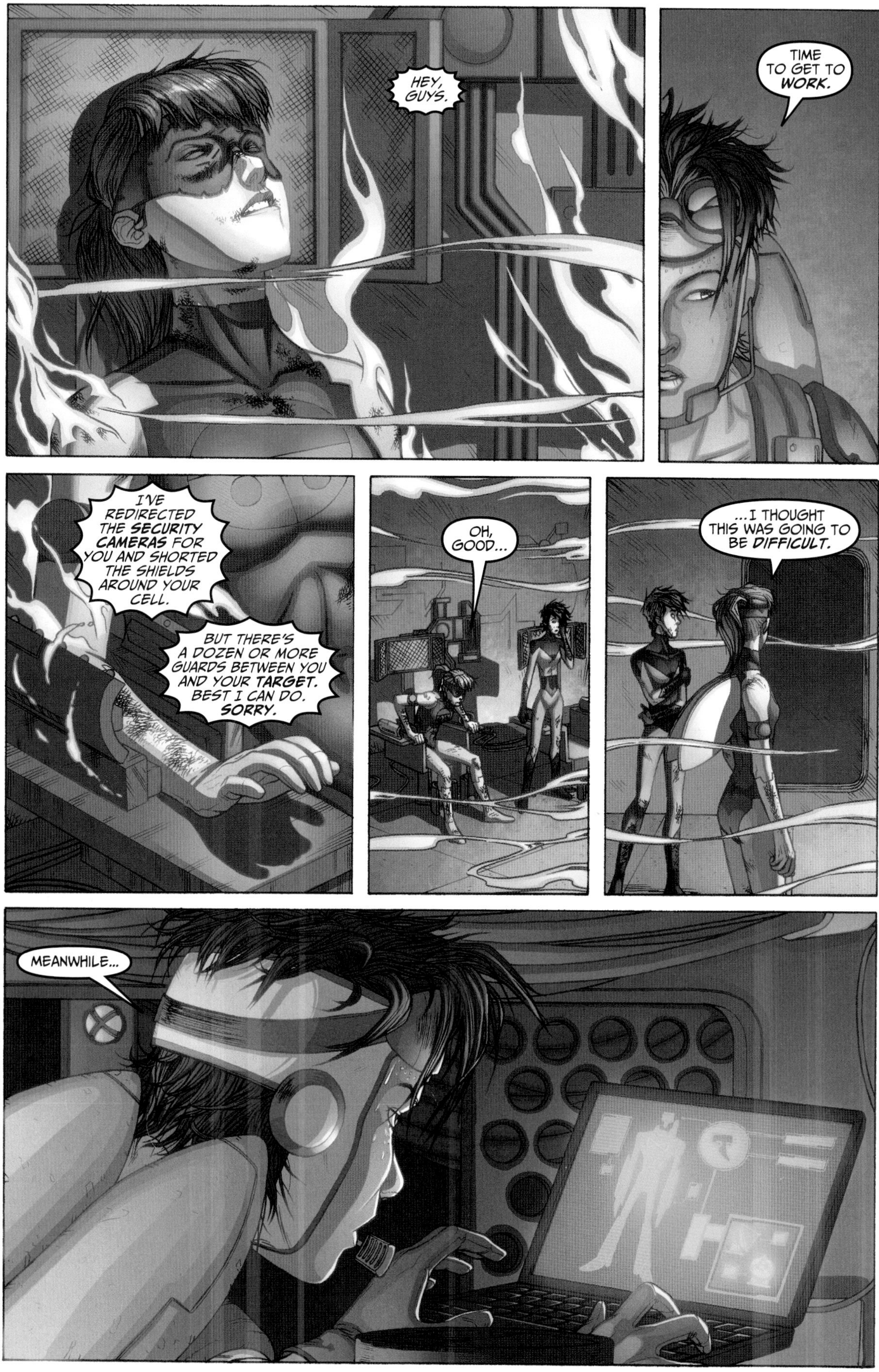
HEY, GUYS.
TIME TO GET TO WORK.
I'VE REDIRECTED THE SECURITY CAMERAS FOR YOU AND SHORTED THE SHIELDS AROUND YOUR CELL.
BUT THERE'S A DOZEN OR MORE GUARDS BETWEEN YOU AND YOUR TARGET. BEST I CAN DO. SORRY.
OH, GOOD...
...I THOUGHT THIS WAS GOING TO BE DIFFICULT.
MEANWHILE...

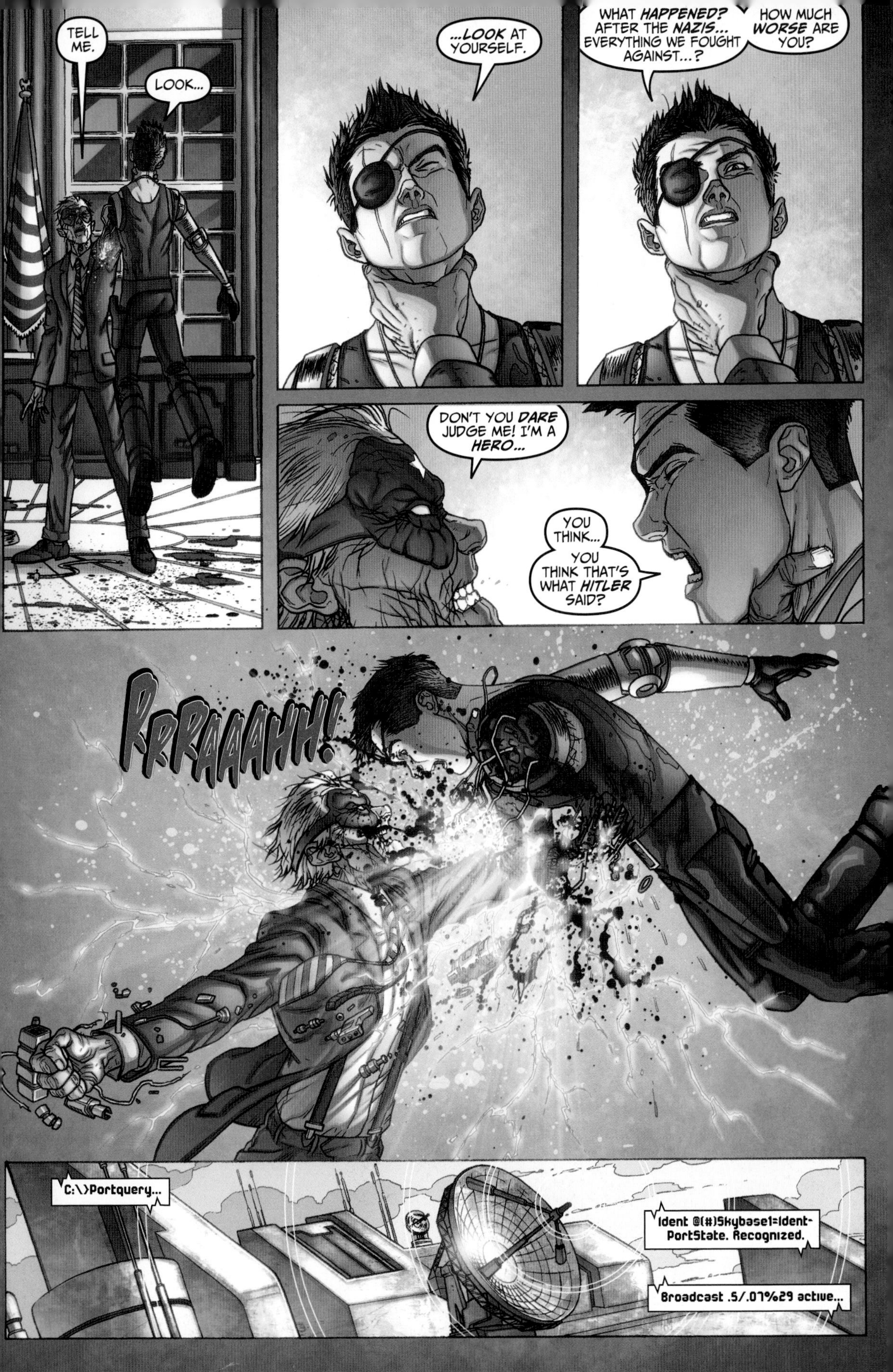
TELL ME.
LOOK...
...LOOK AT YOURSELF.
WHAT HAPPENED? AFTER THE NAZIS... EVERYTHING WE FOUGHT AGAINST...?
HOW MUCH WORSE ARE YOU?
DON'T YOU DARE JUDGE ME! I'M A HERO...
YOU THINK...
YOU THINK THAT'S WHAT HITLER SAID?
RRRAAAAHH!
C:\>Portquery...
Ident @(#)Skybase1=Ident-PortState. Recognized.
Broadcast .5/.07%29 active...

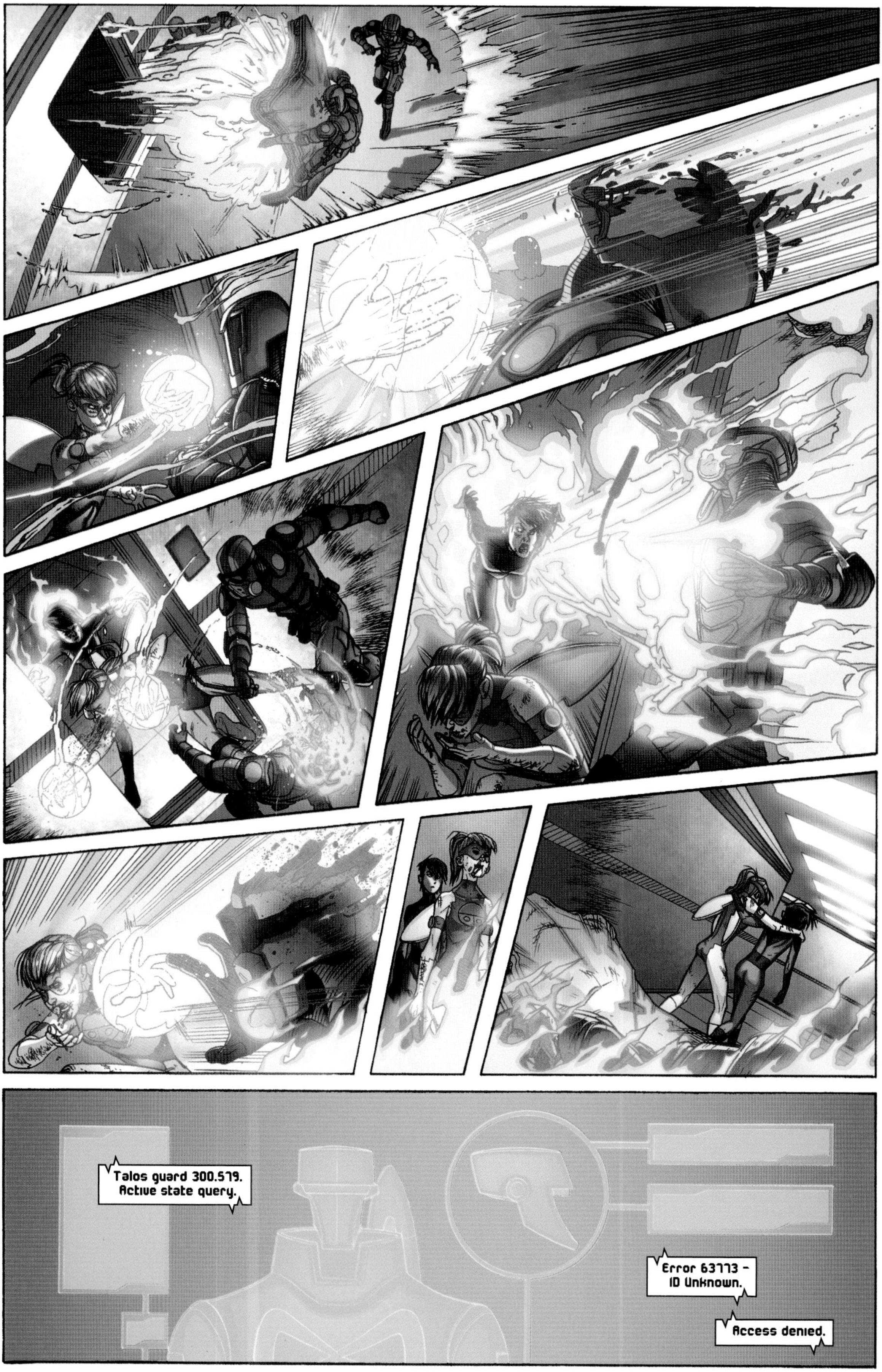
Talos guard 300.579. Active state query.
Error 63773 – ID Unknown.
Access denied.

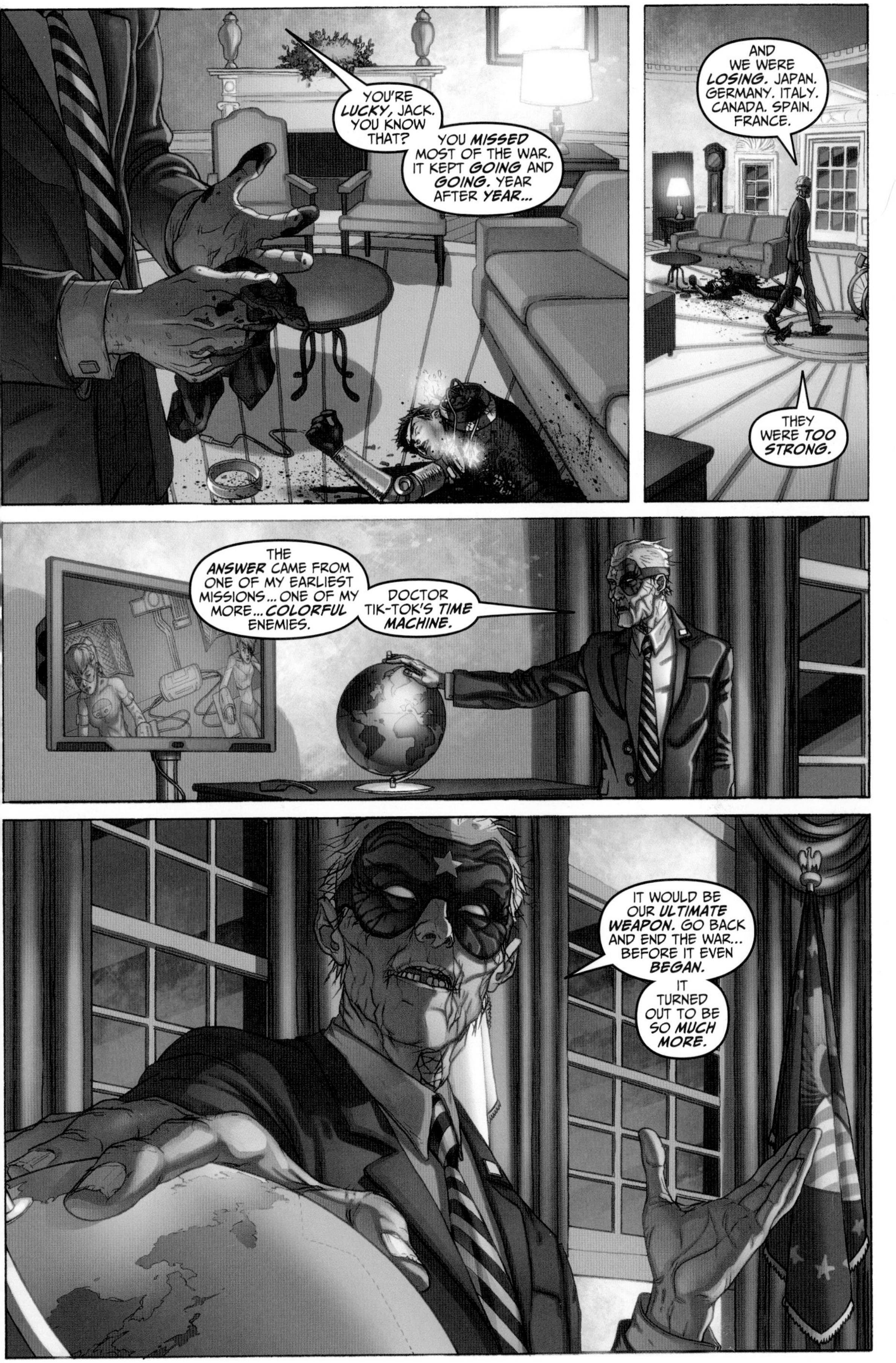
YOU'RE LUCKY, JACK. YOU KNOW THAT?
YOU MISSED MOST OF THE WAR. IT KEPT GOING AND GOING. YEAR AFTER YEAR...
AND WE WERE LOSING. JAPAN. GERMANY. ITALY. CANADA. SPAIN. FRANCE.
THEY WERE TOO STRONG.
THE ANSWER CAME FROM ONE OF MY EARLIEST MISSIONS... ONE OF MY MORE... COLORFUL ENEMIES.
DOCTOR TIK-TOK'S TIME MACHINE.
IT WOULD BE OUR ULTIMATE WEAPON. GO BACK AND END THE WAR... BEFORE IT EVEN BEGAN.
IT TURNED OUT TO BE SO MUCH MORE.

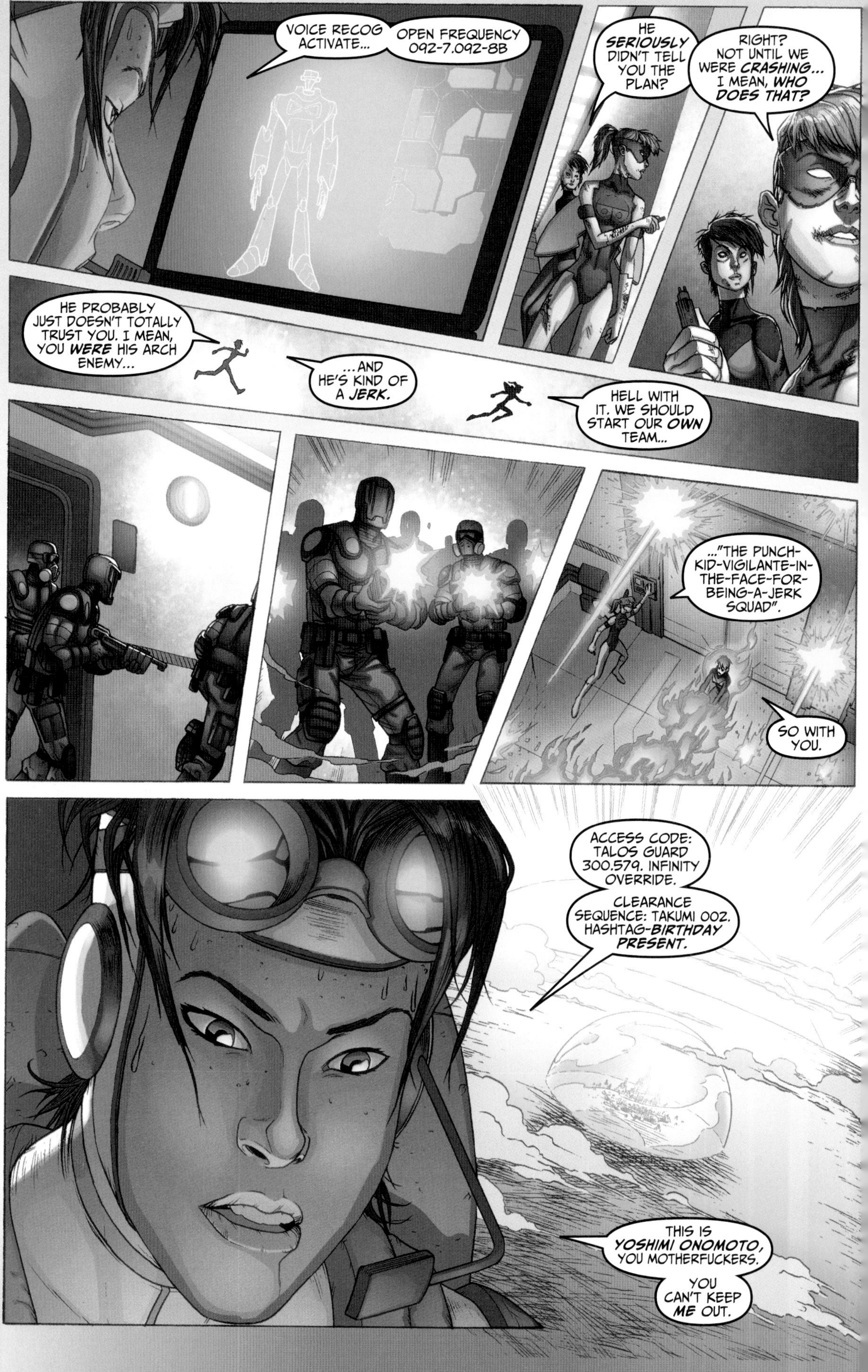
VOICE RECOG ACTIVATE...
OPEN FREQUENCY 092-7.092-8B
HE SERIOUSLY DIDN'T TELL YOU THE PLAN?
RIGHT? NOT UNTIL WE WERE CRASHING... I MEAN, WHO DOES THAT?
HE PROBABLY JUST DOESN'T TOTALLY TRUST YOU. I MEAN, YOU WERE HIS ARCH ENEMY...
...AND HE'S KIND OF A JERK.
HELL WITH IT. WE SHOULD START OUR OWN TEAM...
..."THE PUNCH-KID-VIGILANTE-IN-THE-FACE-FOR-BEING-A-JERK SQUAD".
SO WITH YOU.
ACCESS CODE: TALOS GUARD 300.579. INFINITY OVERRIDE.
CLEARANCE SEQUENCE: TAKUMI 002. HASHTAG-BIRTHDAY PRESENT.
THIS IS YOSHIMI ONOMOTO, YOU MOTHERFUCKERS.
YOU CAN'T KEEP ME OUT.

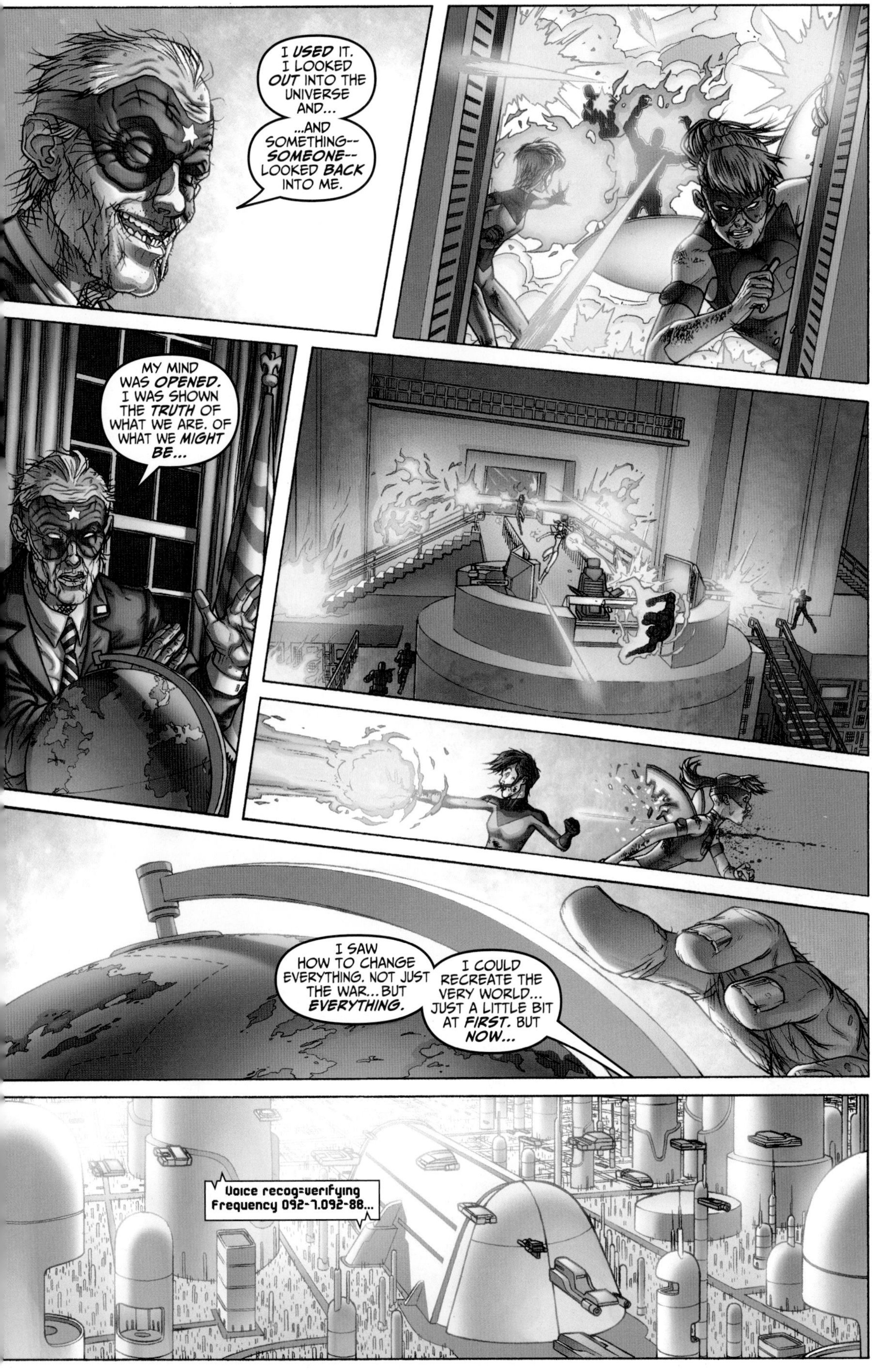
I USED IT. I LOOKED OUT INTO THE UNIVERSE AND...
...AND SOMETHING-- SOMEONE-- LOOKED BACK INTO ME.
MY MIND WAS OPENED. I WAS SHOWN THE TRUTH OF WHAT WE ARE. OF WHAT WE MIGHT BE...
I SAW HOW TO CHANGE EVERYTHING. NOT JUST THE WAR... BUT EVERYTHING.
I COULD RECREATE THE VERY WORLD... JUST A LITTLE BIT AT FIRST. BUT NOW...
Voice recog=verifying
Frequency 092-7.092-88...

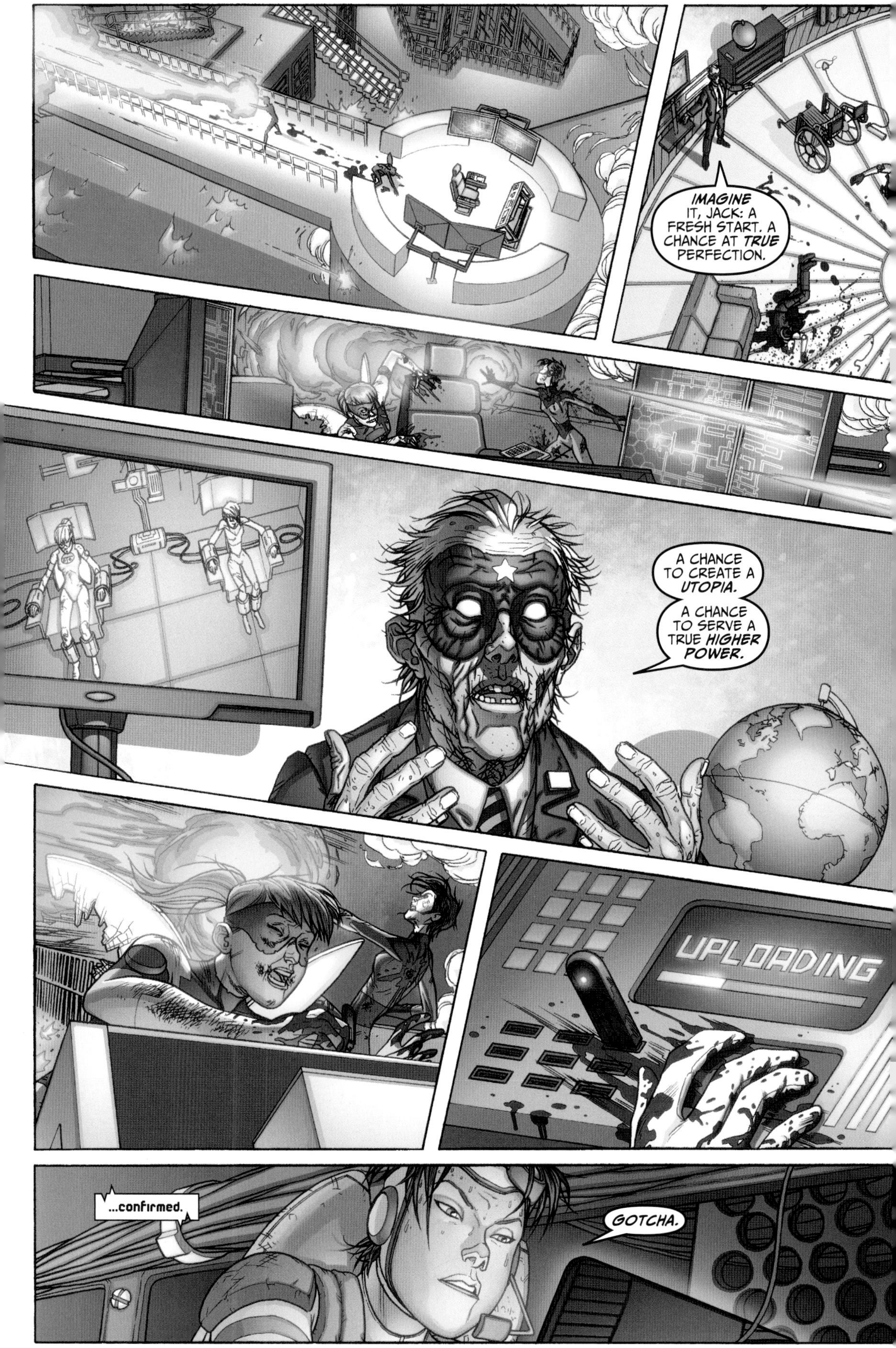
IMAGINE IT, JACK: A FRESH START. A CHANCE AT TRUE PERFECTION.
A CHANCE TO CREATE A UTOPIA.
A CHANCE TO SERVE A TRUE HIGHER POWER.
UPLOADING
...confirmed.
GOTCHA.

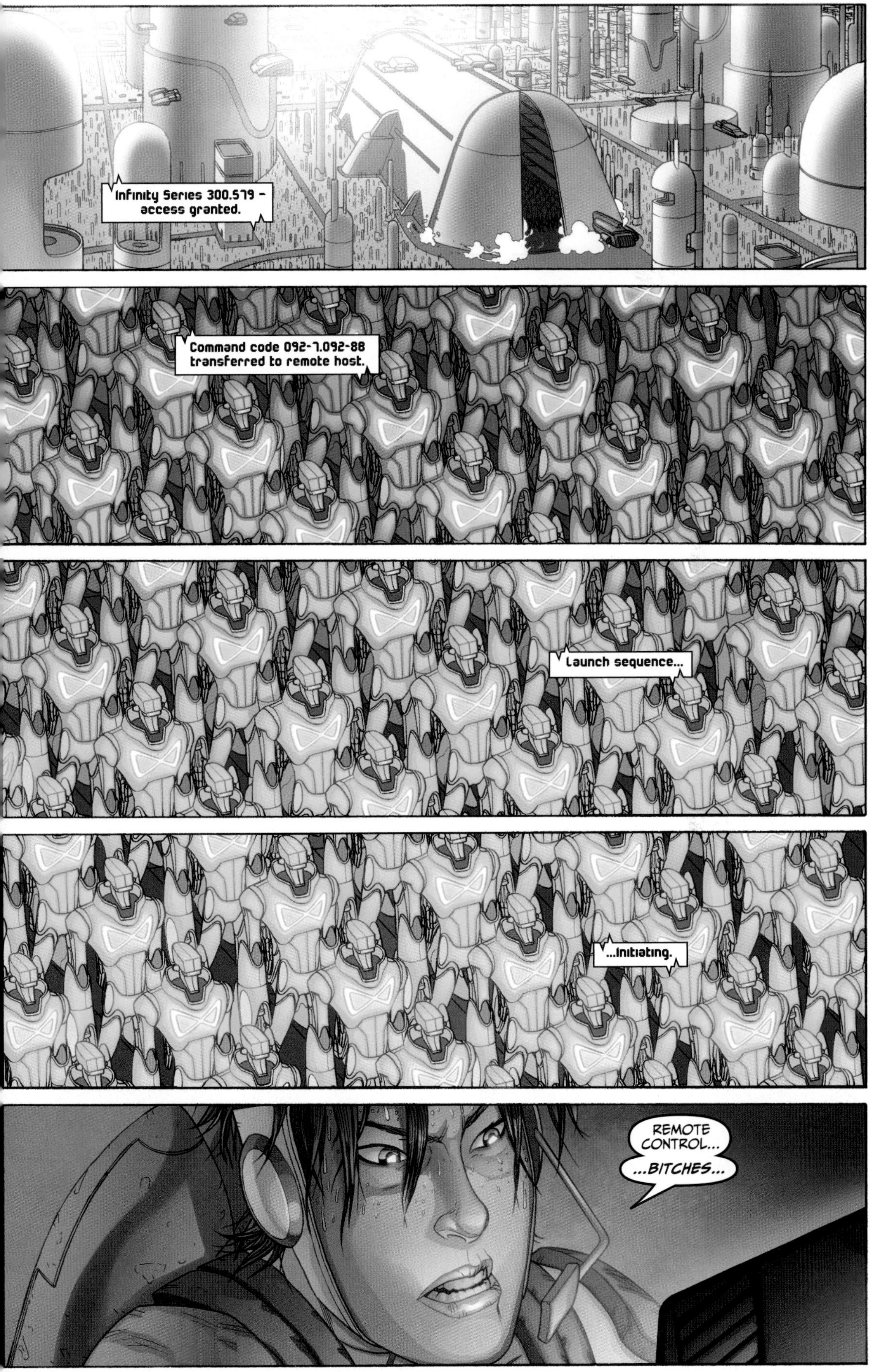
Infinity Series 300.579 – access granted.
Command code 092-7.092-88 transferred to remote host.
Launch sequence...
...initiating.
REMOTE CONTROL...
...BITCHES...

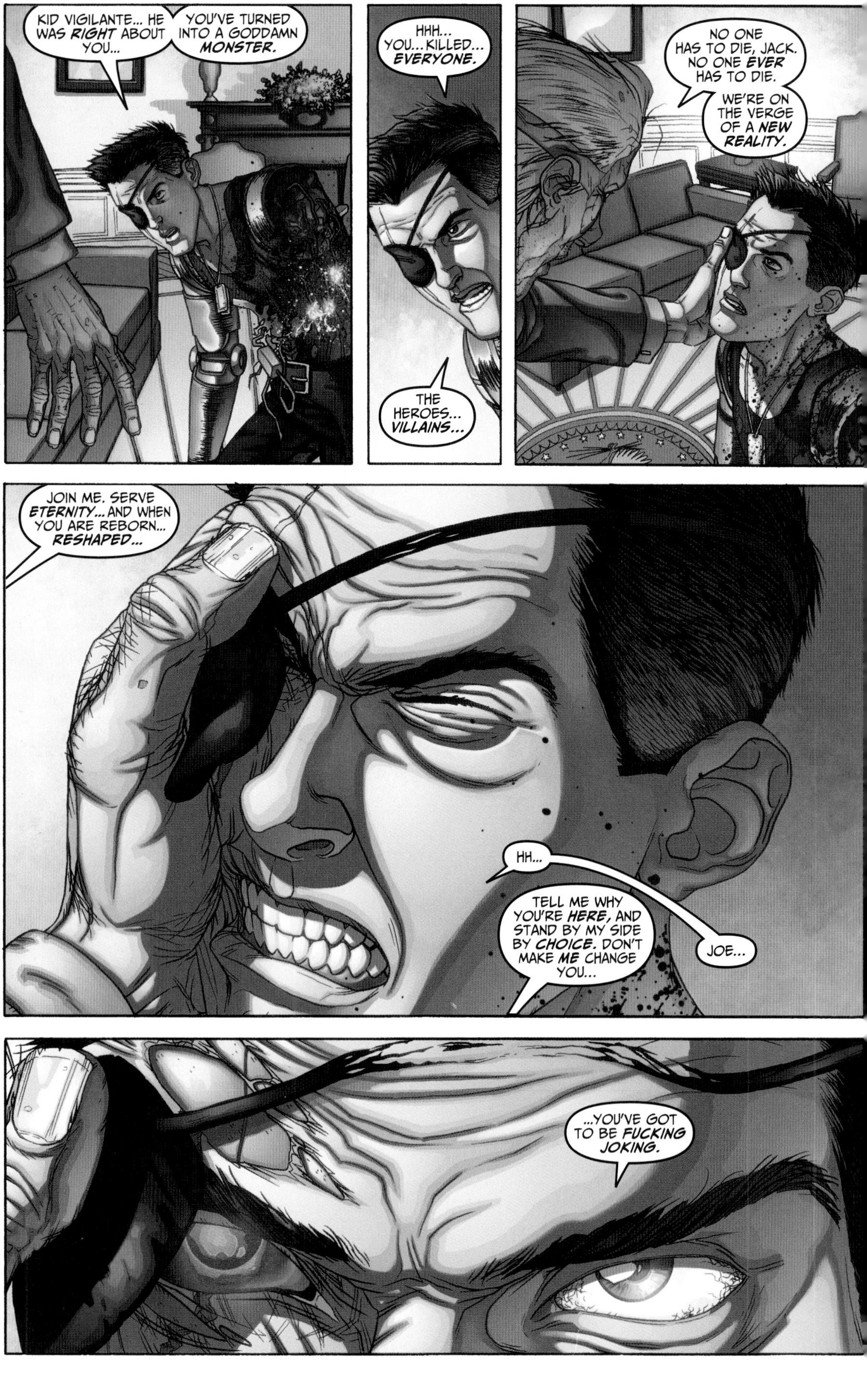
KID VIGILANTE... HE WAS RIGHT ABOUT YOU...
YOU'VE TURNED INTO A GODDAMN MONSTER.
HHH... YOU... KILLED... EVERYONE.
THE HEROES... VILLAINS...
NO ONE HAS TO DIE, JACK. NO ONE EVER HAS TO DIE.
WE'RE ON THE VERGE OF A NEW REALITY.
JOIN ME. SERVE ETERNITY... AND WHEN YOU ARE REBORN... RESHAPED...
HH...
TELL ME WHY YOU'RE HERE, AND STAND BY MY SIDE BY CHOICE. DON'T MAKE ME CHANGE YOU...
JOE...
...YOU'VE GOT TO BE FUCKING JOKING.

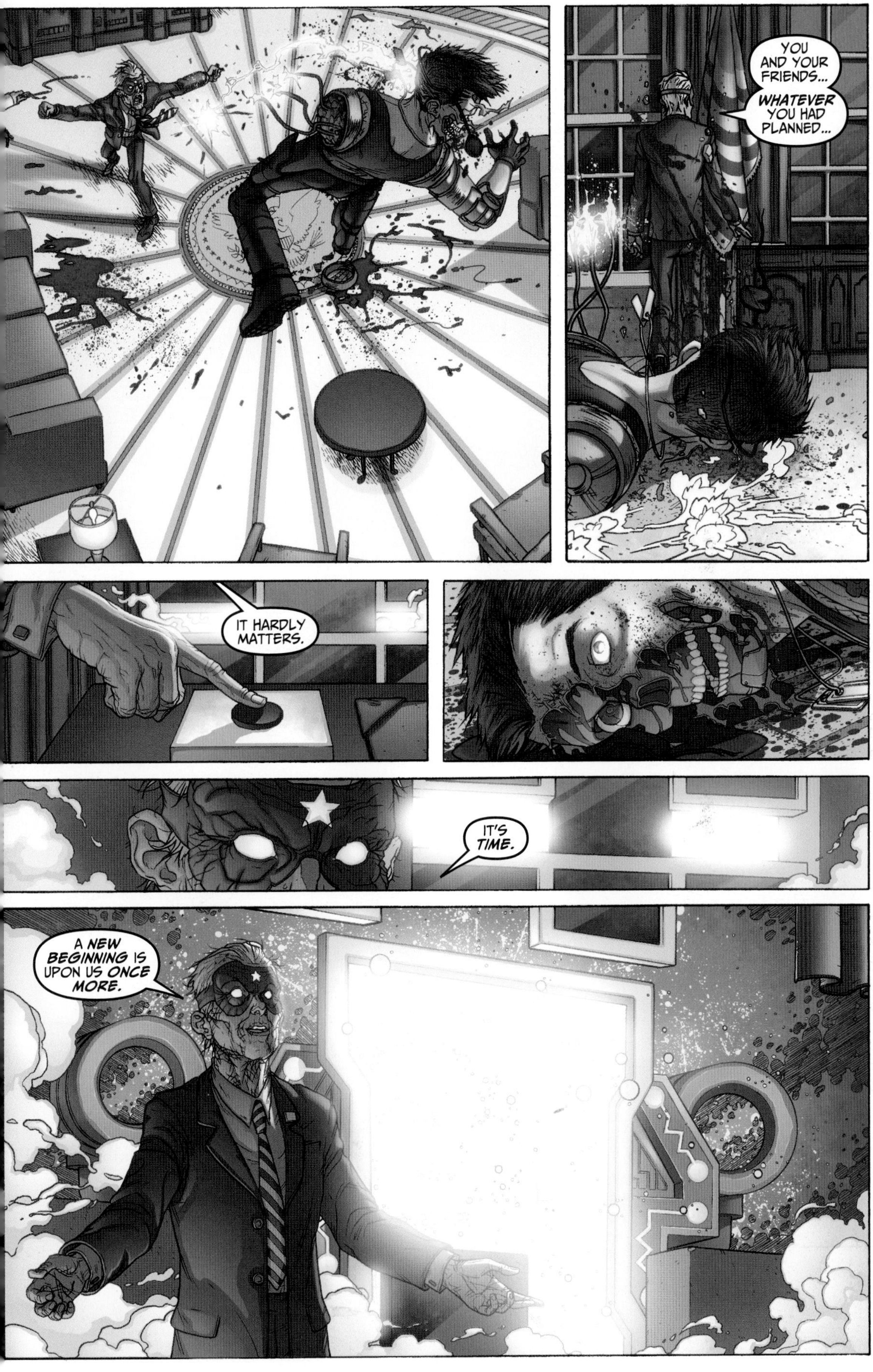
YOU AND YOUR FRIENDS...
WHATEVER YOU HAD PLANNED...
IT HARDLY MATTERS.
IT'S TIME.
A NEW BEGINNING IS UPON US ONCE MORE.

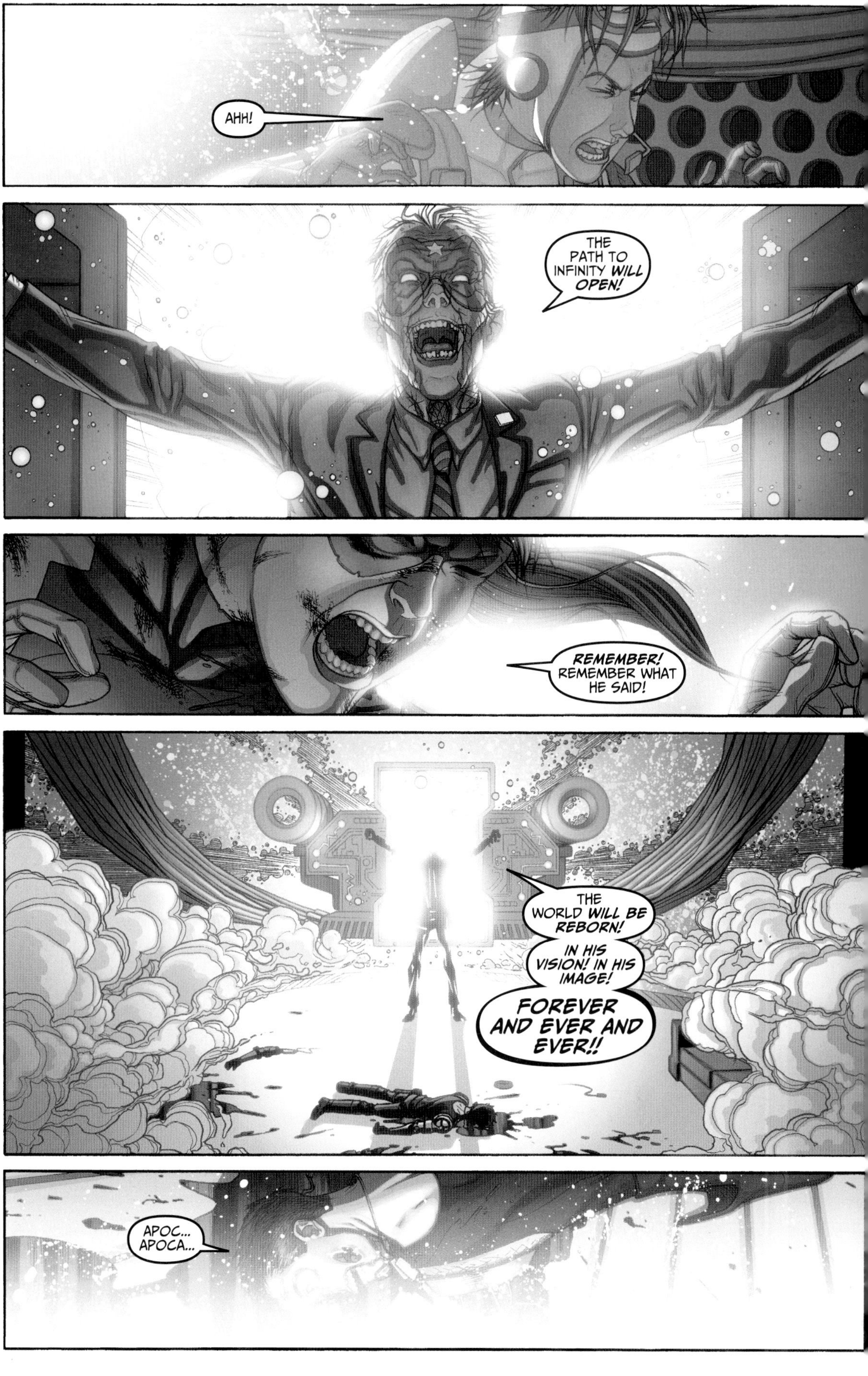
AHH!
THE PATH TO INFINITY WILL OPEN!
REMEMBER! REMEMBER WHAT HE SAID!
THE WORLD WILL BE REBORN!
IN HIS VISION! IN HIS IMAGE!
FOREVER AND EVER AND EVER!!
APOC... APOCA...

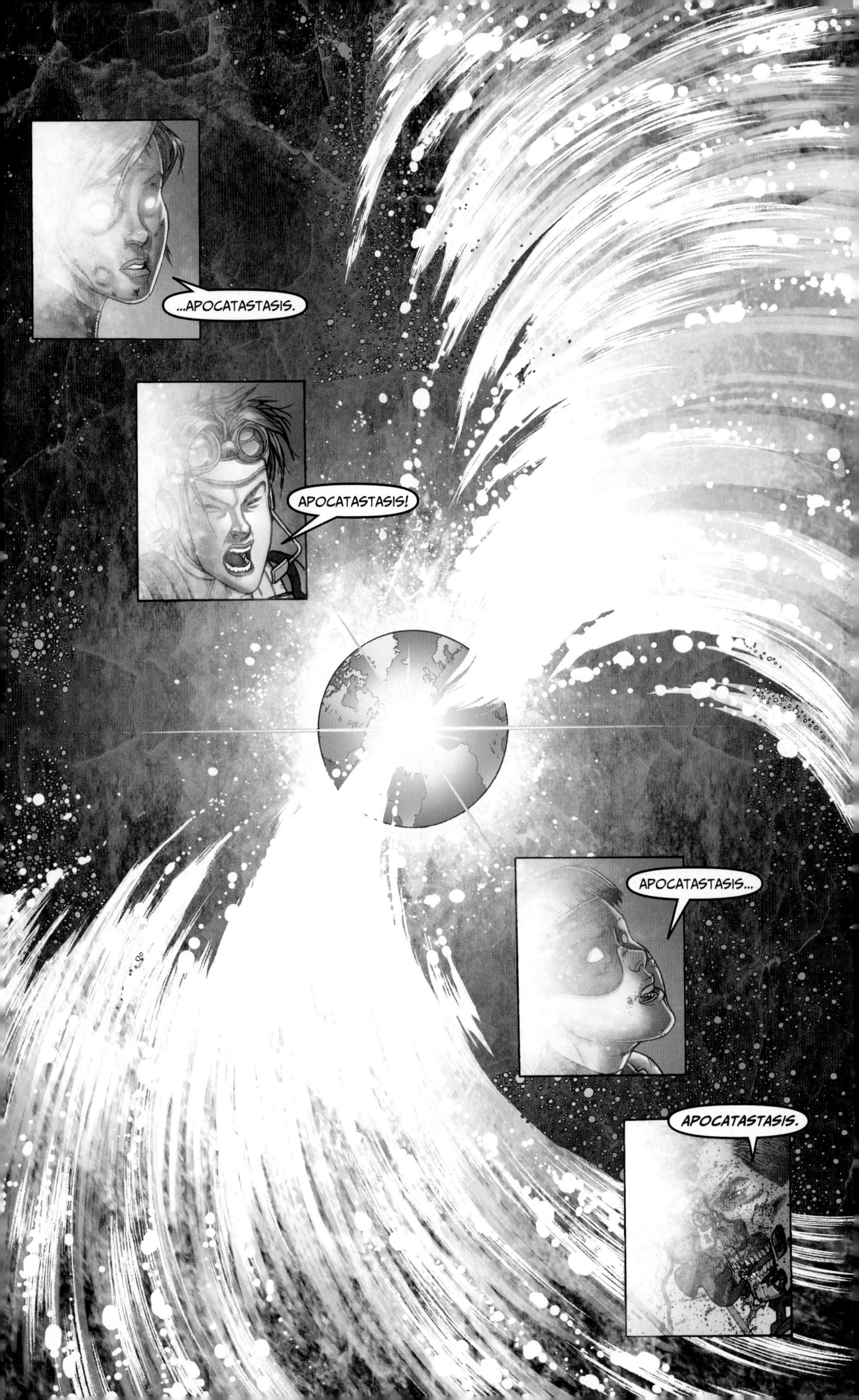
...APOCATASTASIS.
APOCATASTASIS!
APOCATASTASIS...
APOCATASTASIS.

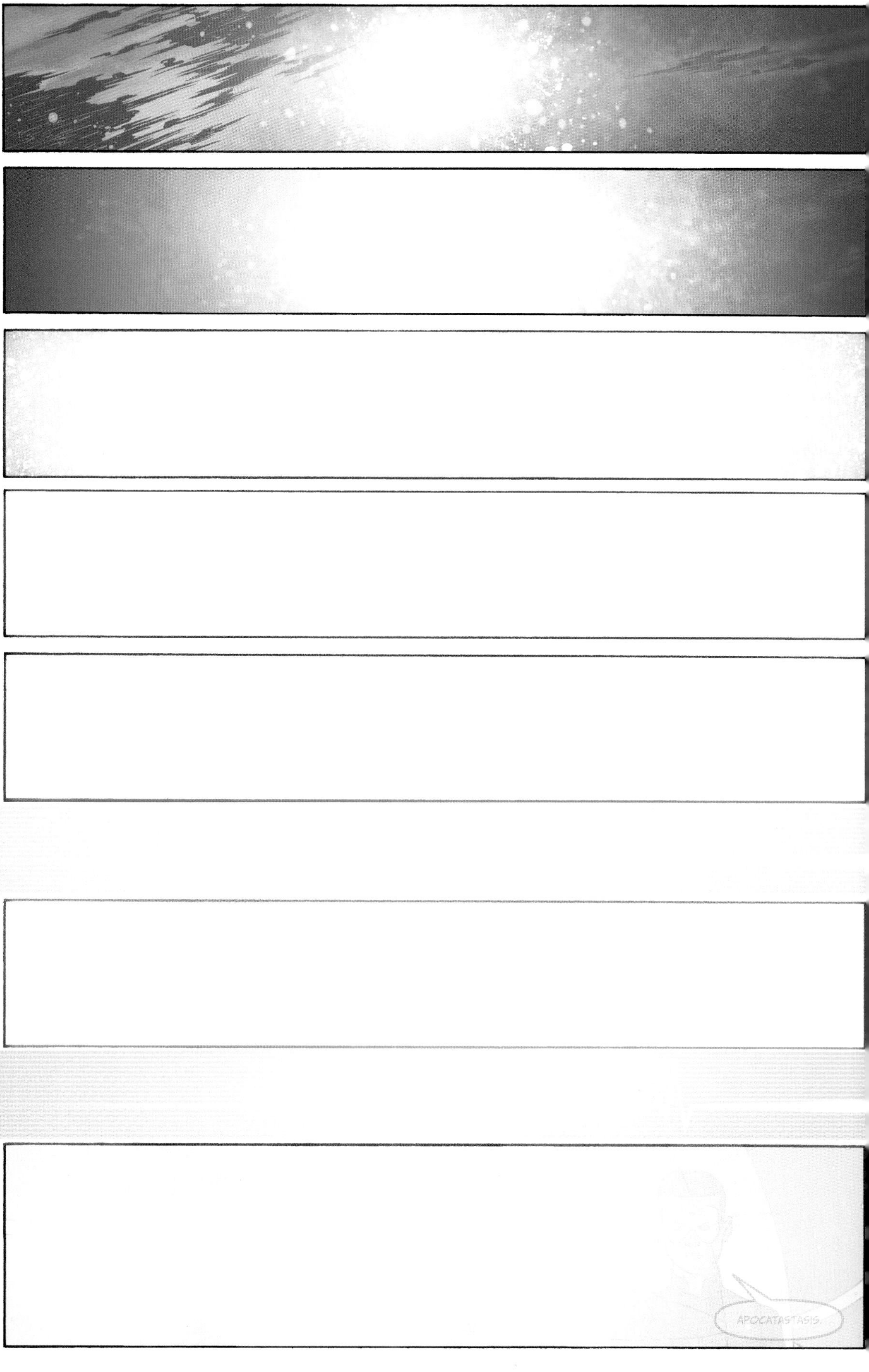

APOCATASTASIS.

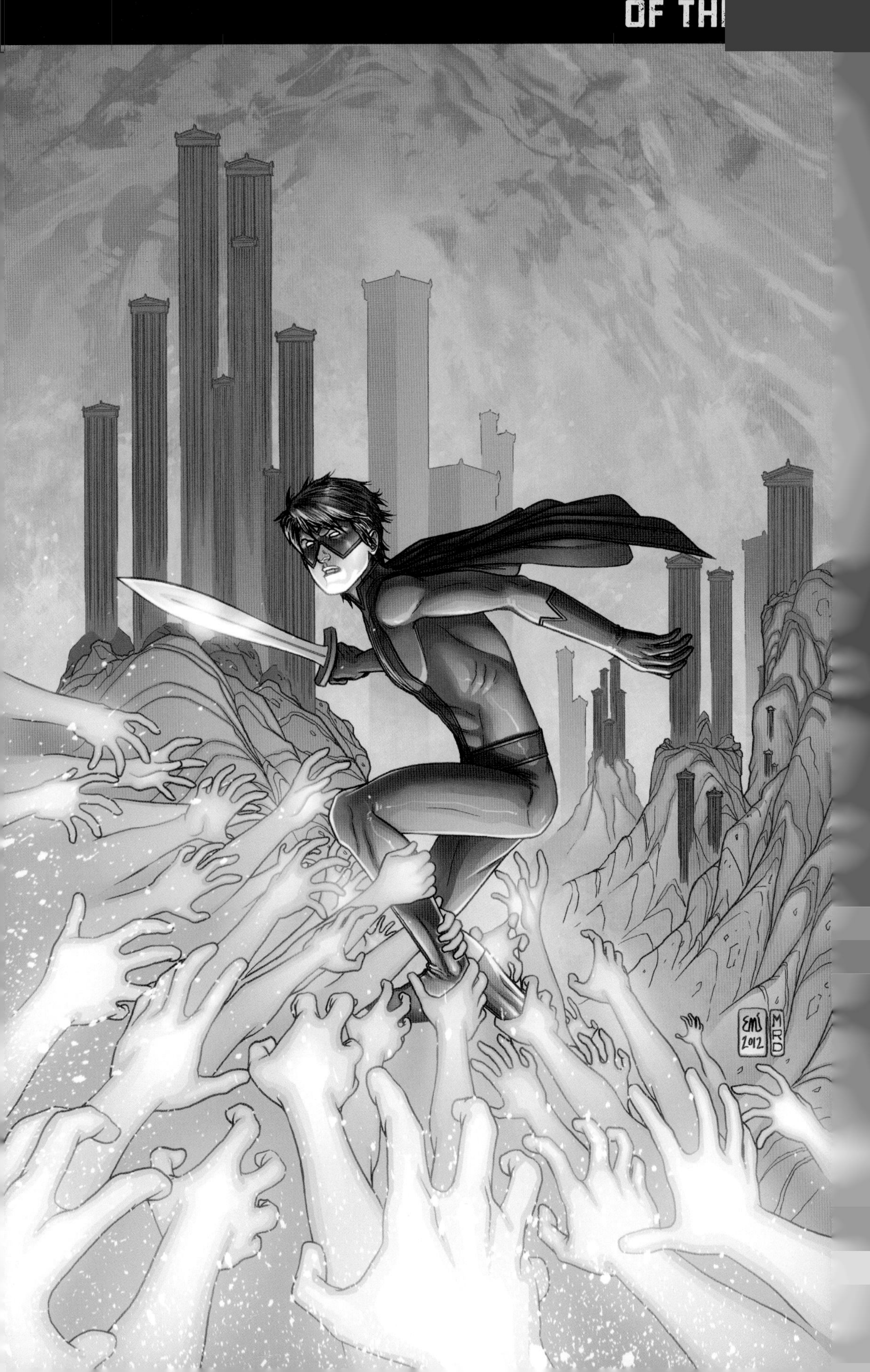
OF TH

They came to us thousands of years ago.
Gods. Aliens. Refugees of a fallen civilization.

For centuries they ruled, intermingling with humanity.
Creating generation after generation of daemons,
faeries, and demigods.

The first generation of heroes and villains.

And then one day, something happened. Something
terrible followed our rulers from their lost home world.

The Gods fell, defending the Earth. Their empire
crumbled, and only the most remote spark of their seed
survived within our species.

And they never told us what it was they had been running from.

They never told us what it was that could frighten a god.

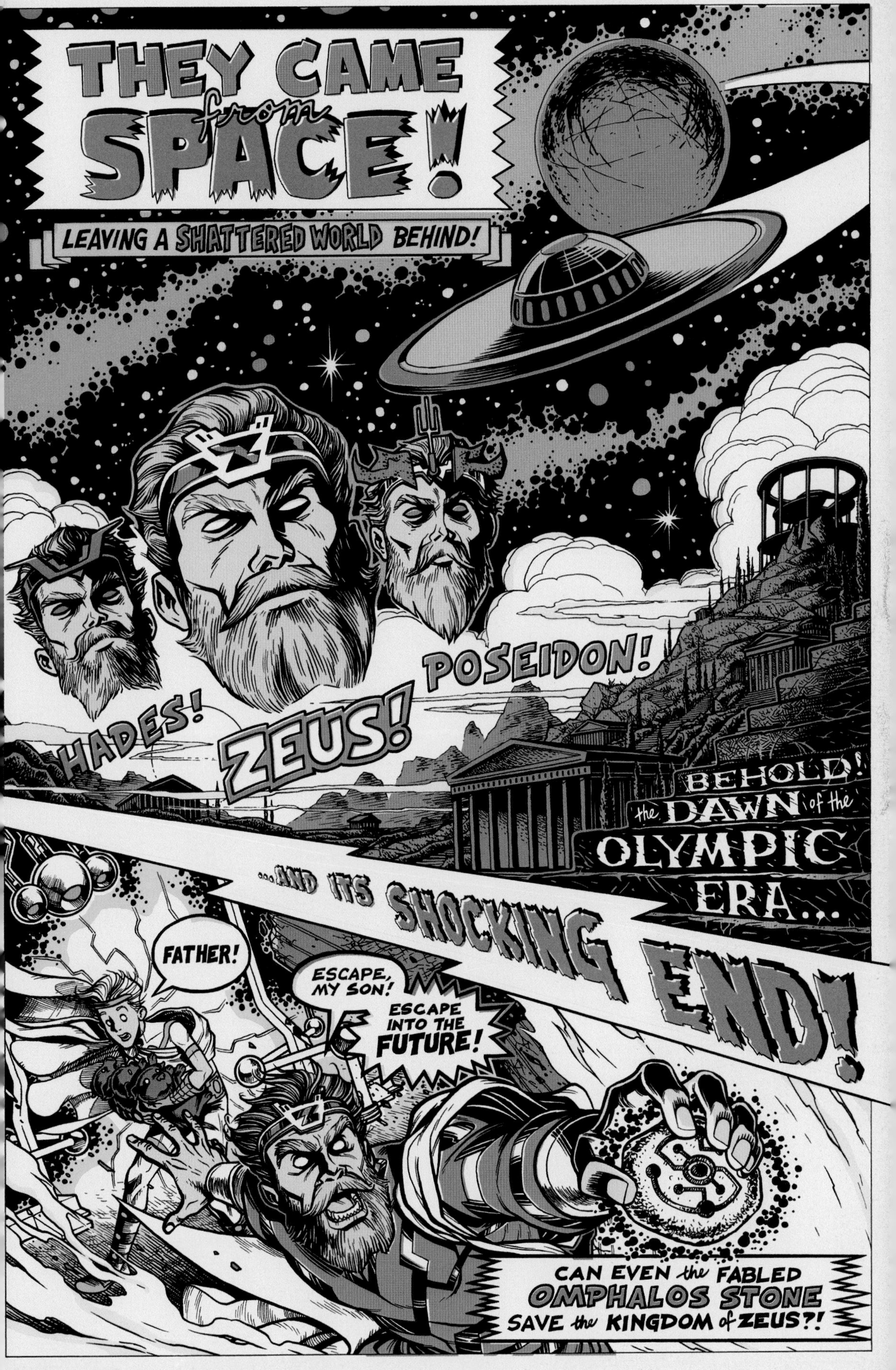
THEY CAME from SPACE!
LEAVING A SHATTERED WORLD BEHIND!
HADES!
ZEUS!
POSEIDON!
BEHOLD! the DAWN of the OLYMPIC ERA...
...AND ITS SHOCKING END!
FATHER!
ESCAPE, MY SON!
ESCAPE INTO THE FUTURE!
CAN EVEN the FABLED OMPHALOS STONE SAVE the KINGDOM of ZEUS?!

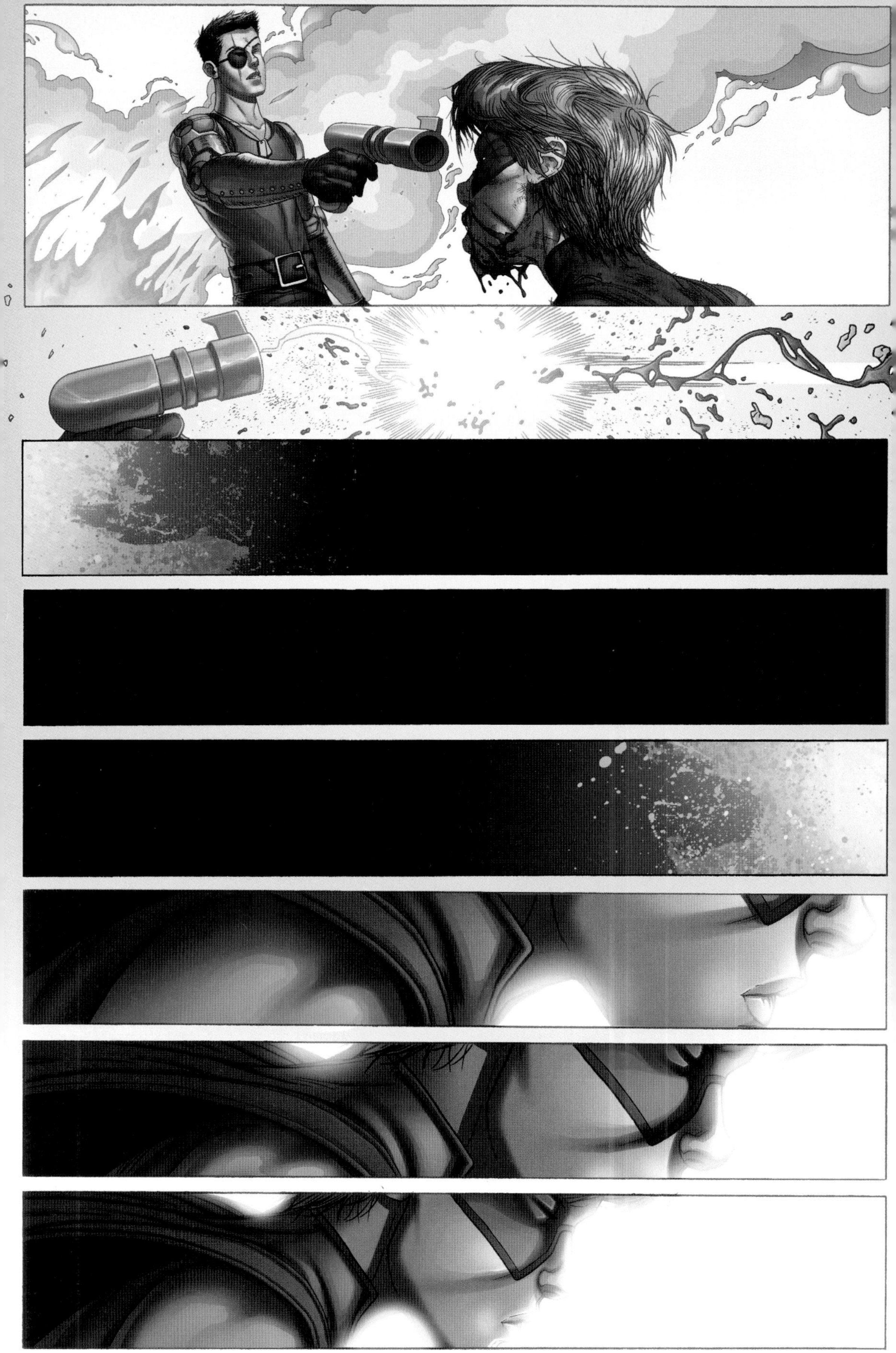

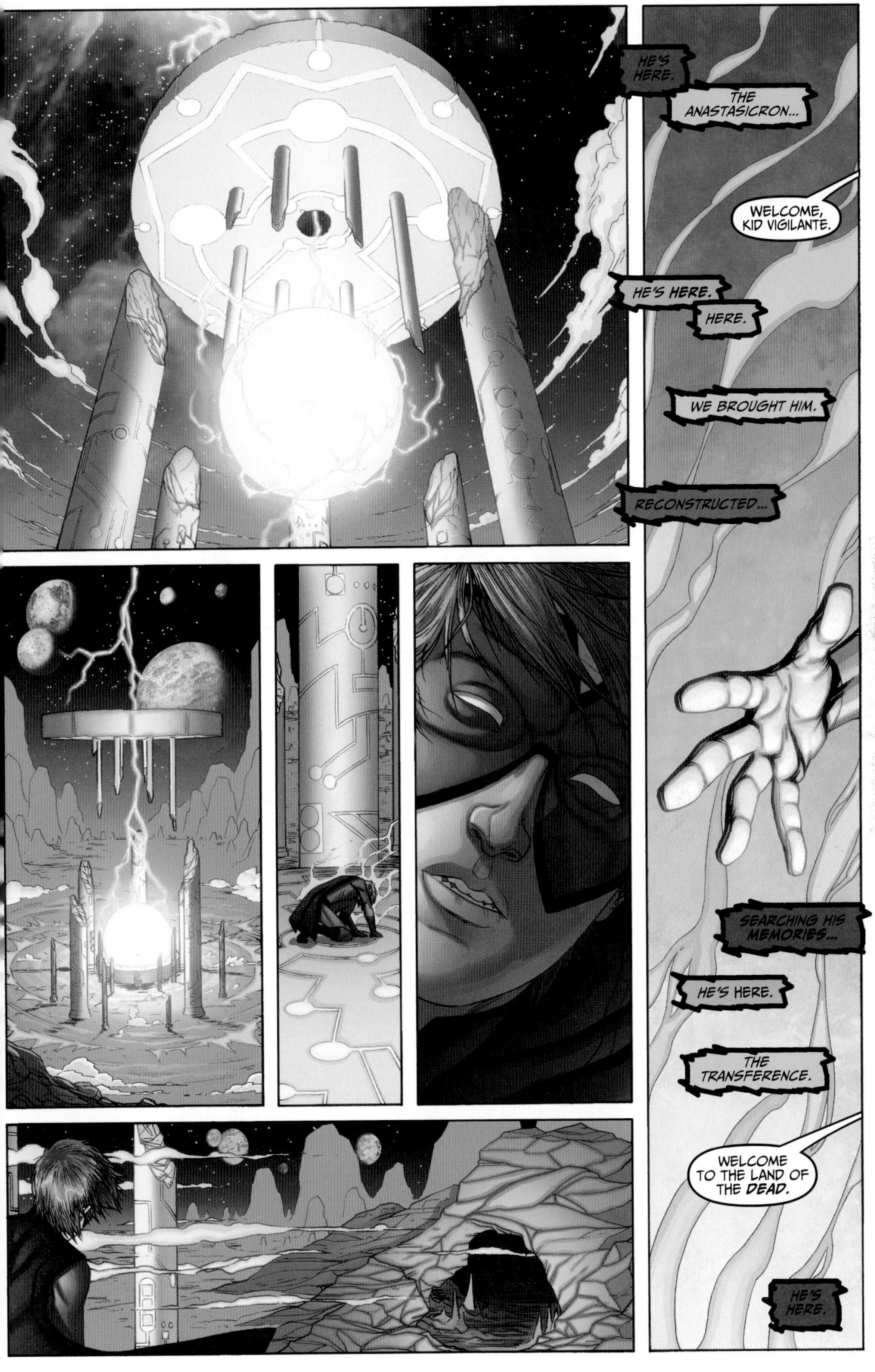
HE'S HERE.
THE ANASTASICRON...
WELCOME, KID VIGILANTE.
HE'S HERE.
HERE.
WE BROUGHT HIM.
RECONSTRUCTED...
SEARCHING HIS MEMORIES...
HE'S HERE.
THE TRANSFERENCE.
WELCOME TO THE LAND OF THE DEAD.
HE'S HERE.

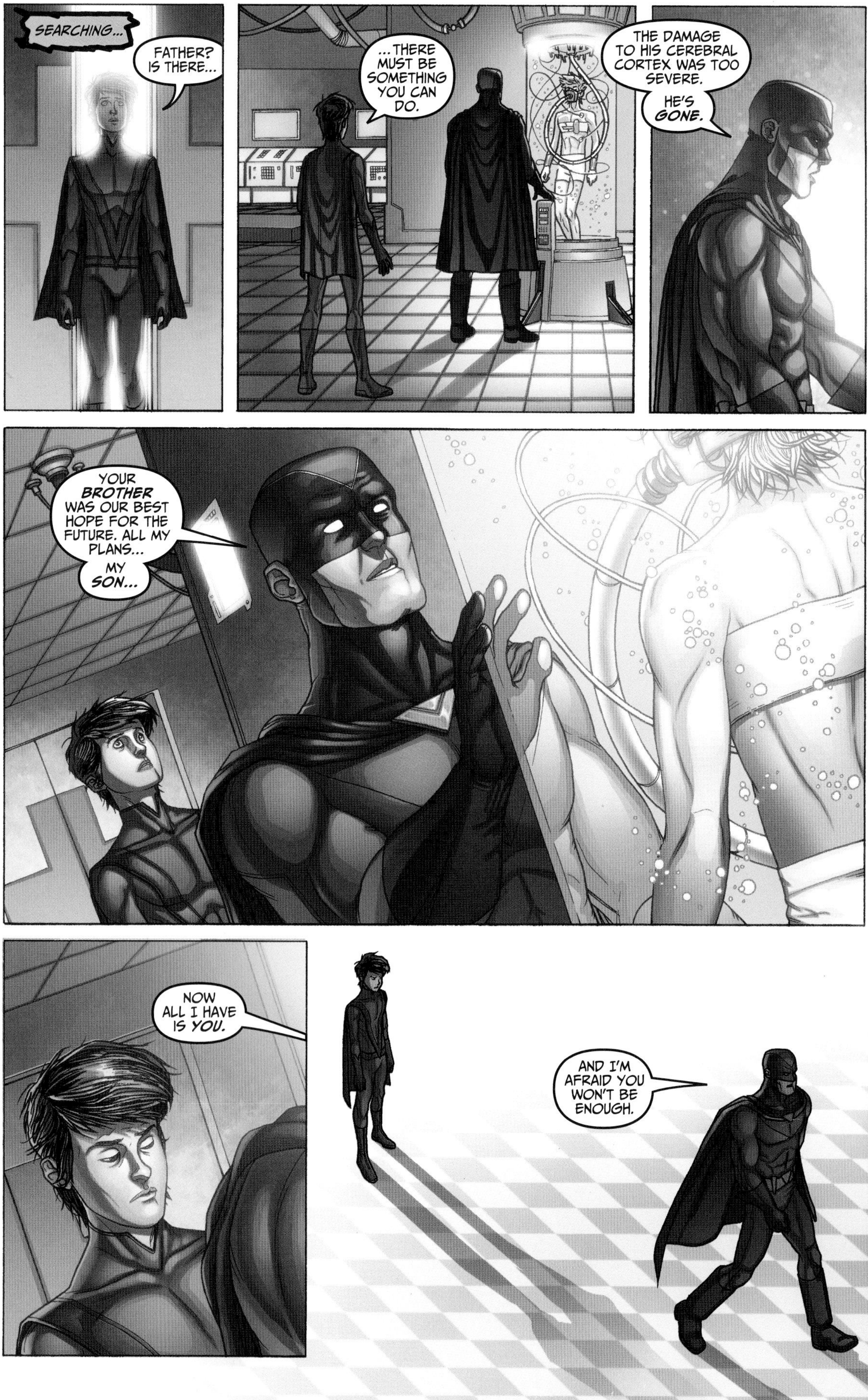
SEARCHING...
FATHER? IS THERE...
...THERE MUST BE SOMETHING YOU CAN DO.
THE DAMAGE TO HIS CEREBRAL CORTEX WAS TOO SEVERE.
HE'S GONE.
YOUR BROTHER WAS OUR BEST HOPE FOR THE FUTURE. ALL MY PLANS...
MY SON...
NOW ALL I HAVE IS YOU.
AND I'M AFRAID YOU WON'T BE ENOUGH.

KID VIGILANTE.

I KNOW YOU CAN HEAR ME.

DID YOU THINK DEATH WOULD PROTECT YOU FROM MY WRATH?

PERHAPS *NOW* YOU UNDERSTAND THE TRUE POWER AT MY DISPOSAL.

YOUR LIFE. YOUR DEATH. YOU EXIST ONLY AS LONG AS *I* WILL IT.

YOU SHOULD BE ON YOUR KNEES! *BEGGING* ME FOR MERCY! *PLEADING* FOR FORGIVENESS!

DO SO AND I *MIGHT* SPARE YOU THE ETERNAL SUFFERING OF TARTARUS.

DON'T YOU *UNDERSTAND?*

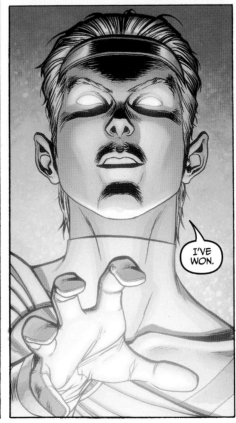

I'VE WON.

AND YOU...

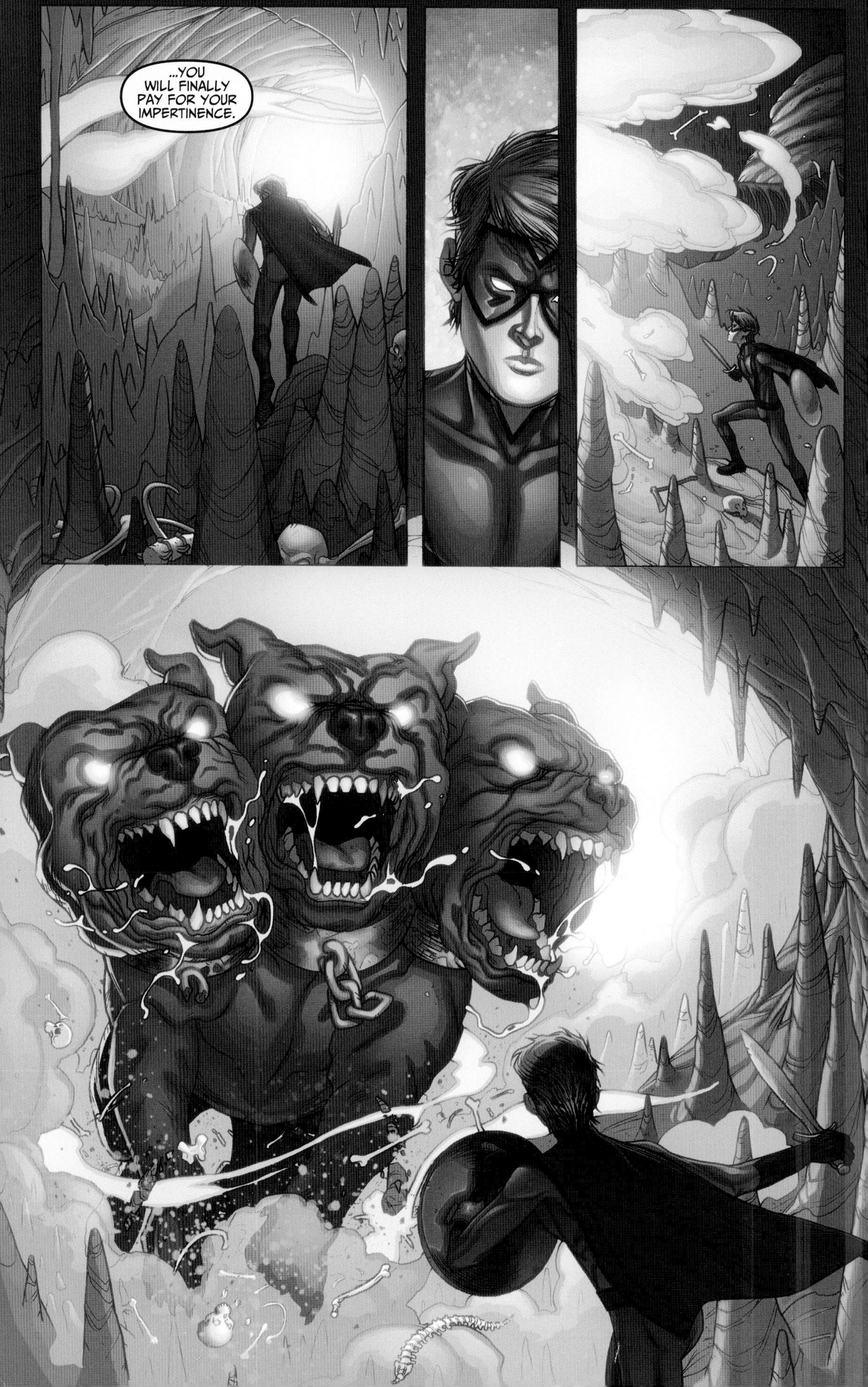
...YOU WILL FINALLY PAY FOR YOUR IMPERTINENCE.

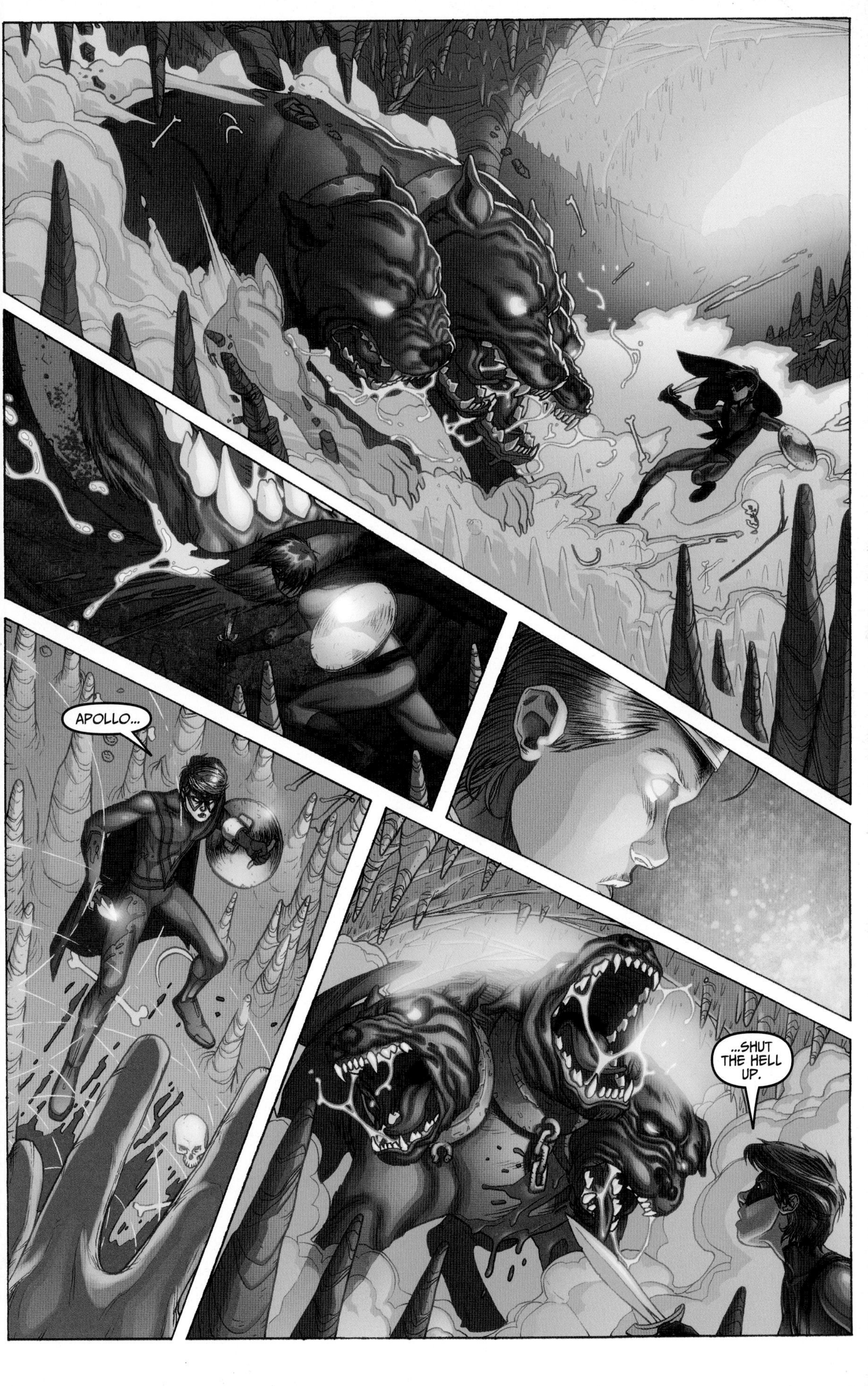
APOLLO...
...SHUT THE HELL UP.

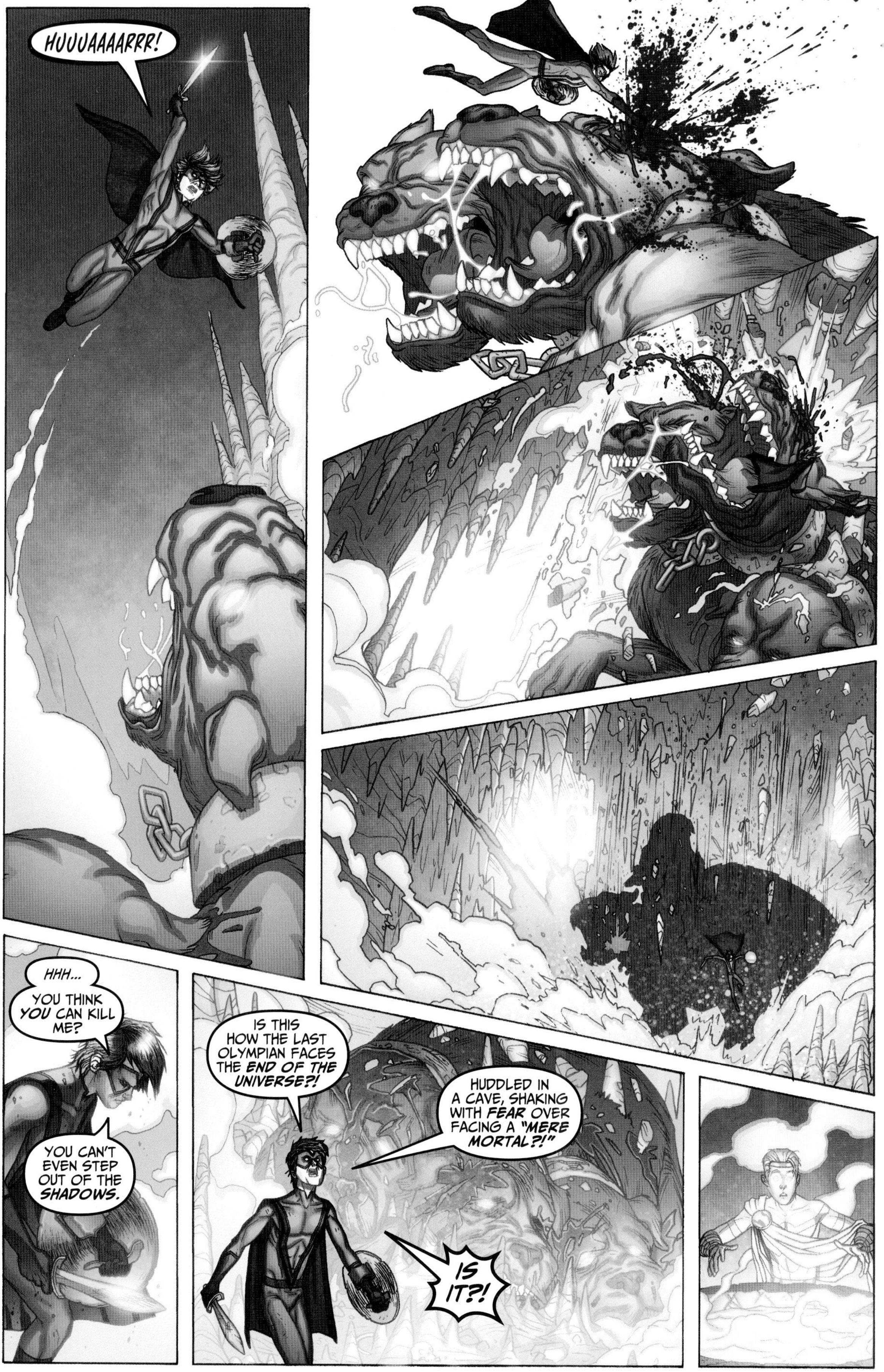
HUUUAAAARRR!
HHH... YOU THINK YOU CAN KILL ME?
YOU CAN'T EVEN STEP OUT OF THE SHADOWS.
IS THIS HOW THE LAST OLYMPIAN FACES THE END OF THE UNIVERSE?!
HUDDLED IN A CAVE, SHAKING WITH FEAR OVER FACING A "MERE MORTAL?!"
IS IT?!

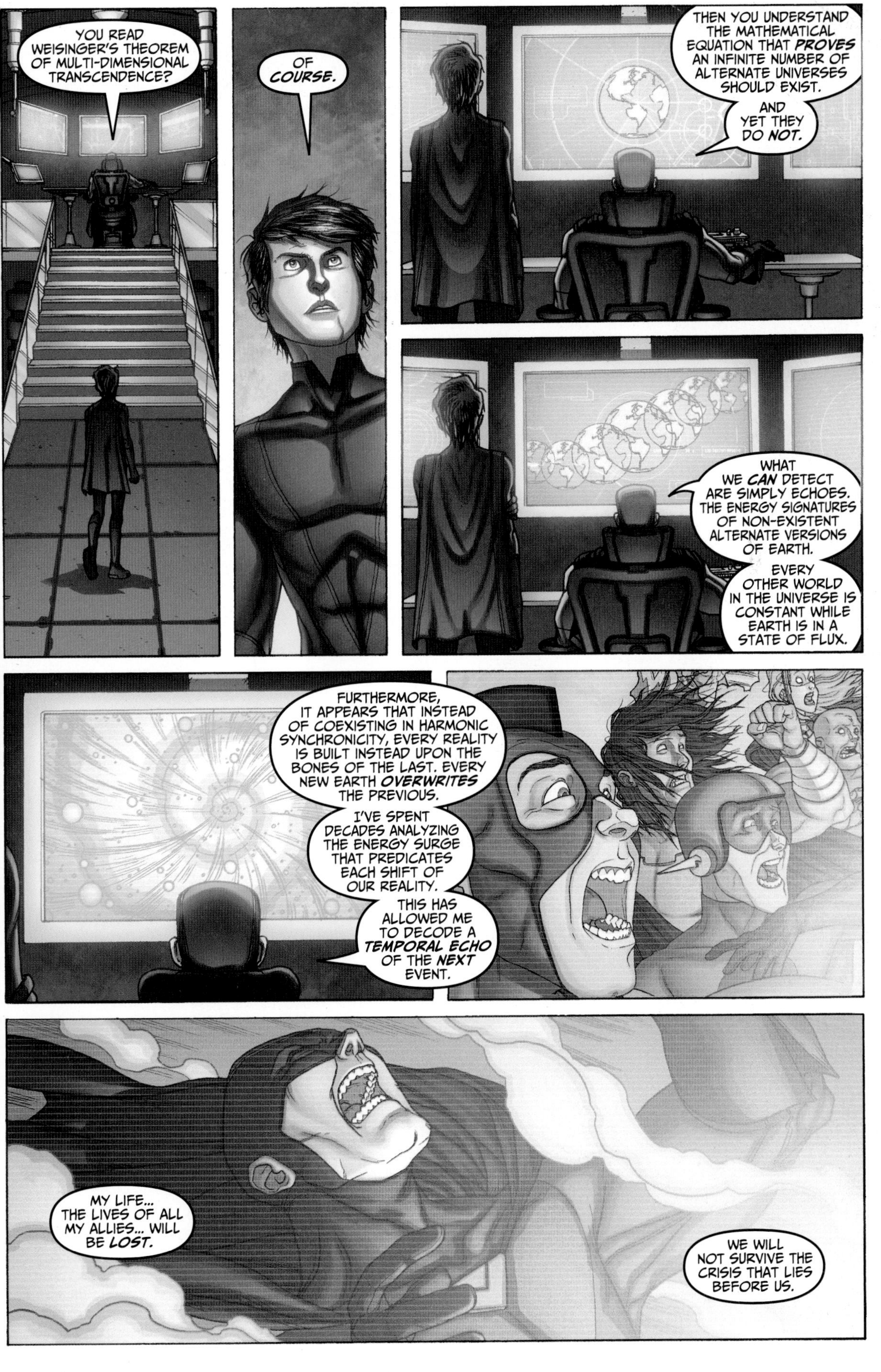
YOU READ WEISINGER'S THEOREM OF MULTI-DIMENSIONAL TRANSCENDENCE?
OF *COURSE.*
THEN YOU UNDERSTAND THE MATHEMATICAL EQUATION THAT *PROVES* AN INFINITE NUMBER OF ALTERNATE UNIVERSES SHOULD EXIST.
AND YET THEY DO *NOT.*
WHAT WE *CAN* DETECT ARE SIMPLY ECHOES. THE ENERGY SIGNATURES OF NON-EXISTENT ALTERNATE VERSIONS OF EARTH.
EVERY OTHER WORLD IN THE UNIVERSE IS CONSTANT WHILE EARTH IS IN A STATE OF FLUX.
FURTHERMORE, IT APPEARS THAT INSTEAD OF COEXISTING IN HARMONIC SYNCHRONICITY, EVERY REALITY IS BUILT INSTEAD UPON THE BONES OF THE LAST. EVERY NEW EARTH *OVERWRITES* THE PREVIOUS.
I'VE SPENT DECADES ANALYZING THE ENERGY SURGE THAT PREDICATES EACH SHIFT OF OUR REALITY.
THIS HAS ALLOWED ME TO DECODE A *TEMPORAL ECHO* OF THE *NEXT* EVENT.
MY LIFE... THE LIVES OF ALL MY ALLIES... WILL BE *LOST.*
WE WILL NOT SURVIVE THE CRISIS THAT LIES BEFORE US.

NOT MUCH ELSE CAME THROUGH... BUT THERE WAS ENOUGH DATA TO ALLOW A *FEW* DEDUCTIONS.

THE ENERGY CASCADE THAT WILL CONSUME ME IS A FORM OF CHRONALLY-CHARGED ANTI-MATTER...

I'VE BEEN ABLE TO TRACE THE ENERGY SIGNATURE *BACKWARDS* IN TIME AS FAR AS OCTOBER OF 1956.

THE DAY THAT TOKYO WAS MINIATURIZED AND THE WAR *ENDED.*

BETWEEN THEN AND NOW, THIS FLUCTUATION OF ANTI-MATTER HAS APPEARED AT LEAST *FIFTY ONE* TIMES.

BUT EACH TIME IT APPEARS, ITS EFFECT INCREASES EXPONENTIALLY.

AT THIS RATE, THE ENERGY LEVEL WILL REACH A CRITICAL STAGE WITHIN FOUR MONTHS *AFTER* MY DEATH.

WHICH MEANS THAT IT WILL NO LONGER BE CONTAINED TO OUR WORLD. IT WILL ENGULF THE ENTIRE *UNIVERSE.*

EVERYTHING AND *EVERYONE* WILL CEASE TO EXIST.

YOU'RE GOING TO DIE...?

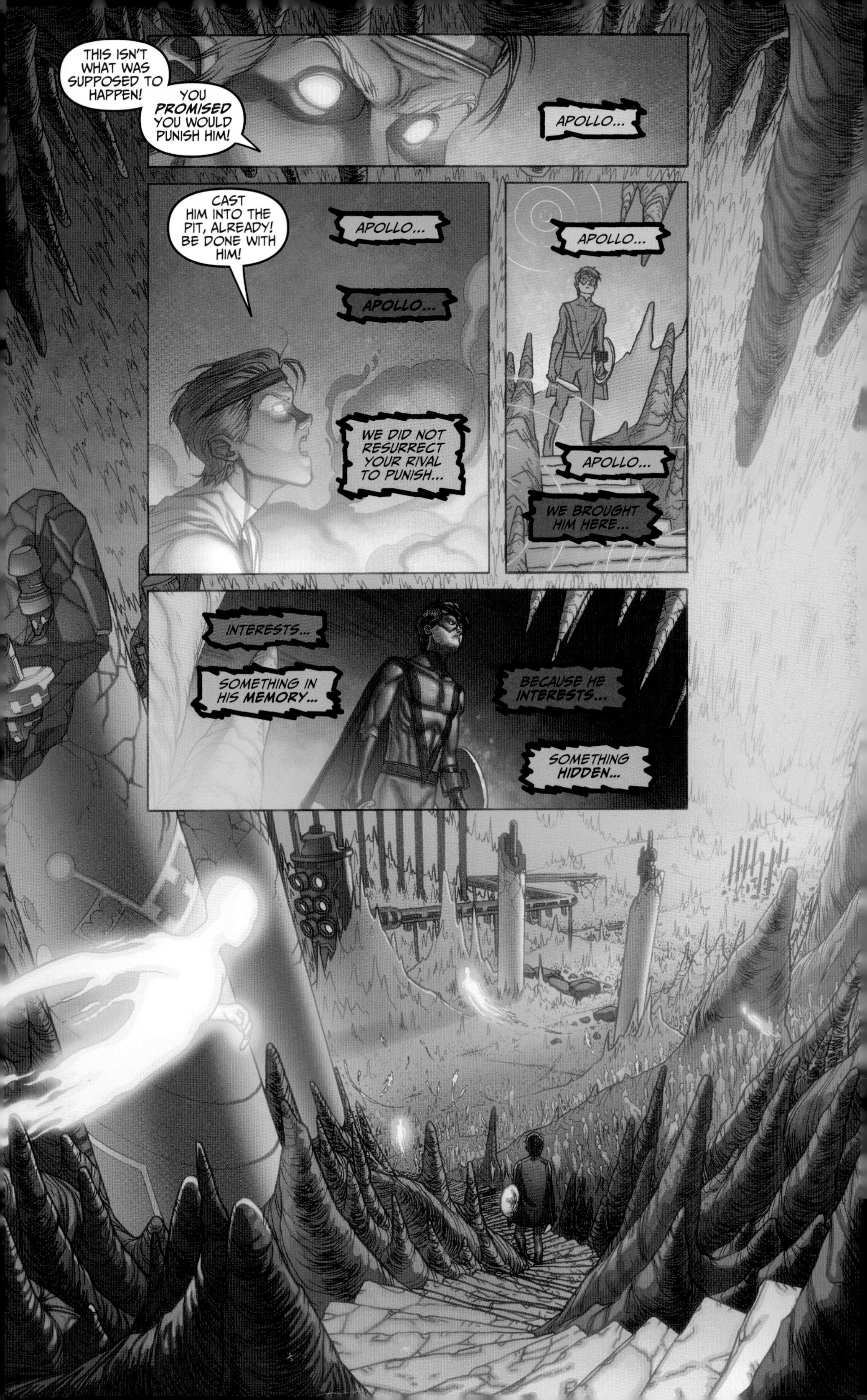
THIS ISN'T WHAT WAS SUPPOSED TO HAPPEN!
YOU PROMISED YOU WOULD PUNISH HIM!
APOLLO...
CAST HIM INTO THE PIT, ALREADY! BE DONE WITH HIM!
APOLLO...
APOLLO...
WE DID NOT RESURRECT YOUR RIVAL TO PUNISH...
APOLLO...
APOLLO...
WE BROUGHT HIM HERE...
INTERESTS...
SOMETHING IN HIS MEMORY...
BECAUSE HE INTERESTS...
SOMETHING HIDDEN...

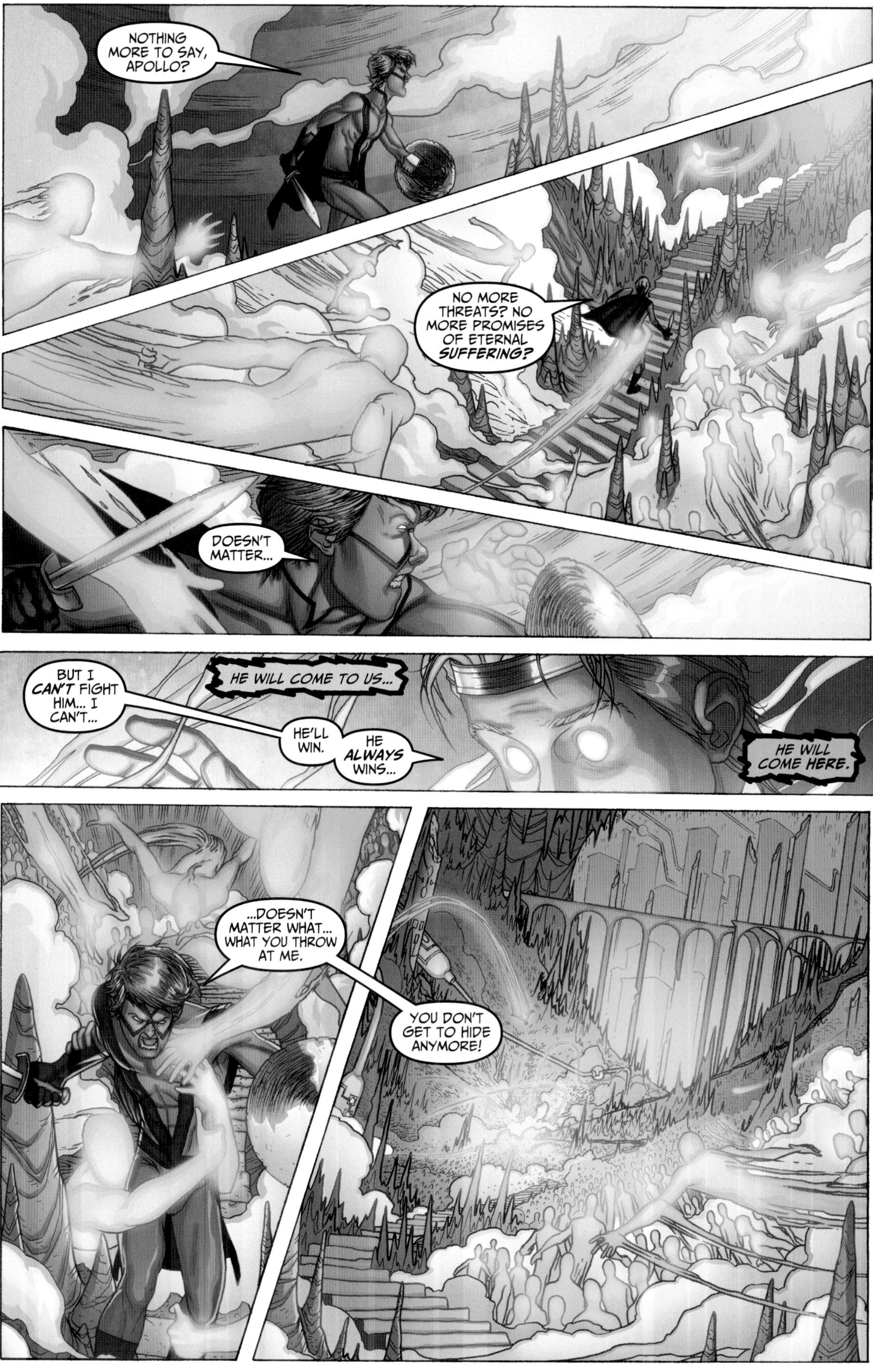

NOTHING MORE TO SAY, APOLLO?
NO MORE THREATS? NO MORE PROMISES OF ETERNAL SUFFERING?
DOESN'T MATTER...
BUT I CAN'T FIGHT HIM... I CAN'T...
HE WILL COME TO US...
HE'LL WIN.
HE ALWAYS WINS...
HE WILL COME HERE.
...DOESN'T MATTER WHAT... WHAT YOU THROW AT ME.
YOU DON'T GET TO HIDE ANYMORE!

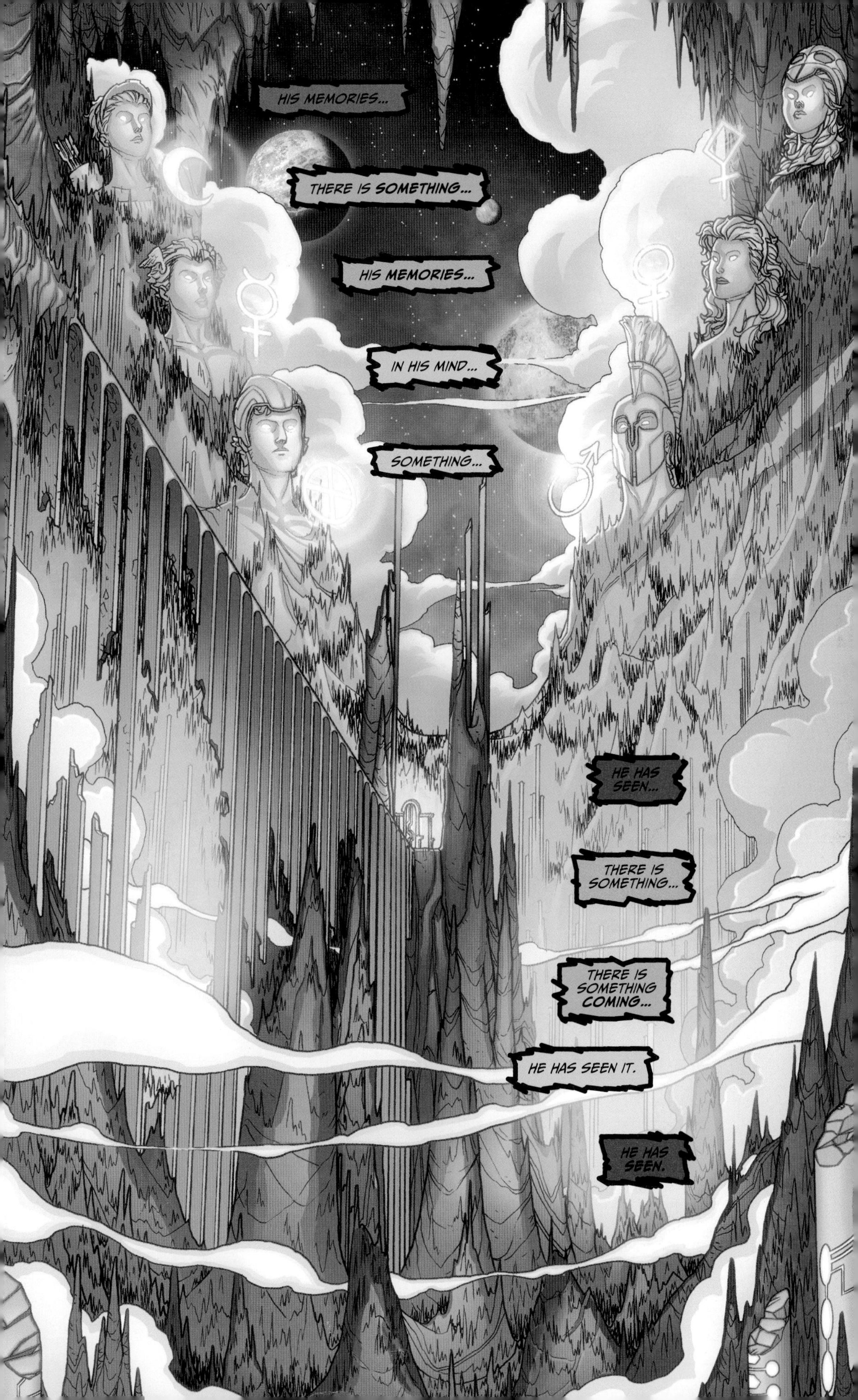
HIS MEMORIES...
THERE IS SOMETHING...
HIS MEMORIES...
IN HIS MIND...
SOMETHING...
HE HAS SEEN...
THERE IS SOMETHING...
THERE IS SOMETHING COMING...
HE HAS SEEN IT.
HE HAS SEEN.

AS YOU'VE ALREADY SEEN, THE ANTI-MATTER WAVE IS STRONG ENOUGH THAT IT IS SENDING TEMPORAL ECHOES *BACKWARDS* THROUGH THE TIME STREAM.

IT TOOK YEARS, BUT I WAS ABLE TO MODIFY A HUMAN BRAIN IN UTERO, SO THAT IT COULD *ABSORB* THIS ENERGY.

THIS WAS MEANT TO BE YOUR BROTHER'S MISSION. WHEN I CLONED YOU BOTH, *HIS* DNA WAS ALTERED; HIS BRAIN MUTATED SO THAT HE COULD *SLOWLY* PROCESS THE TEMPORAL DATA.

SINCE YOU'RE HIS TWIN, THE SAME CAN BE DONE FOR YOU, *BUT...*

YOUR CREATION WAS *NOT* INTENDED. YOUR MIND WILL NOT EASILY ADAPT TO THE INFLUX OF INFORMATION.

IT WILL TAKE YOU TIME. TIME *YOU WILL NOT HAVE.*

THIS IS THE ONLY WEAPON I CAN GIVE YOU TO FIGHT THE ONCOMING CRISIS: THE GIFT OF *FORESIGHT.*

YOU UNDERSTAND NOW WHAT IS AT STAKE. ARE YOU READY?

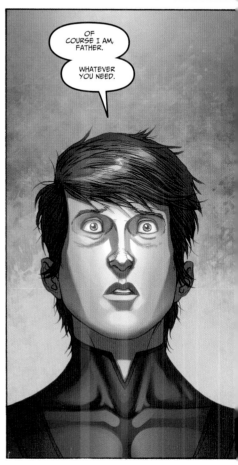

OF COURSE I AM, FATHER.

WHATEVER YOU NEED.

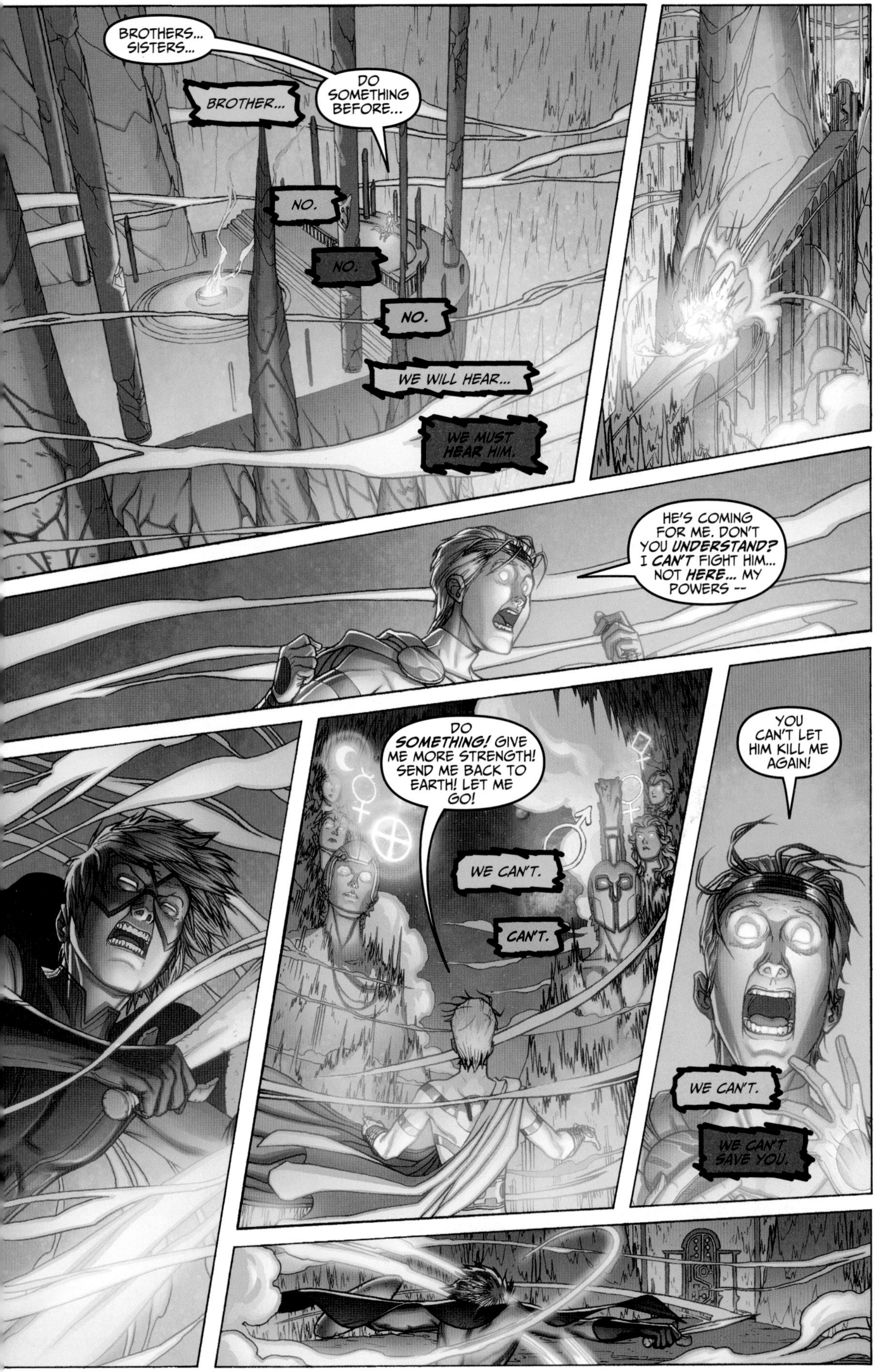
BROTHERS... SISTERS...
BROTHER...
DO SOMETHING BEFORE...
NO.
NO.
NO.
WE WILL HEAR...
WE MUST HEAR HIM.
HE'S COMING FOR ME. DON'T YOU UNDERSTAND? I CAN'T FIGHT HIM... NOT HERE... MY POWERS --
DO SOMETHING! GIVE ME MORE STRENGTH! SEND ME BACK TO EARTH! LET ME GO!
WE CAN'T.
CAN'T.
YOU CAN'T LET HIM KILL ME AGAIN!
WE CAN'T.
WE CAN'T SAVE YOU.

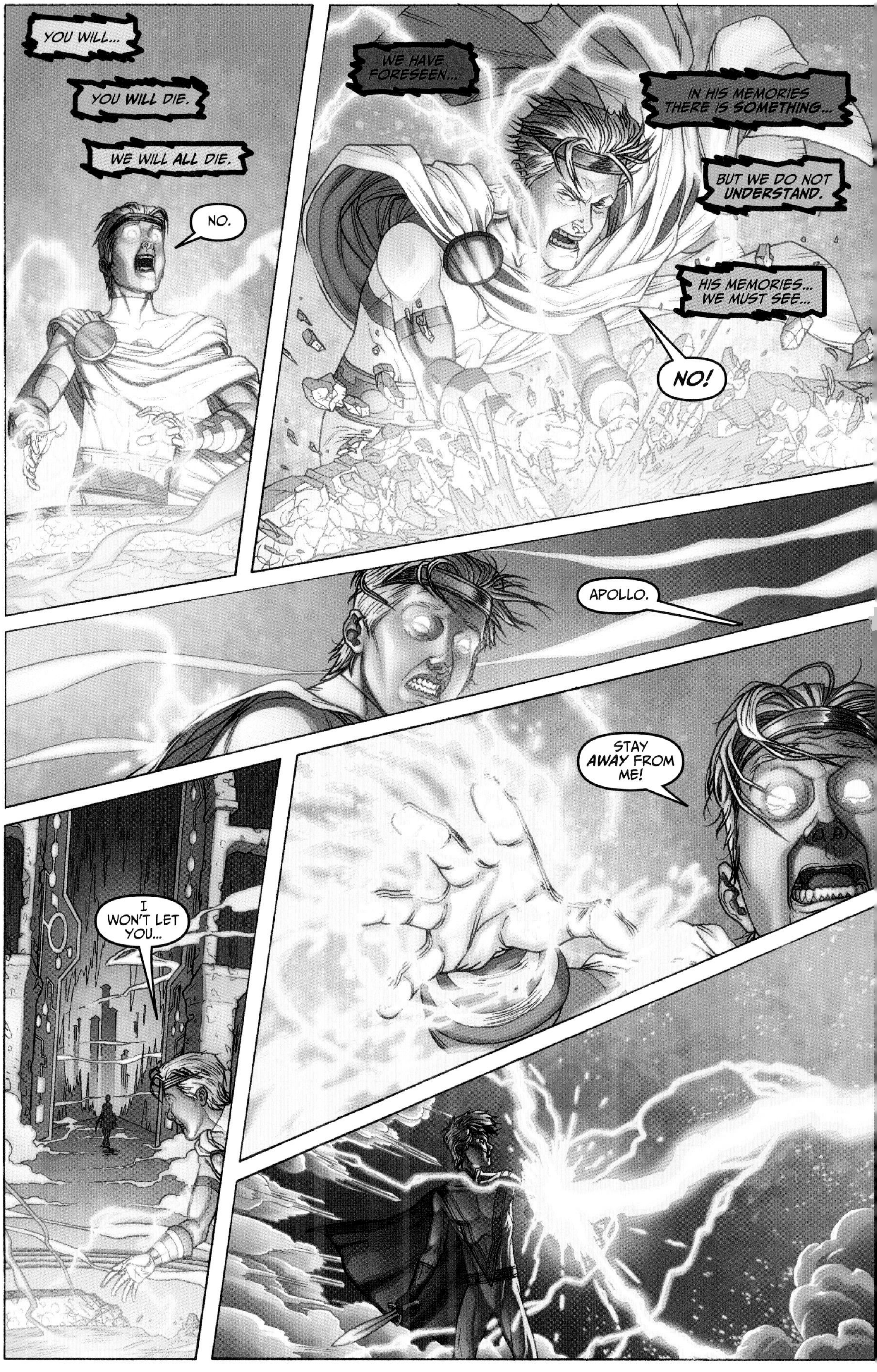
YOU WILL...
YOU WILL DIE.
WE WILL ALL DIE.
NO.
WE HAVE FORESEEN...
IN HIS MEMORIES THERE IS SOMETHING...
BUT WE DO NOT UNDERSTAND.
HIS MEMORIES... WE MUST SEE...
NO!
APOLLO.
STAY AWAY FROM ME!
I WON'T LET YOU...

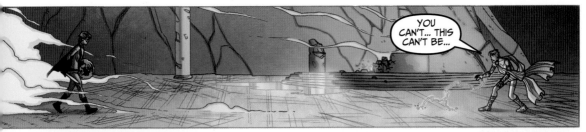

YOU CAN'T... THIS CAN'T BE...

STAY BACK...

PLEASE... ...I DON'T...

PLEASE...

...PLEASE DON'T HURT ME ANYMORE.

I DIDN'T COME HERE TO FIGHT YOU.

I CAME HERE TO SAVE YOU.

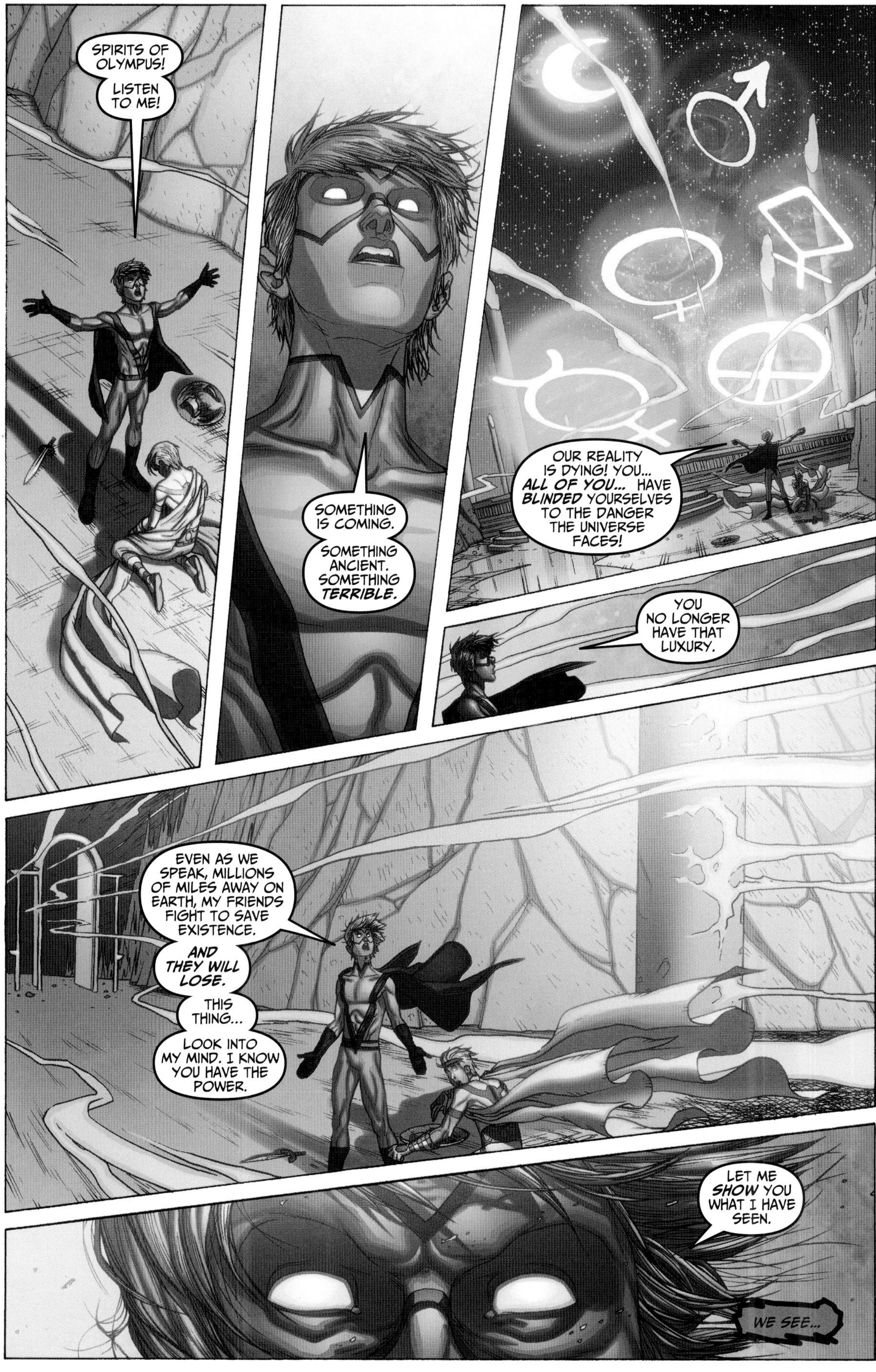
SPIRITS OF OLYMPUS!
LISTEN TO ME!
SOMETHING IS COMING.
SOMETHING ANCIENT. SOMETHING TERRIBLE.
OUR REALITY IS DYING! YOU... ALL OF YOU... HAVE BLINDED YOURSELVES TO THE DANGER THE UNIVERSE FACES!
YOU NO LONGER HAVE THAT LUXURY.
EVEN AS WE SPEAK, MILLIONS OF MILES AWAY ON EARTH, MY FRIENDS FIGHT TO SAVE EXISTENCE.
AND THEY WILL LOSE.
THIS THING...
LOOK INTO MY MIND. I KNOW YOU HAVE THE POWER.
LET ME SHOW YOU WHAT I HAVE SEEN.
WE SEE...

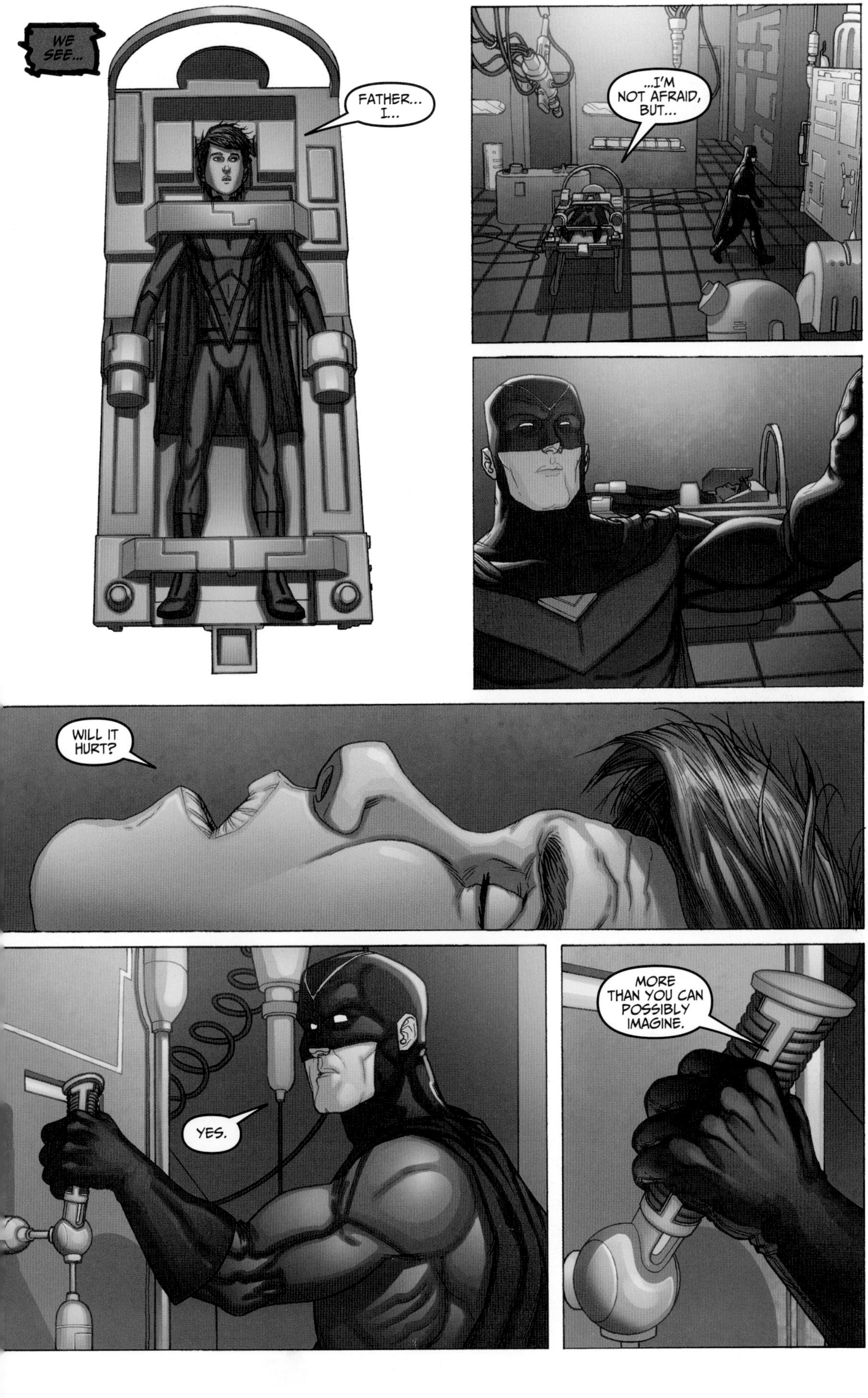
WE SEE...
FATHER... I...
...I'M NOT AFRAID, BUT...
WILL IT HURT?
YES.
MORE THAN YOU CAN POSSIBLY IMAGINE.

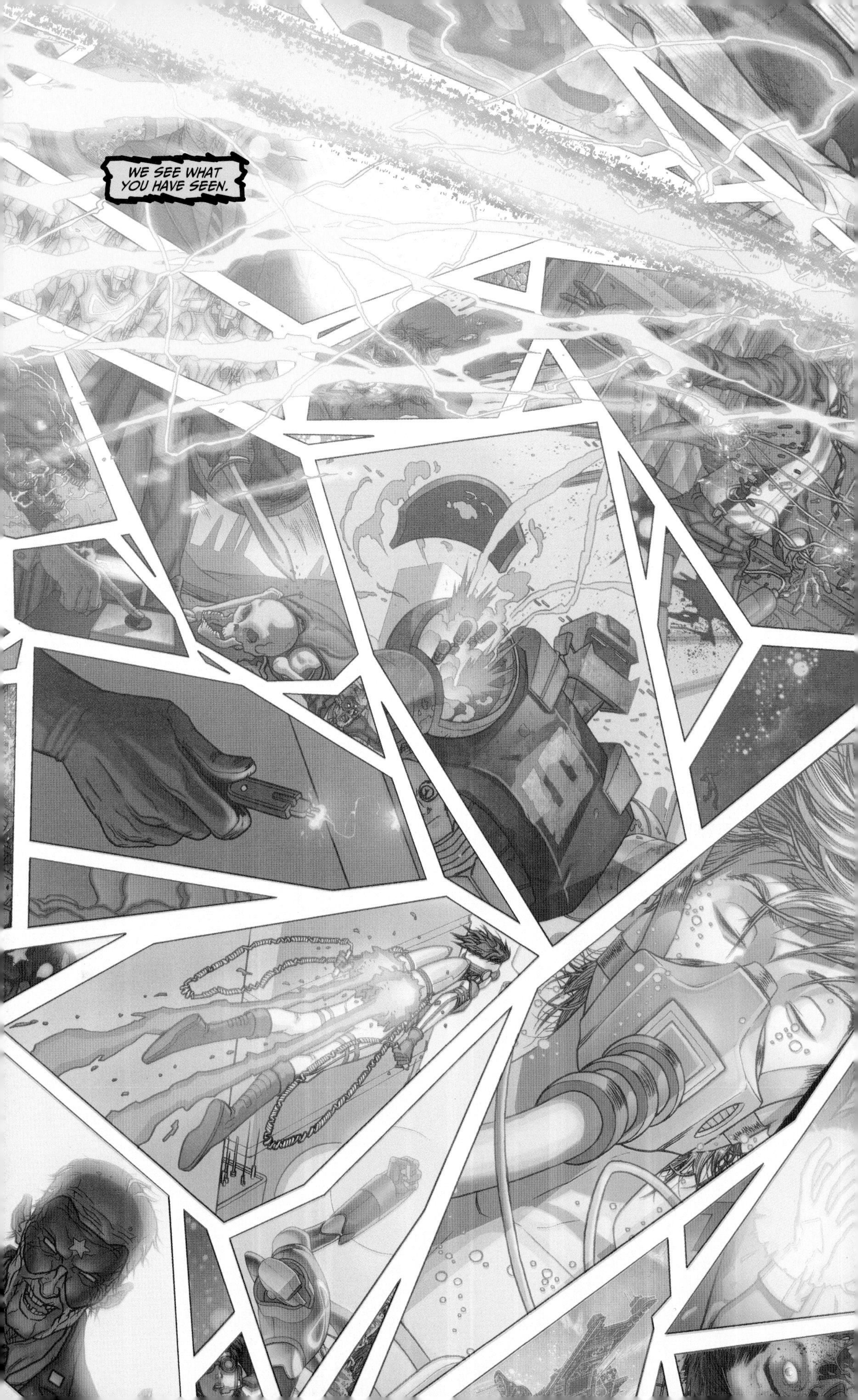
WE SEE WHAT YOU HAVE SEEN.

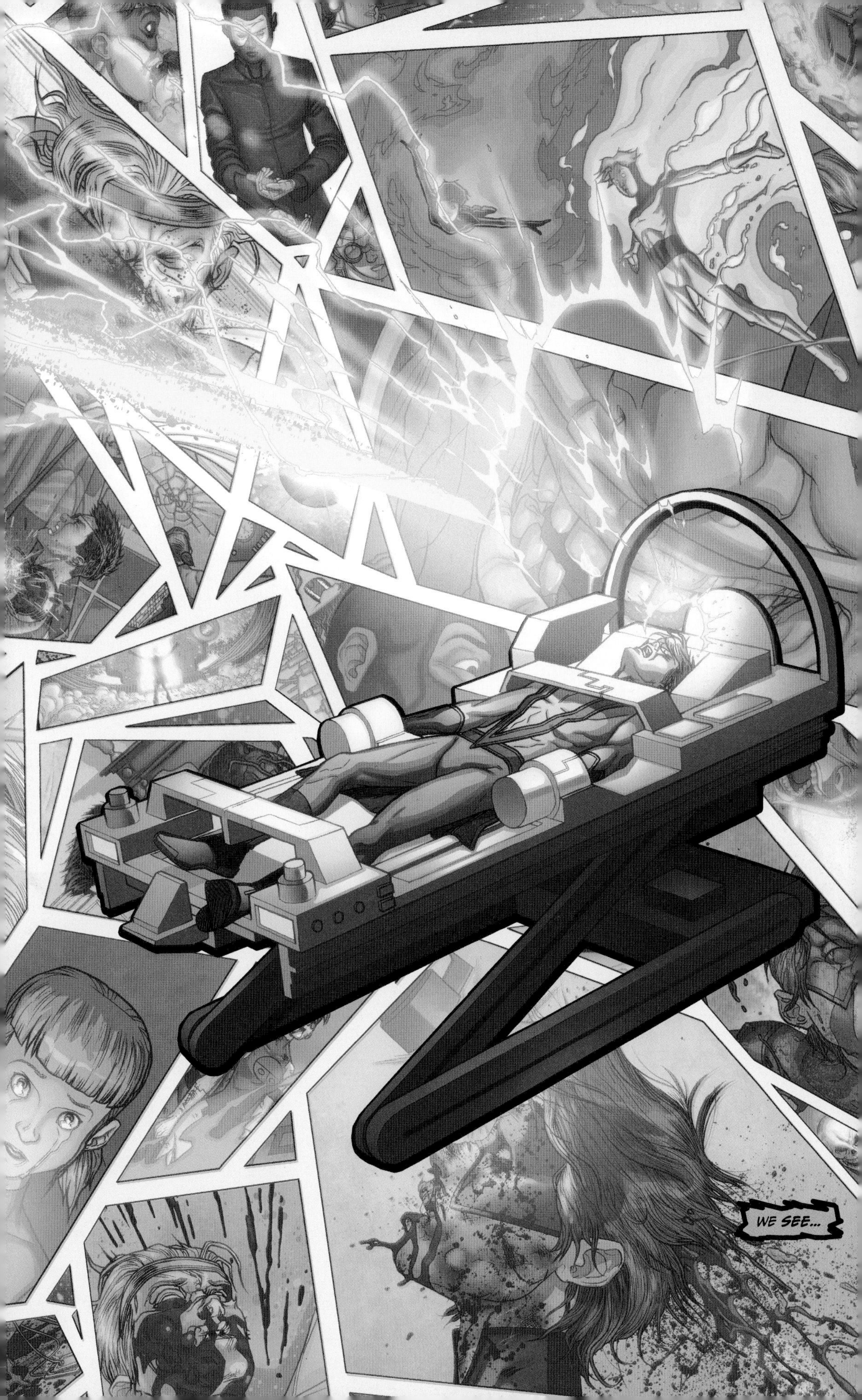
WE SEE...

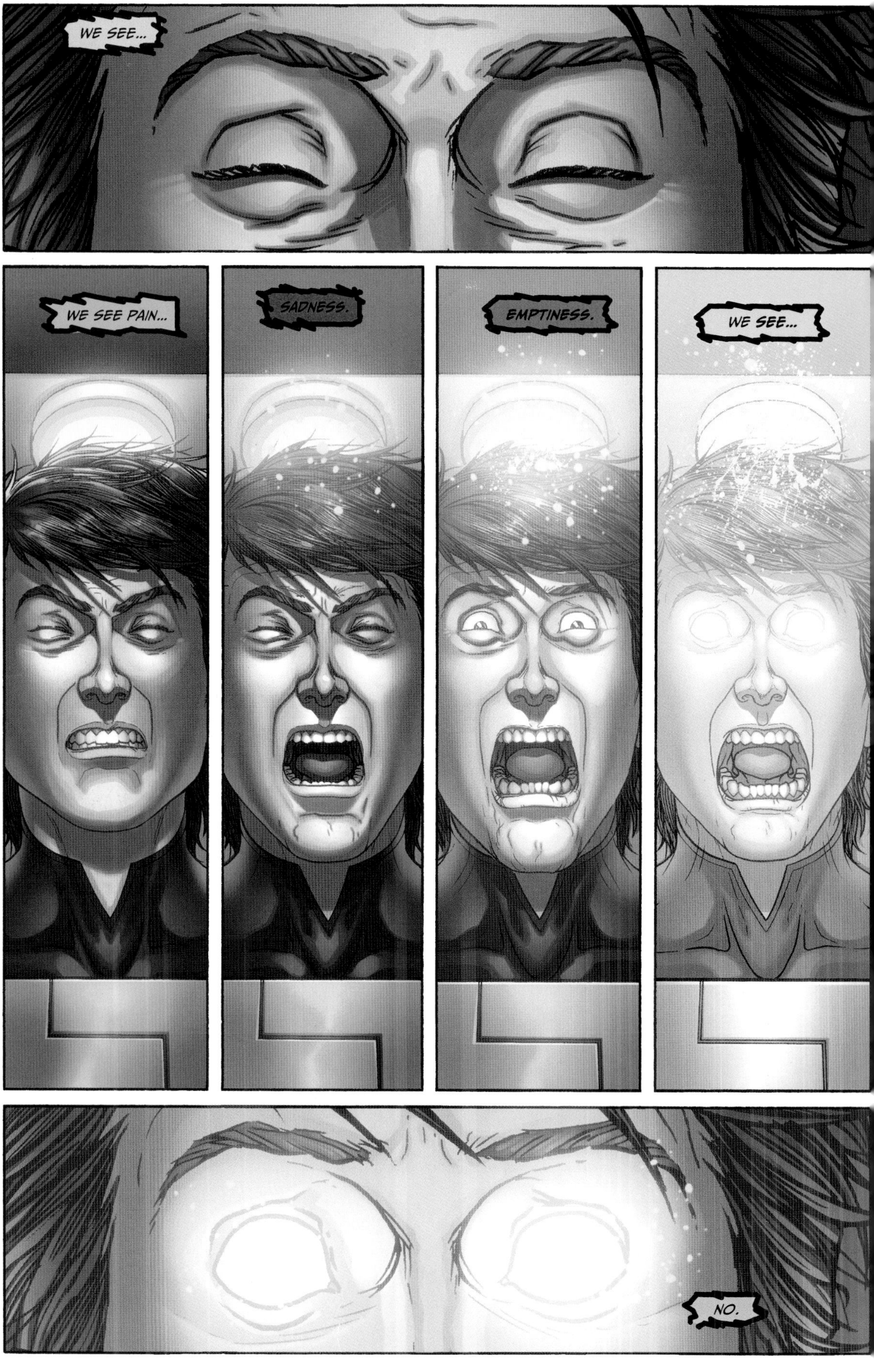
WE SEE...
WE SEE PAIN...
SADNESS.
EMPTINESS.
WE SEE...
NO.

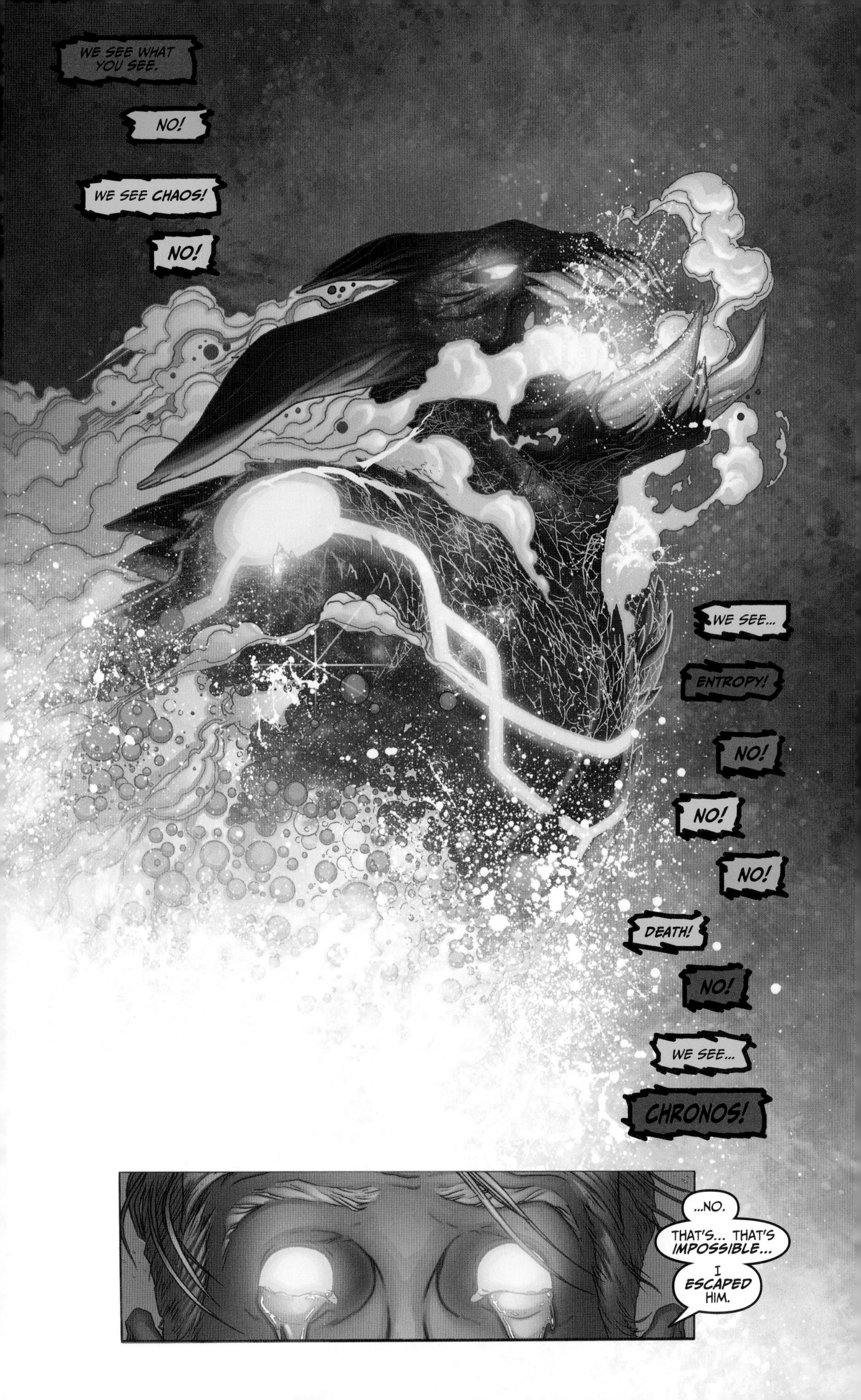
WE SEE WHAT YOU SEE.
NO!
WE SEE CHAOS!
NO!
WE SEE...
ENTROPY!
NO!
NO!
NO!
DEATH!
NO!
WE SEE...
CHRONOS!
...NO.
THAT'S... THAT'S IMPOSSIBLE...
I ESCAPED HIM.

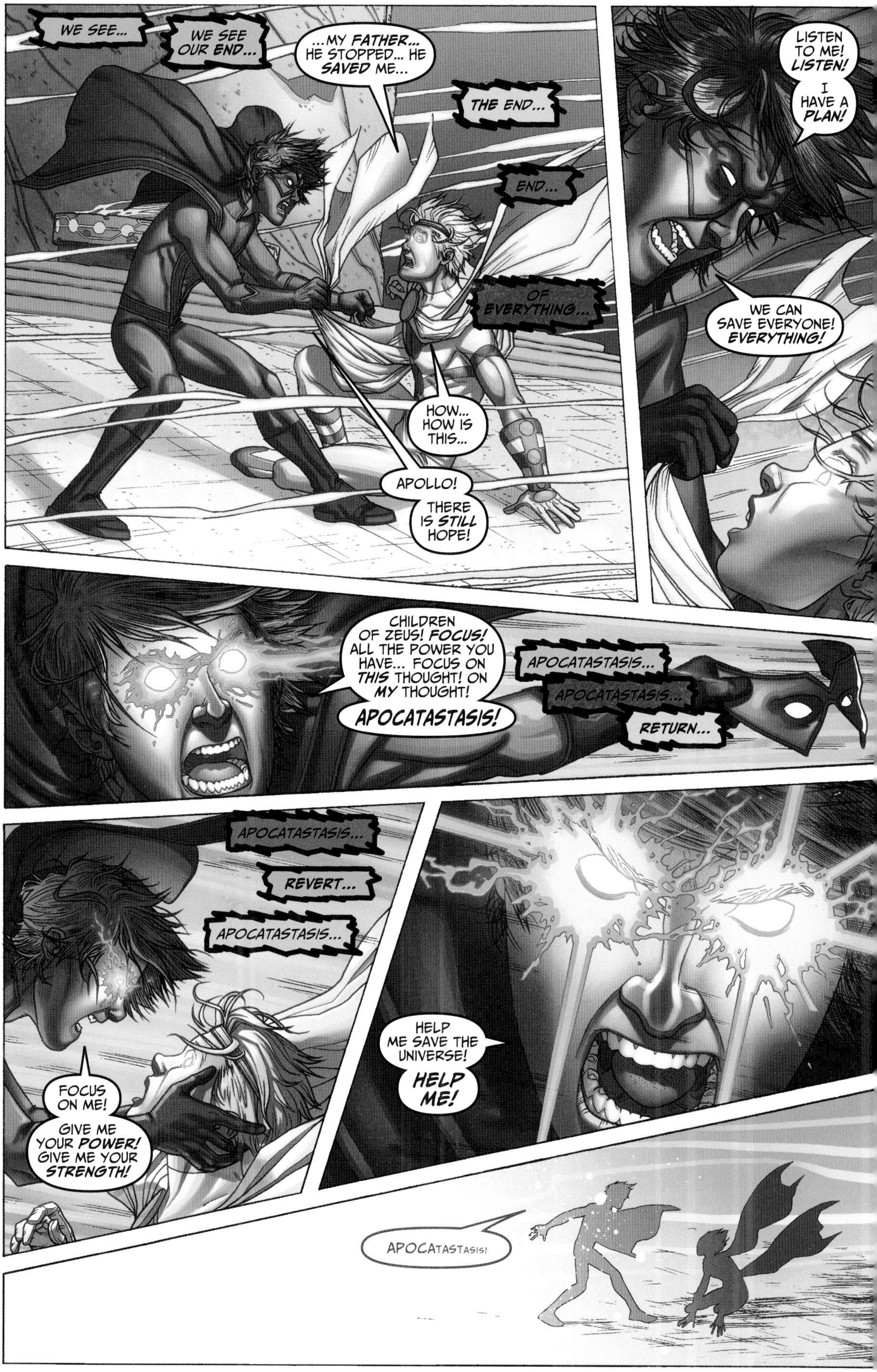
WE SEE...
WE SEE OUR END...
...MY FATHER... HE STOPPED... HE SAVED ME...
THE END...
END...
OF EVERYTHING...
HOW... HOW IS THIS...
APOLLO!
THERE IS STILL HOPE!
LISTEN TO ME! LISTEN!
I HAVE A PLAN!
WE CAN SAVE EVERYONE! EVERYTHING!
CHILDREN OF ZEUS! FOCUS! ALL THE POWER YOU HAVE... FOCUS ON THIS THOUGHT! ON MY THOUGHT!
APOCATASTASIS!
APOCATASTASIS...
APOCATASTASIS...
RETURN...
APOCATASTASIS...
REVERT...
APOCATASTASIS...
FOCUS ON ME!
GIVE ME YOUR POWER! GIVE ME YOUR STRENGTH!
HELP ME SAVE THE UNIVERSE!
HELP ME!
APOCATASTASIS!

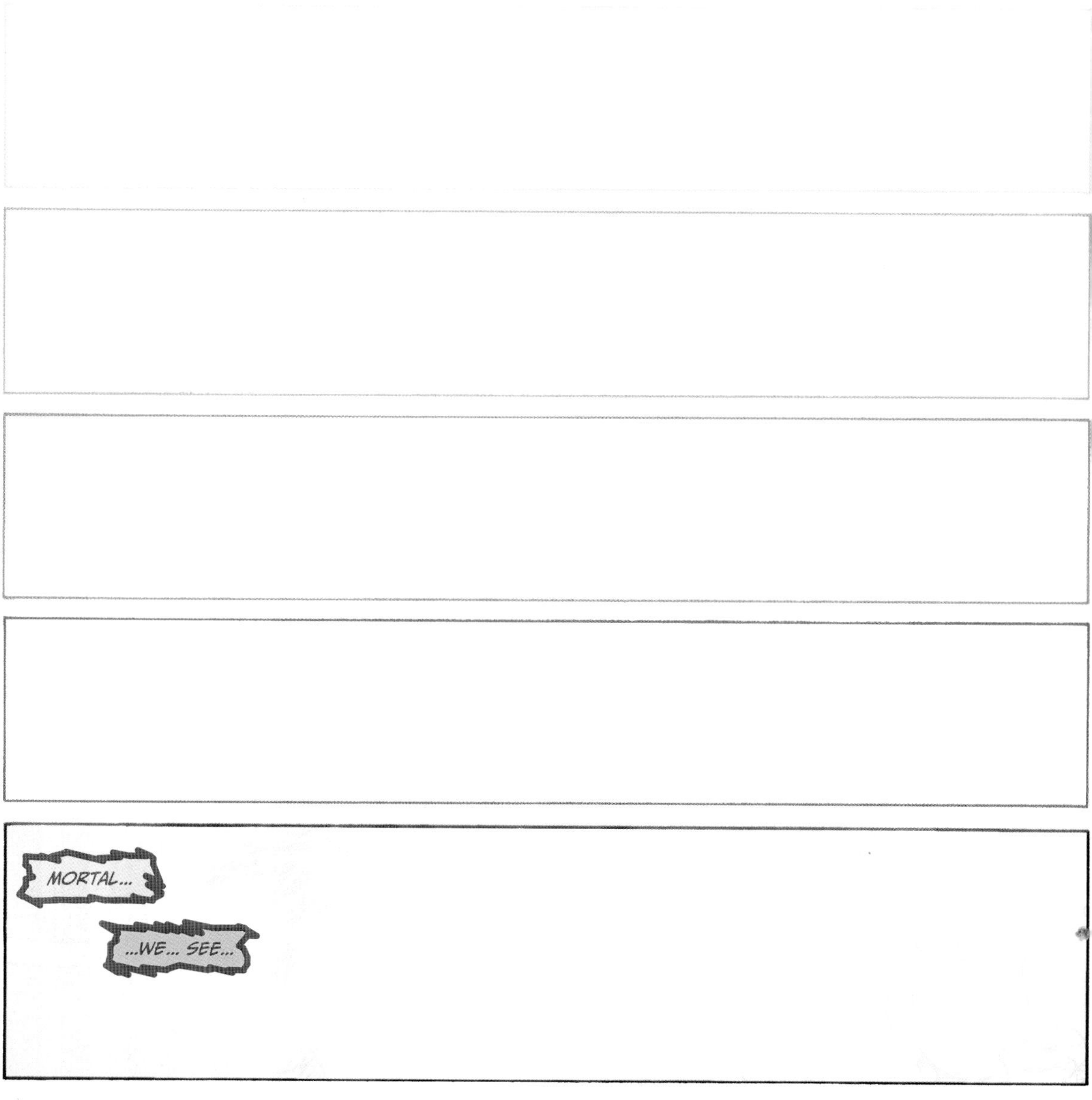
MORTAL...
...WE... SEE...

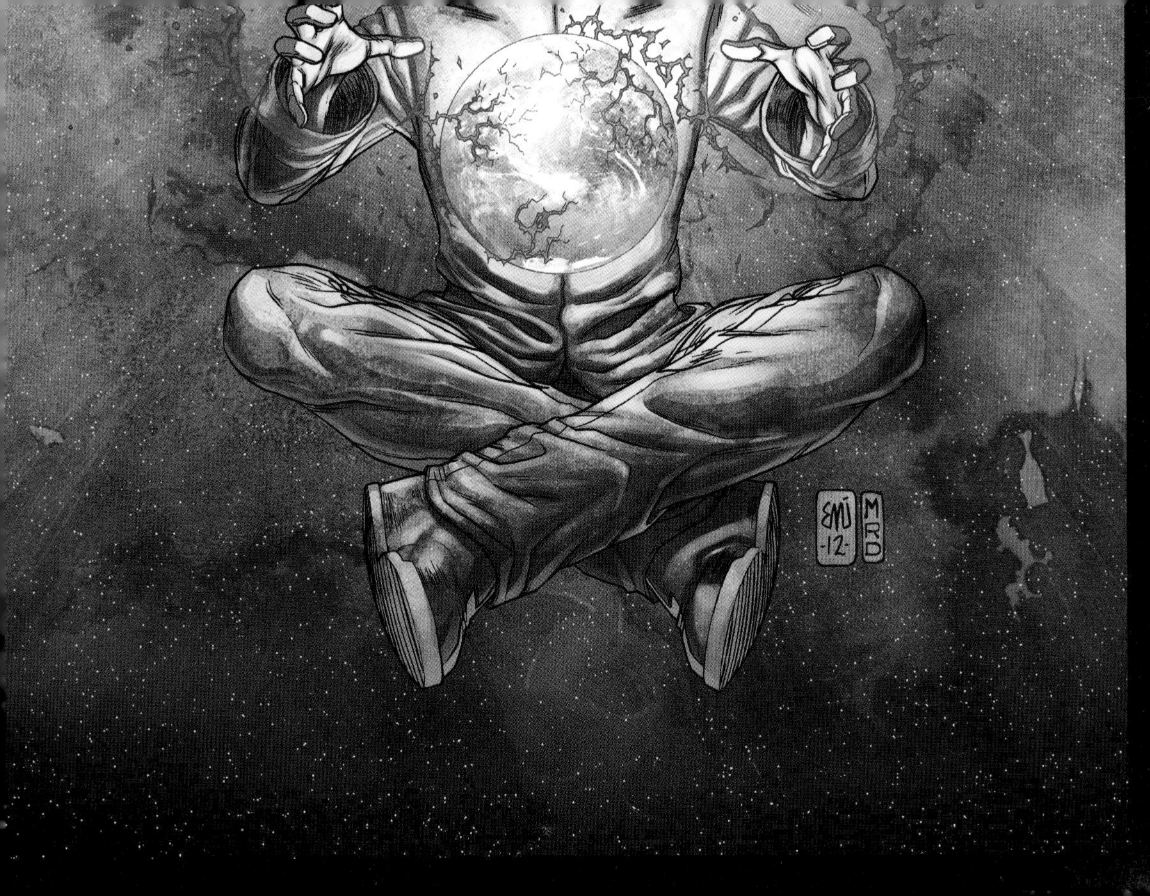
EMÜ -12-
MRD

Everything you remember is wrong.

Three months ago the universe was in deadly peril. Our mentors and our guardians and our parents... they were summoned to battle a great and terrible evil...

They left us in charge...

...and we died.

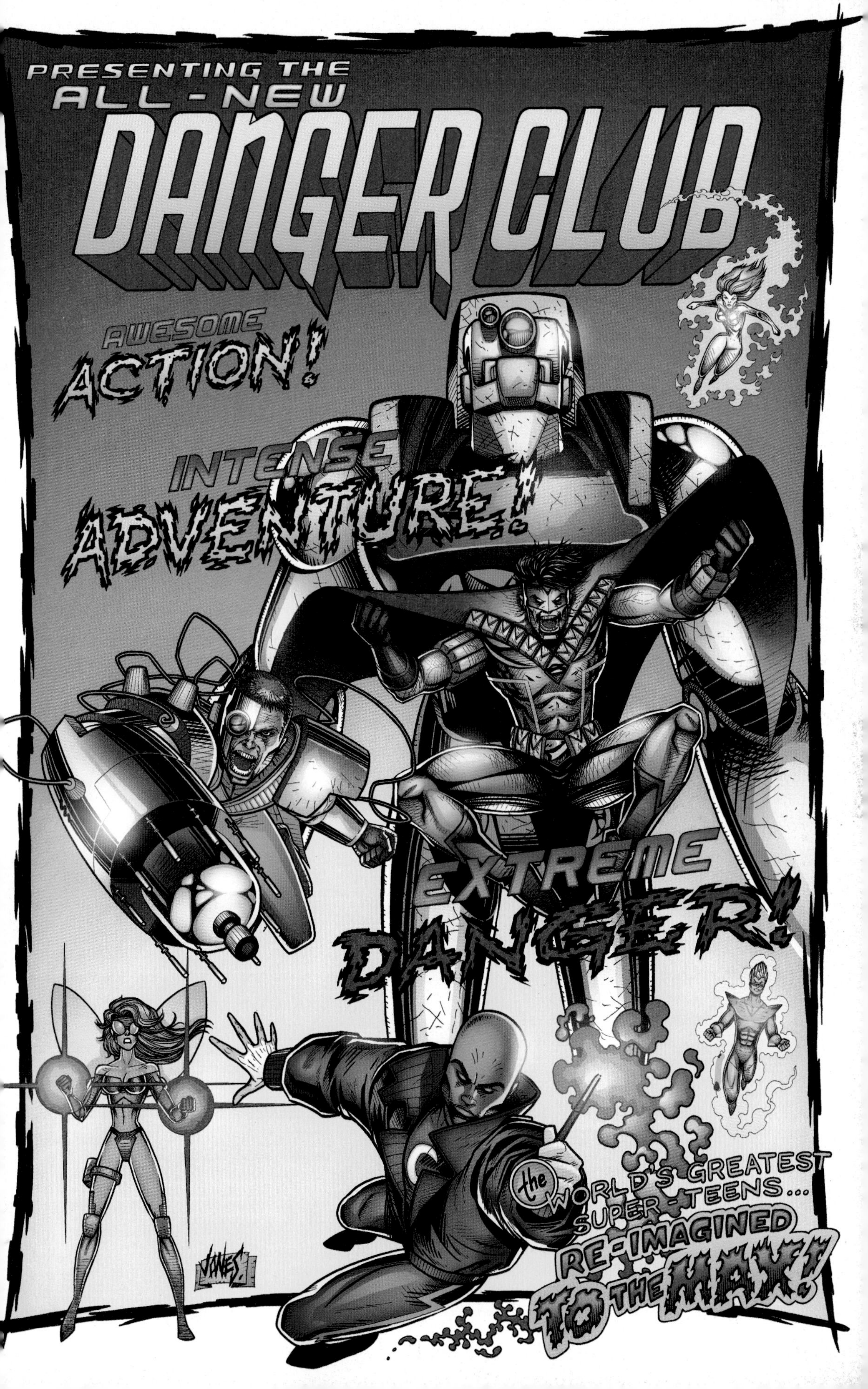

PRESENTING THE
ALL-NEW
DANGER CLUB
AWESOME
ACTION!
INTENSE
ADVENTURE!
EXTREME
DANGER!
the
WORLD'S GREATEST
SUPER-TEENS...
RE-IMAGINED
TO THE MAX!
JONES

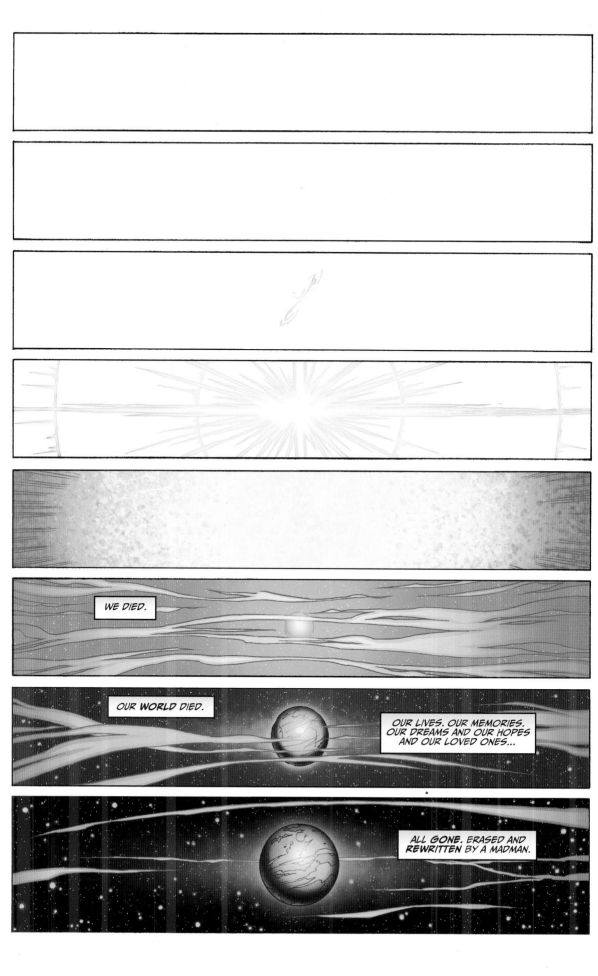

WE DIED.

OUR WORLD DIED.

OUR LIVES. OUR MEMORIES.
OUR DREAMS AND OUR HOPES
AND OUR LOVED ONES...

ALL GONE. ERASED AND
REWRITTEN BY A MADMAN.

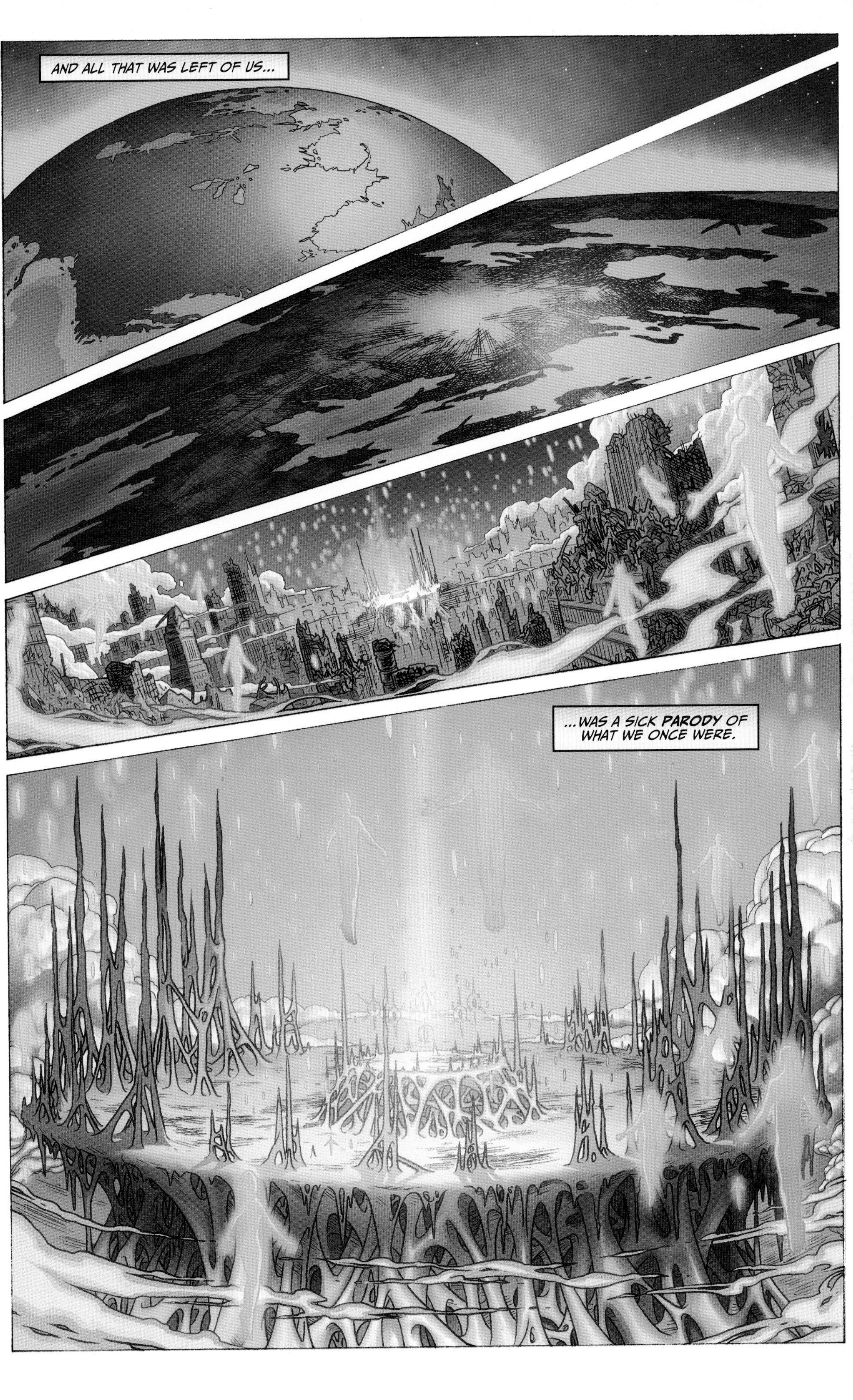
AND ALL THAT WAS LEFT OF US...
...WAS A SICK PARODY OF WHAT WE ONCE WERE.

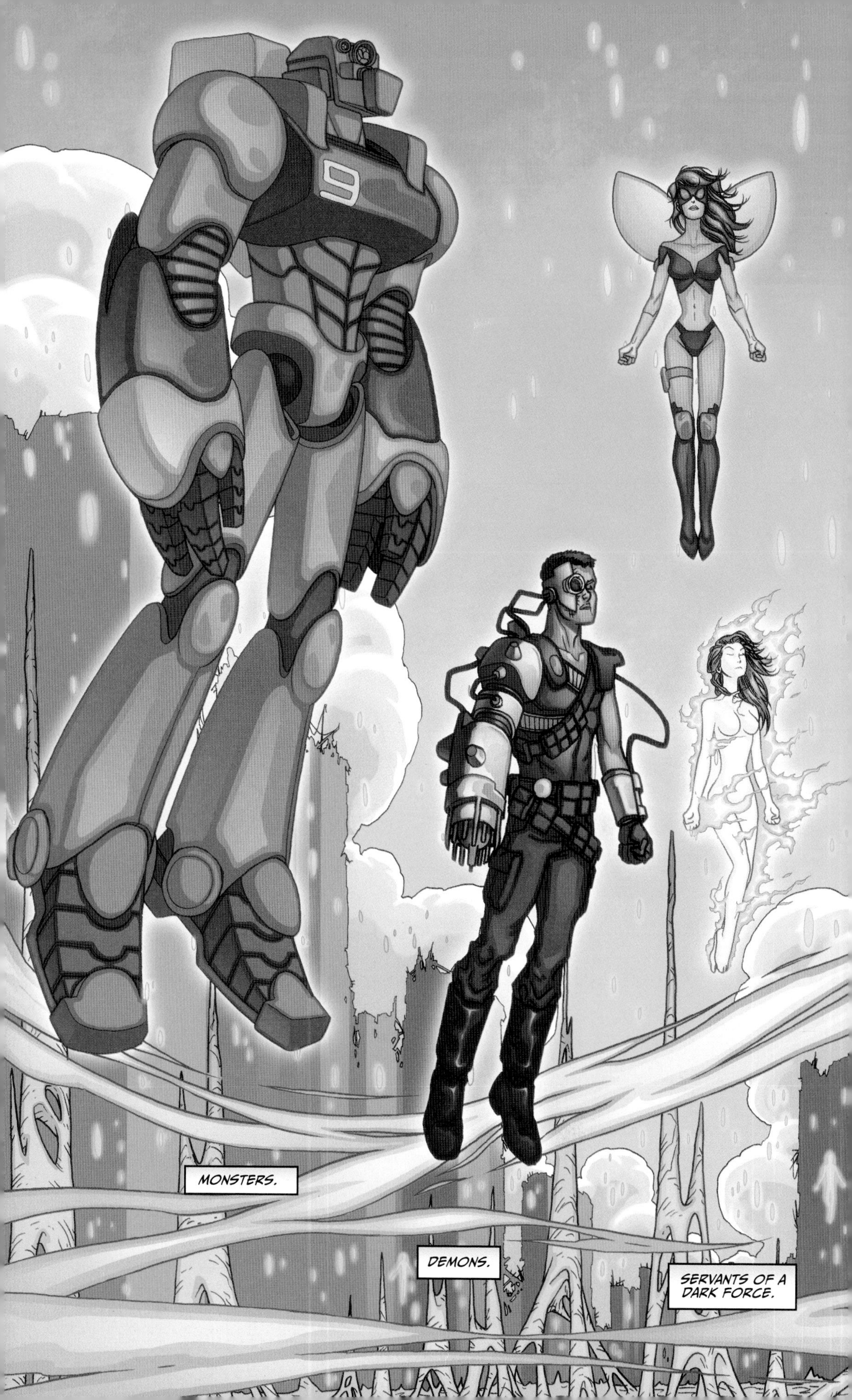
MONSTERS.
DEMONS.
SERVANTS OF A DARK FORCE.

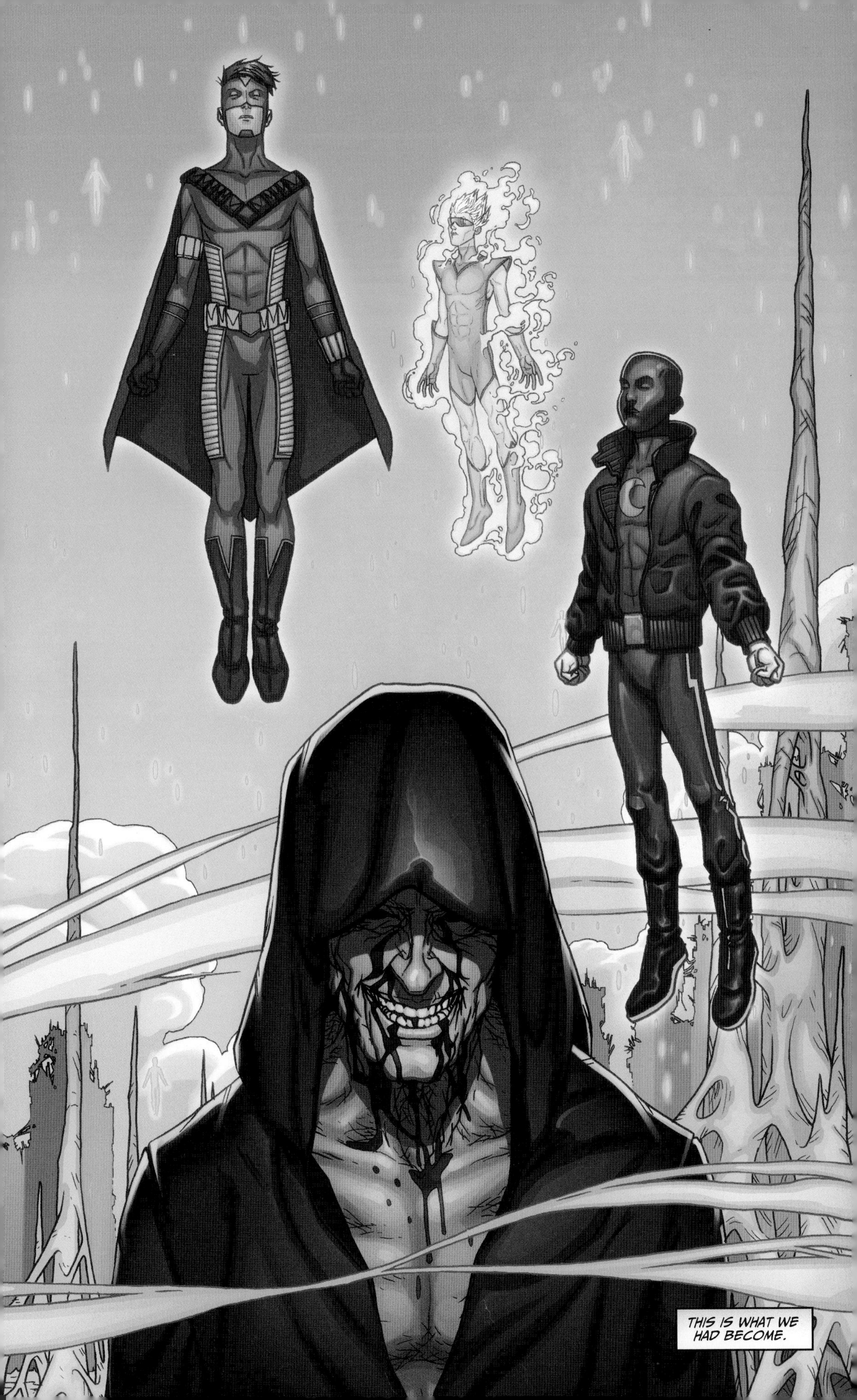
THIS IS WHAT WE HAD BECOME.

IT BEGAN WITH THE END OF THE LONG WAR.

WITH THE SUBJUGATION OF JAPAN.

WE UNLEASHED IMPOSSIBLE WEAPONS ON OUR ENEMY – TRANSFORMING AN ENTIRE **NATION** INTO A **PRISON** CAMP.

IT WAS THE RISE OF THE GLOBAL EMPIRE OF THE UNITED STATES. AND **ANYONE** THAT STOOD IN THE WAY OF THE AMERICAN SPIRIT WOULD FALL. ANYTHING HE COULD NOT DEFEAT...

...WAS **ERASED** FROM EXISTENCE. ERASED FROM THE TIME STREAM.

OVER AND OVER AGAIN, OUR REALITY HAS BEEN **MANIPULATED.** GUIDED BY A MALEVOLENT FORCE WHOSE LUST FOR CRUELTY IS SURPASSED ONLY BY ITS **HUNGER** FOR DEATH.

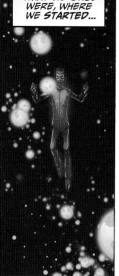

IN THE PROCESS... WHAT WE ONCE WERE, WHERE WE **STARTED**...

... HAS BEEN LOST IN THE SHIFTING SEA OF A LONG-DEAD MULTIVERSE.

AND THROUGH EVERY INCARNATION, EVERY **RE-IMAGINATION** OF OUR IDENTITIES...

...WE HAVE BEEN UNAWARE. BLIND.

UNTIL NOW.

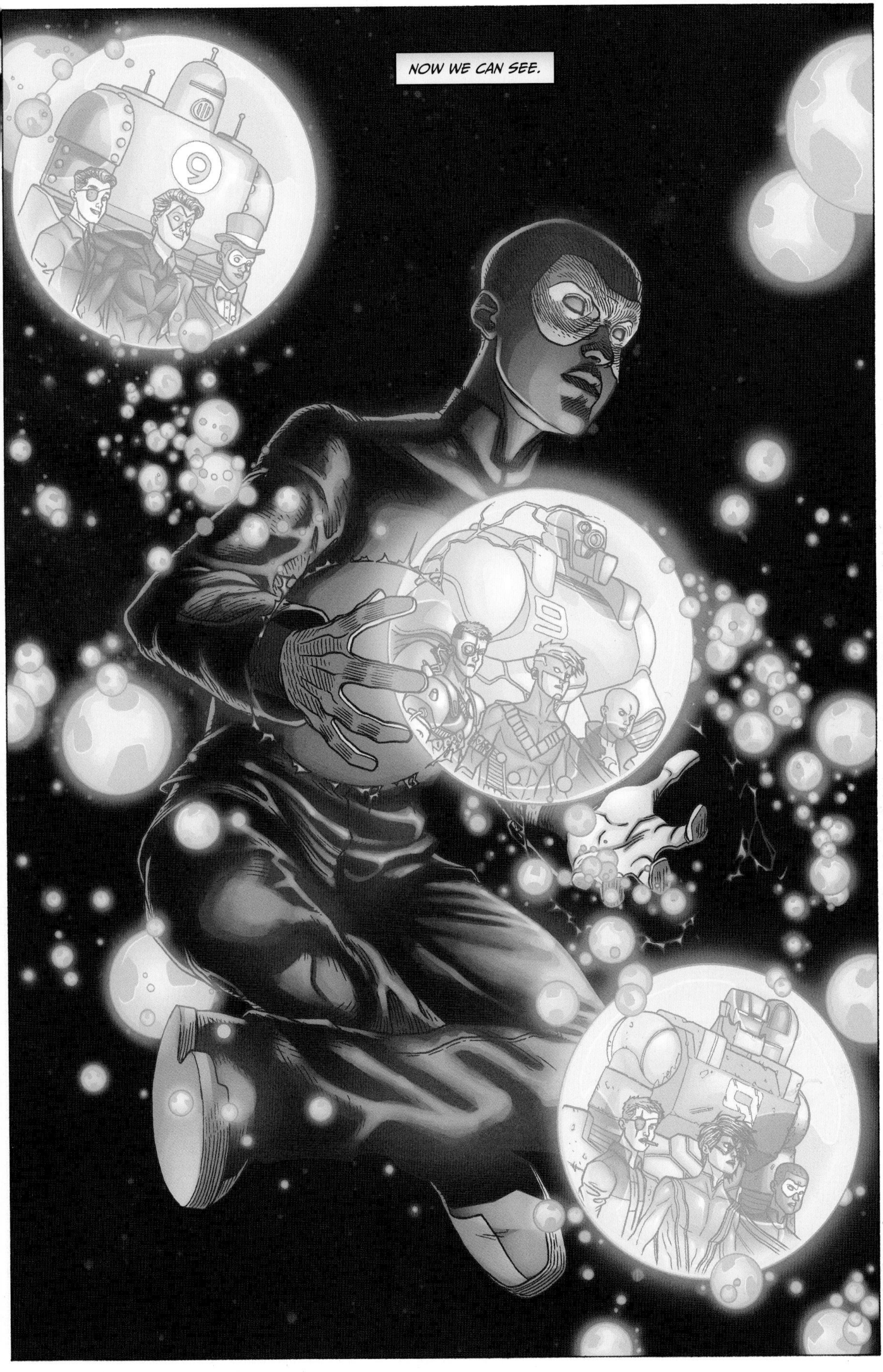
NOW WE CAN SEE.

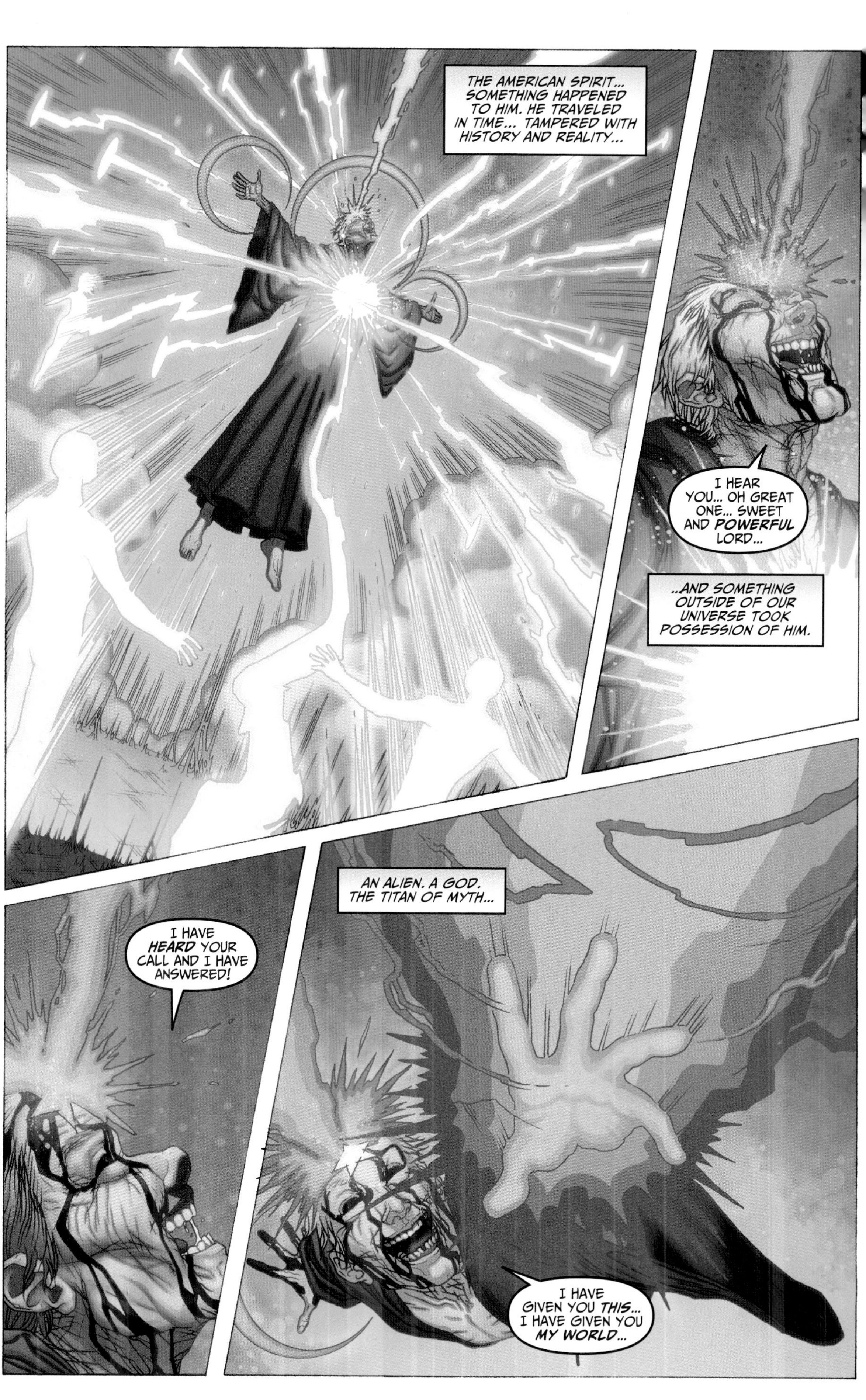
THE AMERICAN SPIRIT... SOMETHING HAPPENED TO HIM. HE TRAVELED IN TIME... TAMPERED WITH HISTORY AND REALITY...
I HEAR YOU... OH GREAT ONE... SWEET AND POWERFUL LORD...
..AND SOMETHING OUTSIDE OF OUR UNIVERSE TOOK POSSESSION OF HIM.
I HAVE HEARD YOUR CALL AND I HAVE ANSWERED!
AN ALIEN. A GOD. THE TITAN OF MYTH...
I HAVE GIVEN YOU THIS... I HAVE GIVEN YOU MY WORLD...

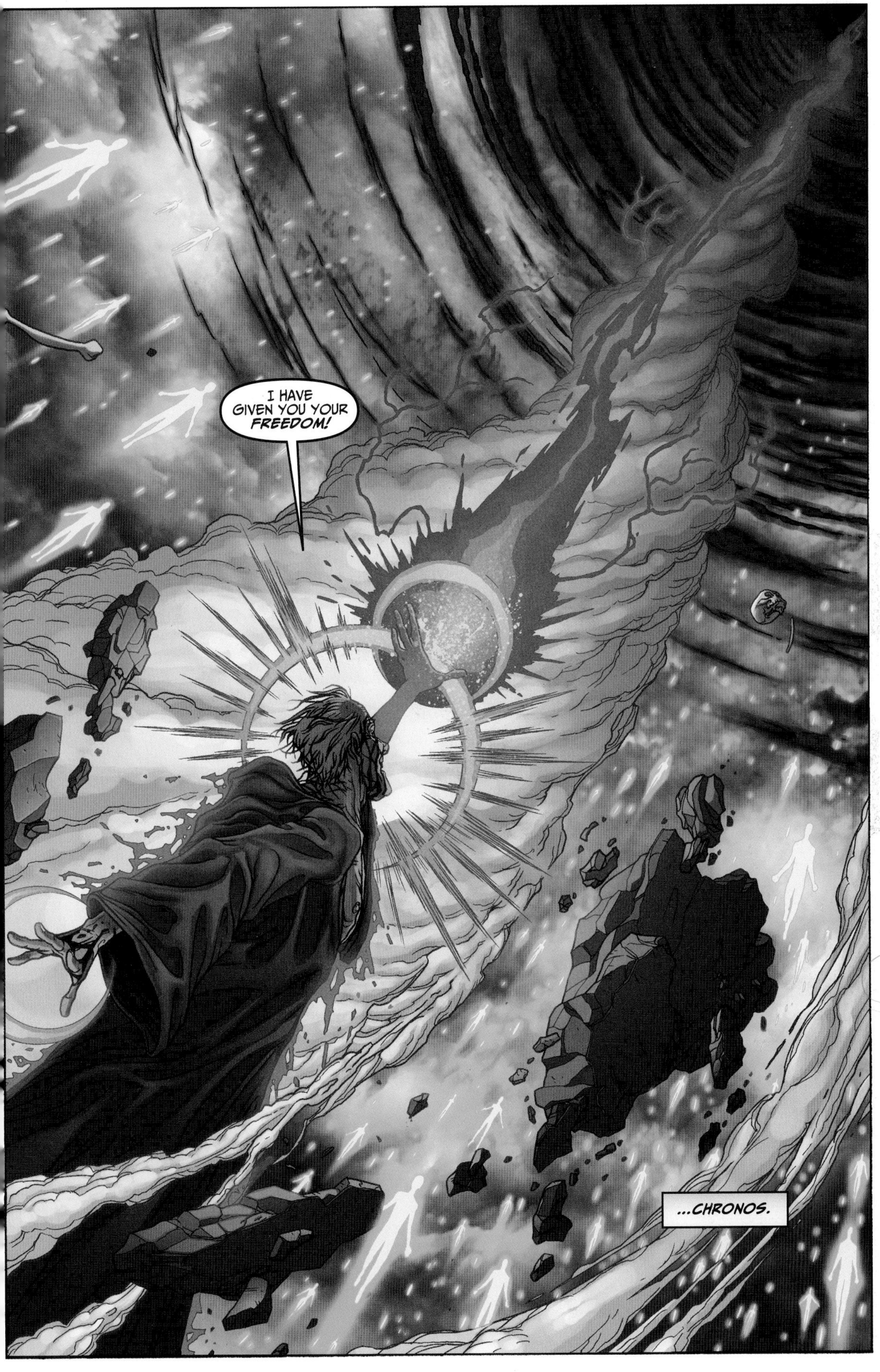
I HAVE GIVEN YOU YOUR *FREEDOM!*
...CHRONOS.

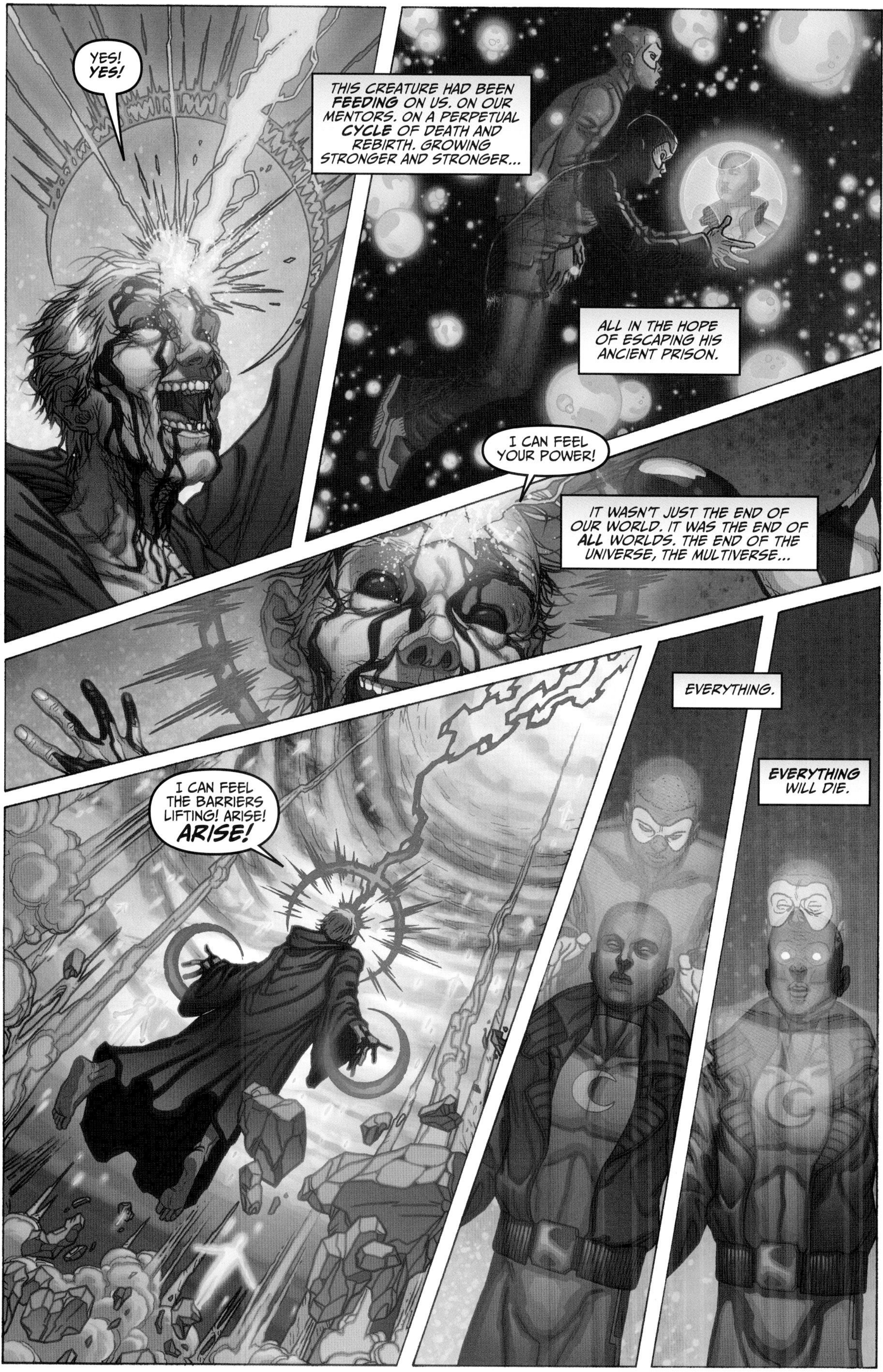
YES! YES!
THIS CREATURE HAD BEEN FEEDING ON US. ON OUR MENTORS. ON A PERPETUAL CYCLE OF DEATH AND REBIRTH. GROWING STRONGER AND STRONGER...
ALL IN THE HOPE OF ESCAPING HIS ANCIENT PRISON.
I CAN FEEL YOUR POWER!
IT WASN'T JUST THE END OF OUR WORLD. IT WAS THE END OF ALL WORLDS. THE END OF THE UNIVERSE, THE MULTIVERSE...
I CAN FEEL THE BARRIERS LIFTING! ARISE! ARISE!
EVERYTHING.
EVERYTHING WILL DIE.

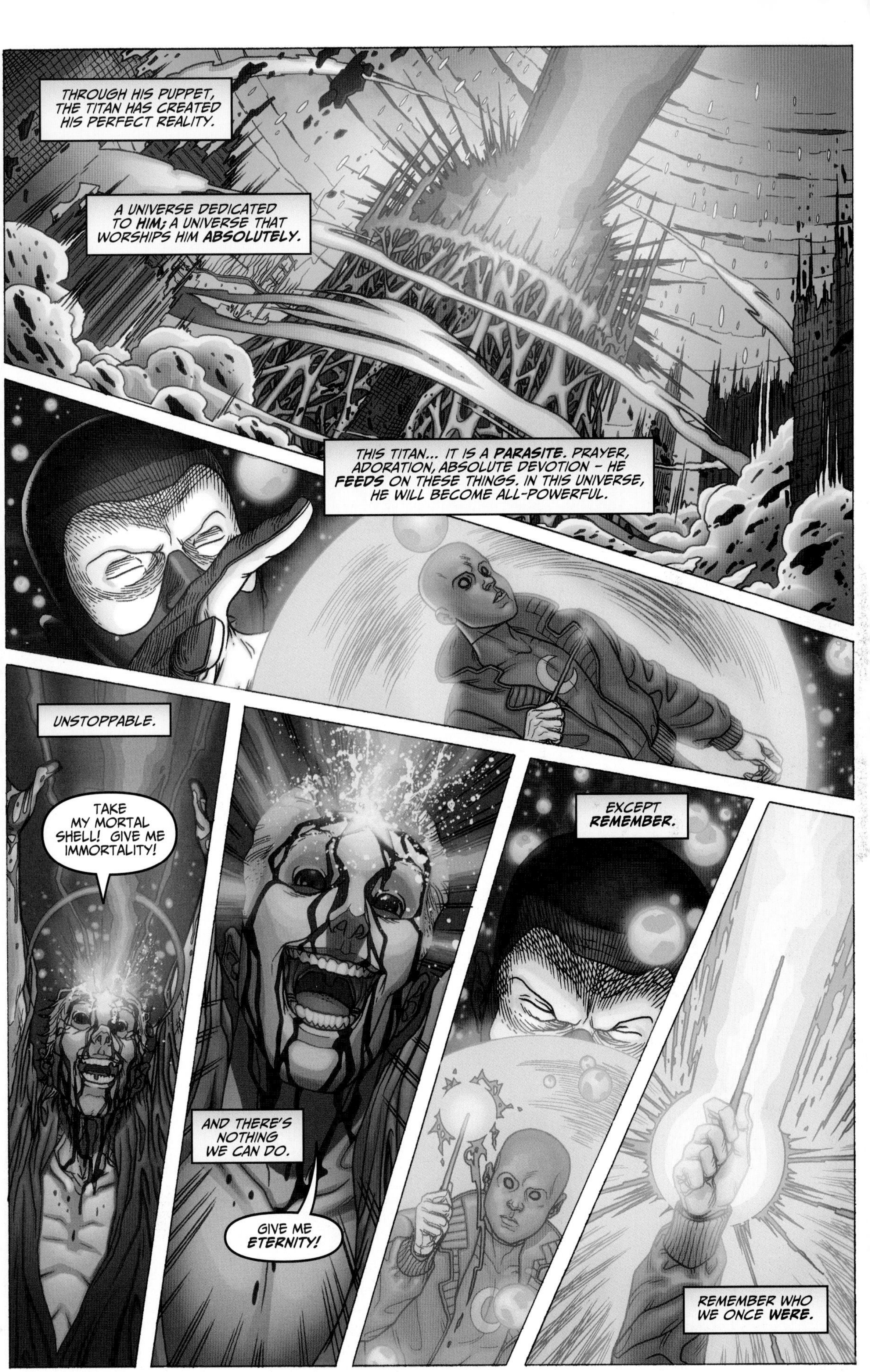
THROUGH HIS PUPPET, THE TITAN HAS CREATED HIS PERFECT REALITY.
A UNIVERSE DEDICATED TO HIM; A UNIVERSE THAT WORSHIPS HIM ABSOLUTELY.
THIS TITAN... IT IS A PARASITE. PRAYER, ADORATION, ABSOLUTE DEVOTION – HE FEEDS ON THESE THINGS. IN THIS UNIVERSE, HE WILL BECOME ALL-POWERFUL.
UNSTOPPABLE.
TAKE MY MORTAL SHELL! GIVE ME IMMORTALITY!
AND THERE'S NOTHING WE CAN DO.
GIVE ME ETERNITY!
EXCEPT REMEMBER.
REMEMBER WHO WE ONCE WERE.

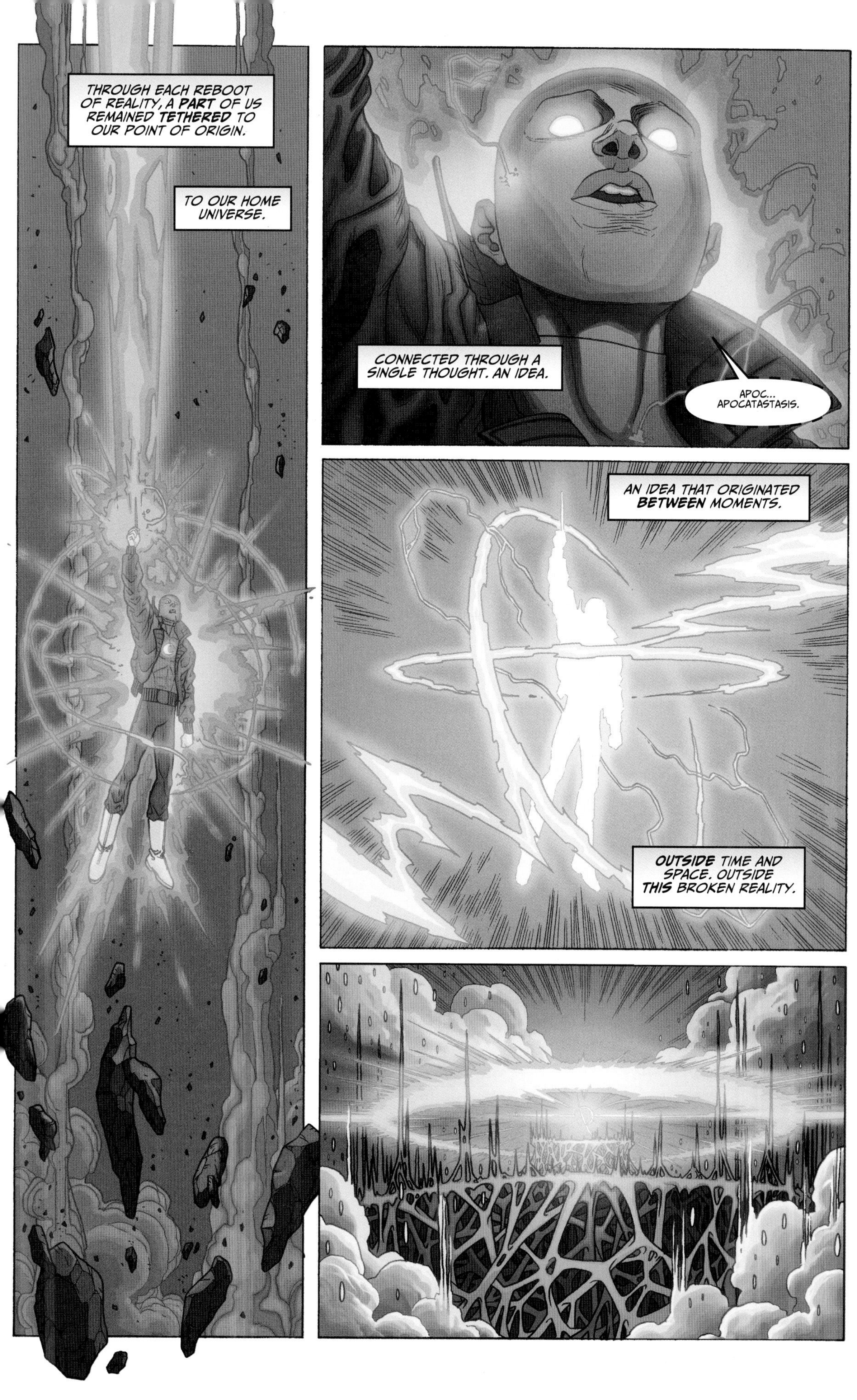
THROUGH EACH REBOOT OF REALITY, A **PART** OF US REMAINED **TETHERED** TO OUR POINT OF ORIGIN.
TO OUR HOME UNIVERSE.
CONNECTED THROUGH A SINGLE THOUGHT. AN IDEA.
APOC... APOCATASTASIS.
AN IDEA THAT ORIGINATED **BETWEEN** MOMENTS.
OUTSIDE TIME AND SPACE. OUTSIDE **THIS** BROKEN REALITY.

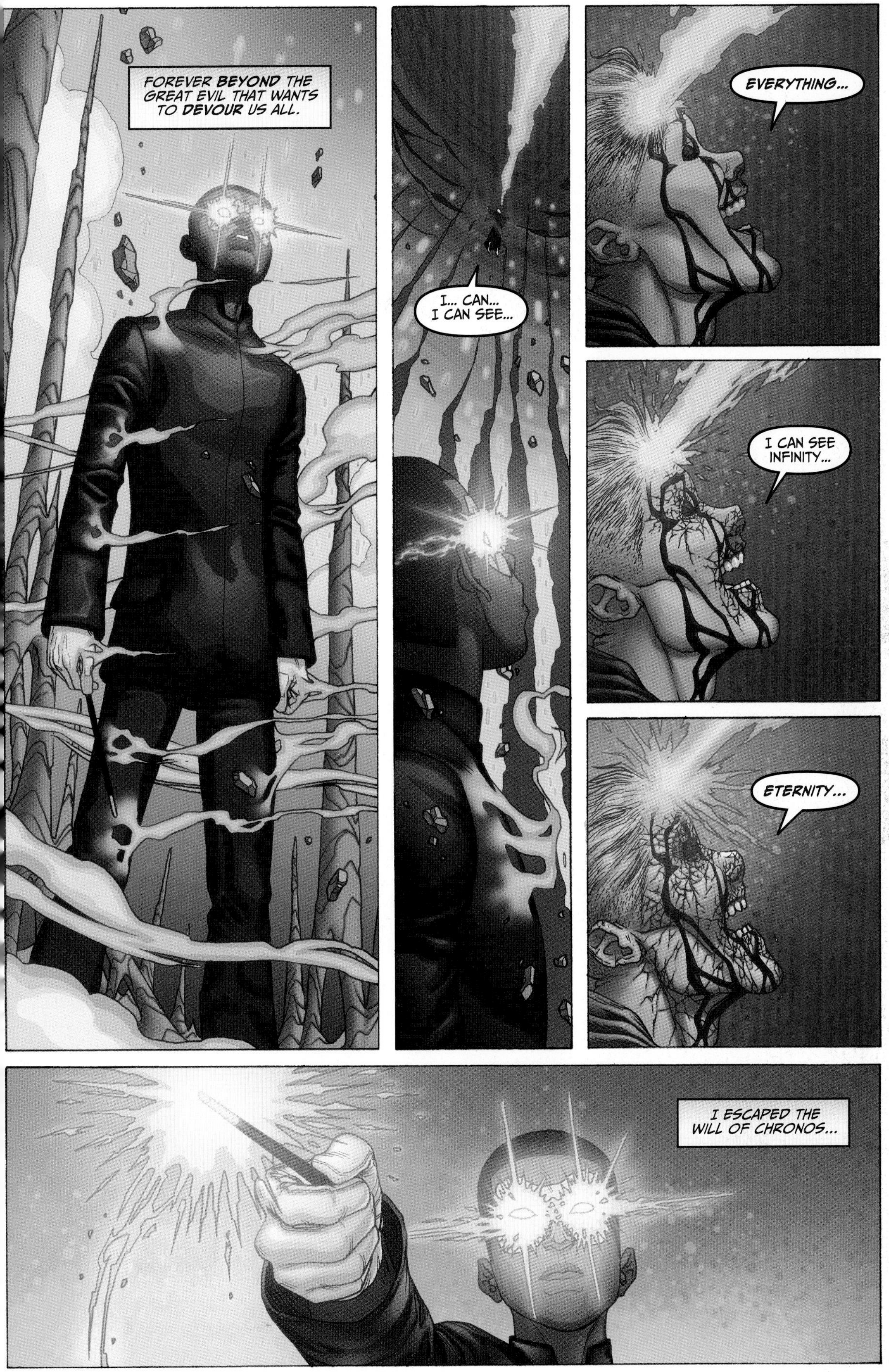
FOREVER BEYOND THE GREAT EVIL THAT WANTS TO DEVOUR US ALL.
I... CAN... I CAN SEE...
EVERYTHING...
I CAN SEE INFINITY...
ETERNITY...
I ESCAPED THE WILL OF CHRONOS...

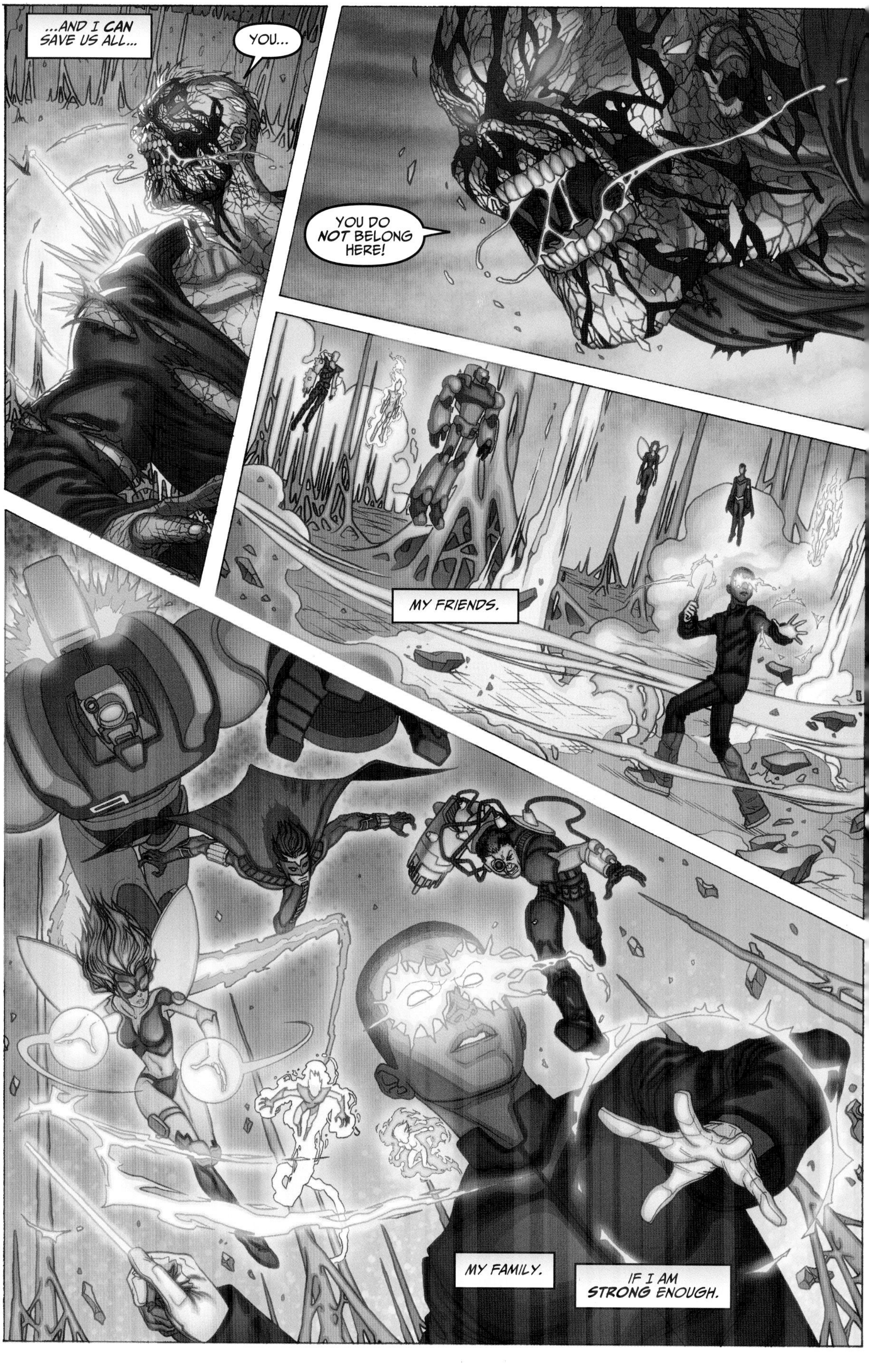
...AND I CAN SAVE US ALL...
YOU...
YOU DO NOT BELONG HERE!
MY FRIENDS.
MY FAMILY.
IF I AM STRONG ENOUGH.

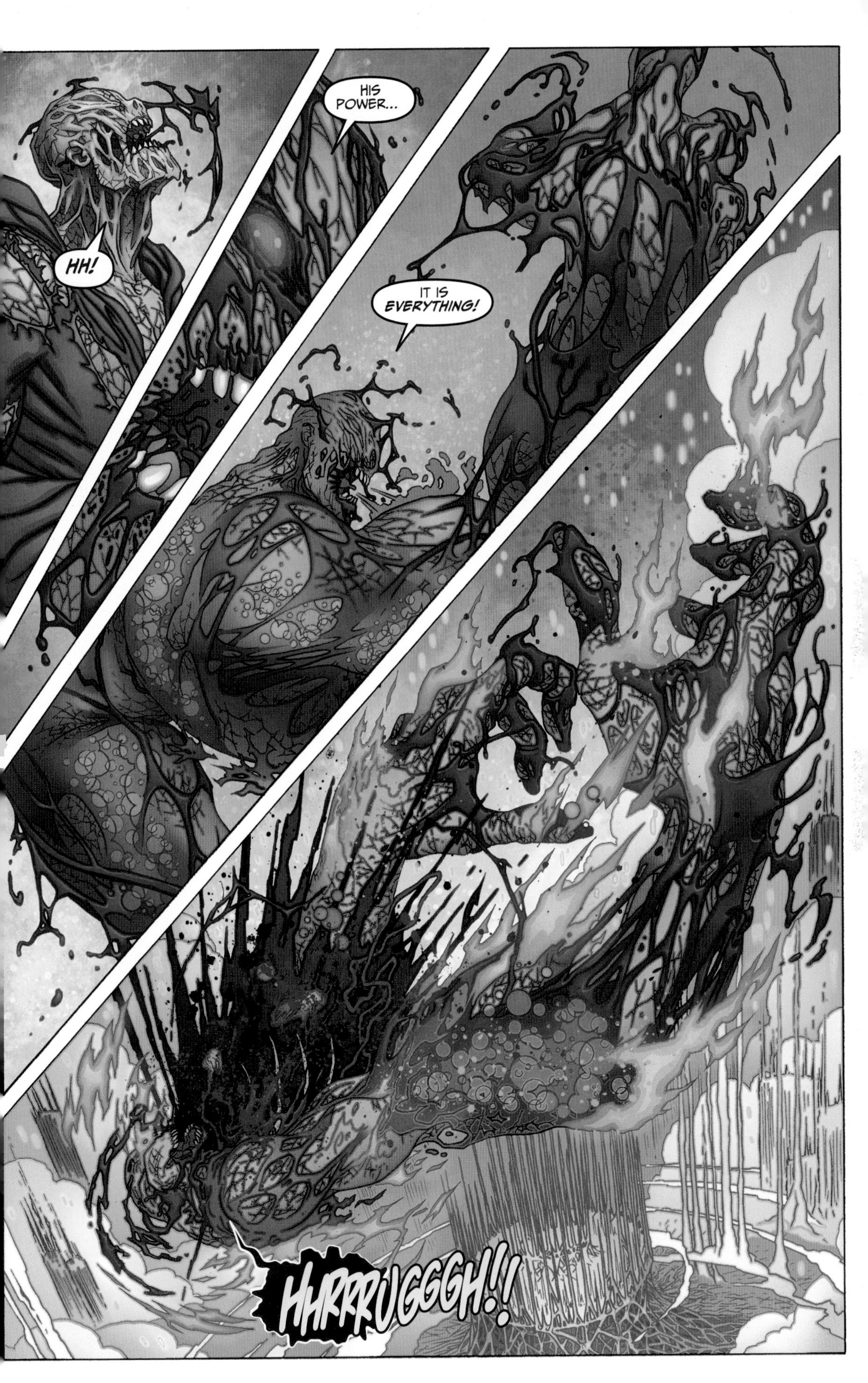
HH!
HIS POWER...
IT IS EVERYTHING!
HHRRRUGGGH!!

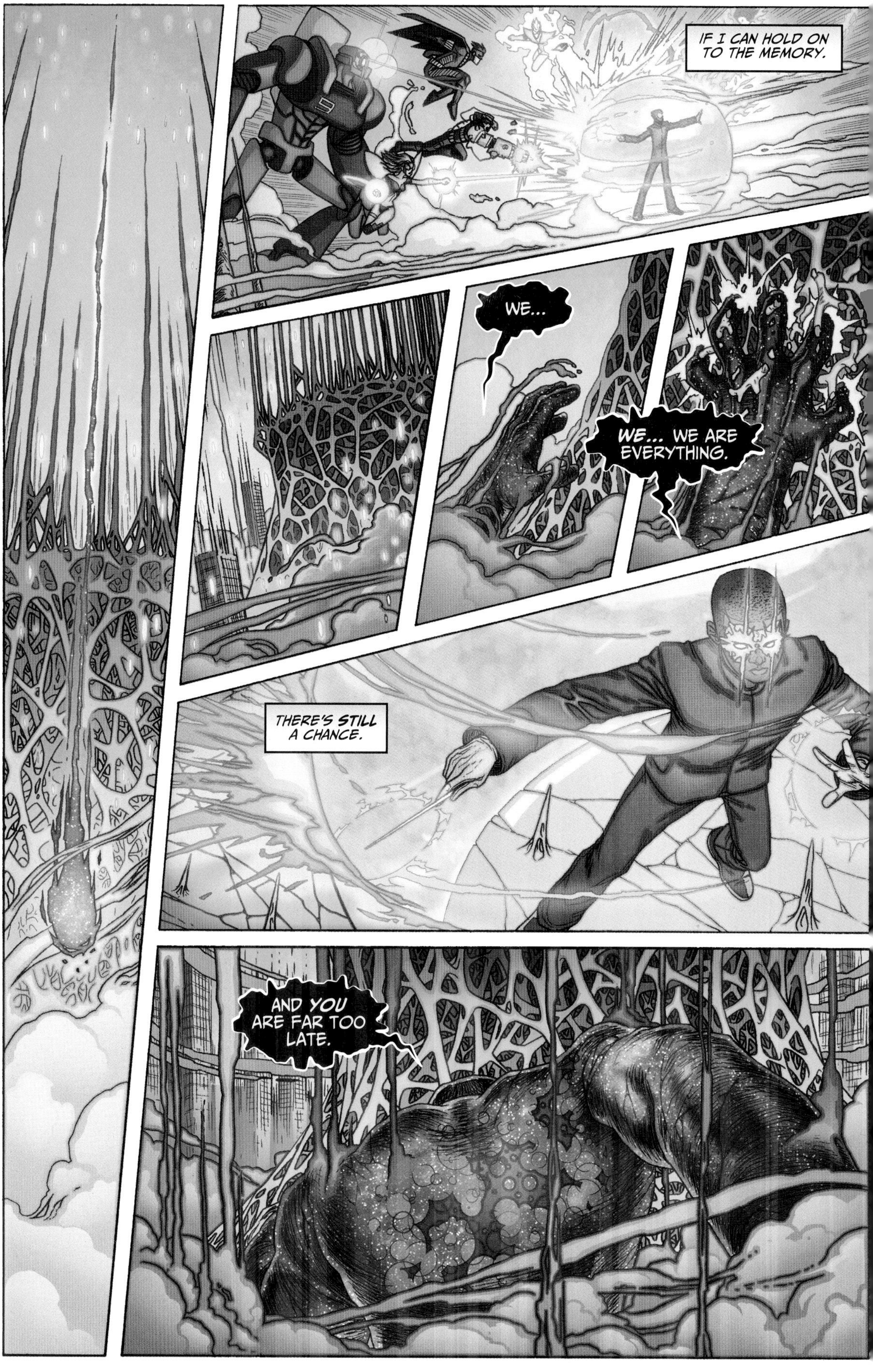
IF I CAN HOLD ON TO THE MEMORY.
WE...
WE... WE ARE EVERYTHING.
THERE'S STILL A CHANCE.
AND YOU ARE FAR TOO LATE.

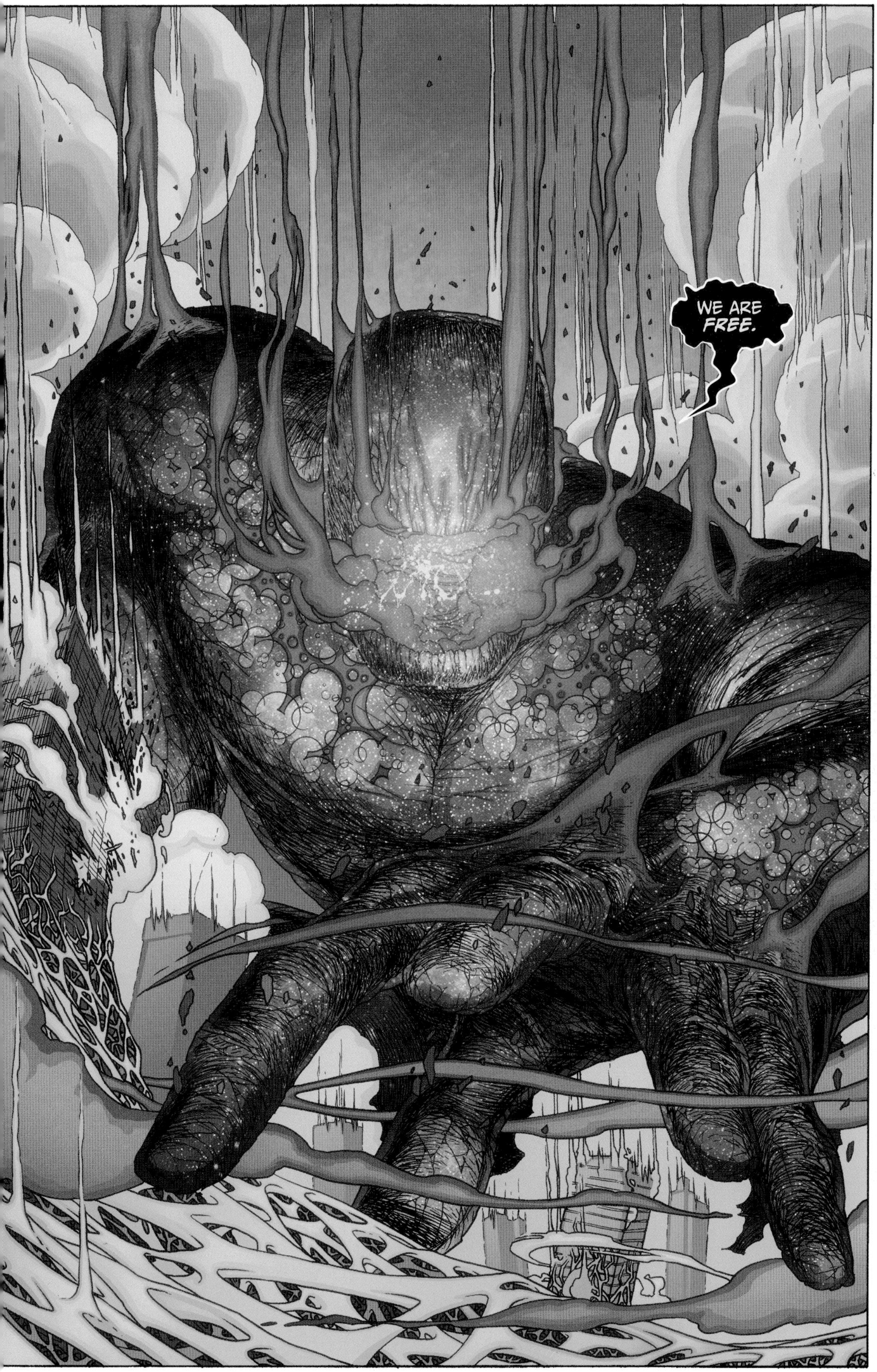
WE ARE FREE.

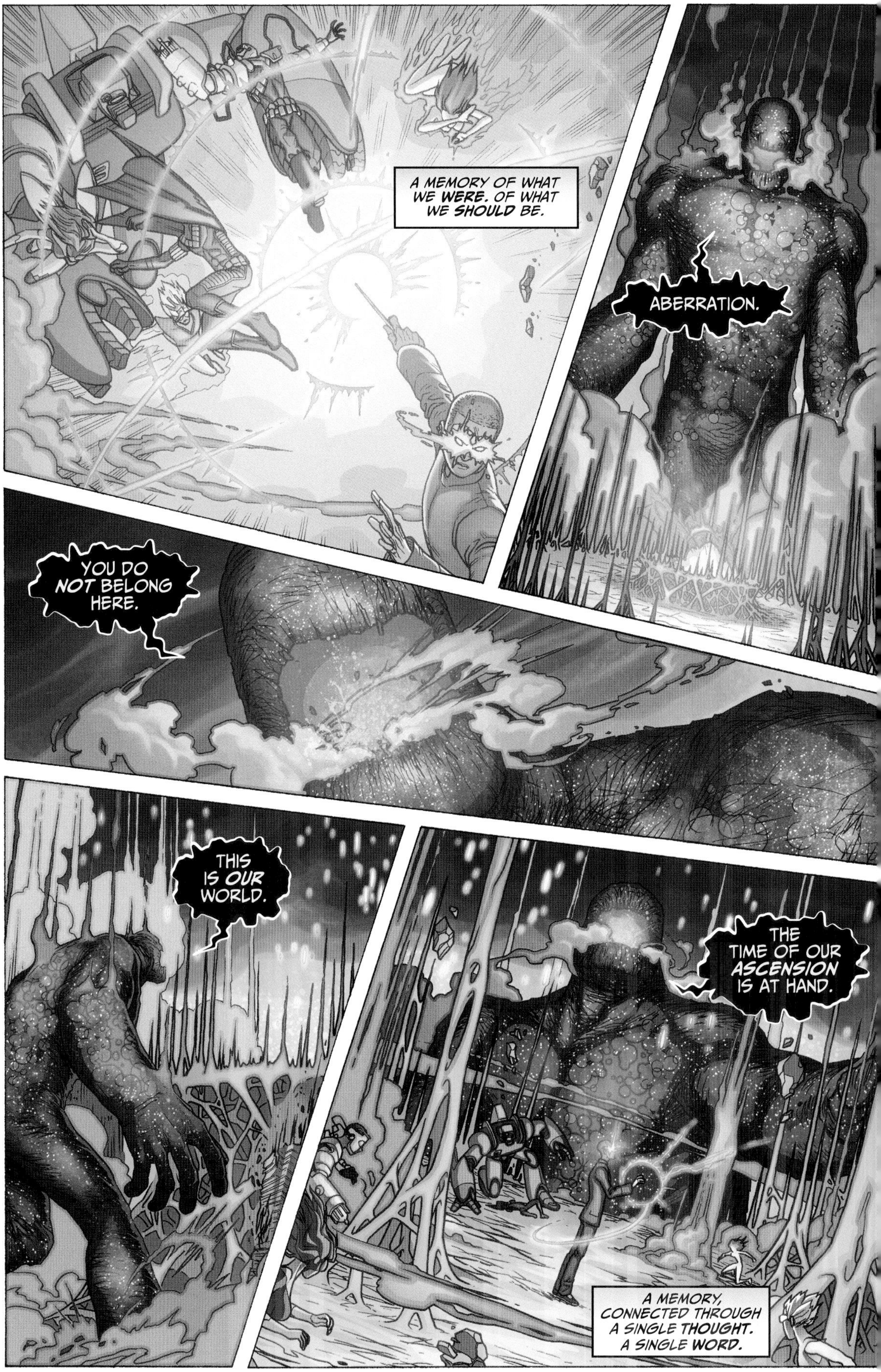
A MEMORY OF WHAT WE WERE. OF WHAT WE SHOULD BE.
ABERRATION.
YOU DO NOT BELONG HERE.
THIS IS OUR WORLD.
THE TIME OF OUR ASCENSION IS AT HAND.
A MEMORY, CONNECTED THROUGH A SINGLE THOUGHT. A SINGLE WORD.

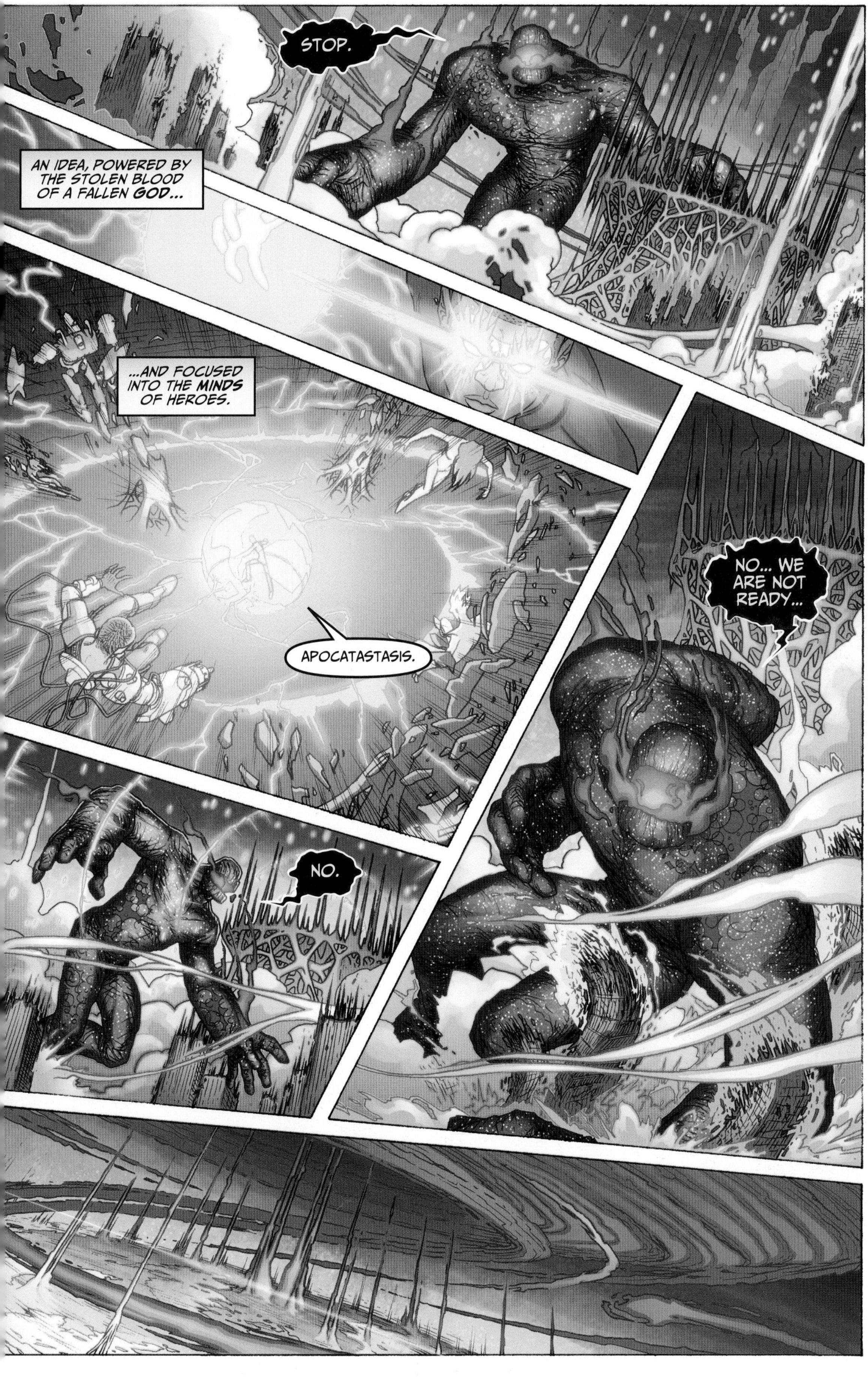
STOP.
AN IDEA, POWERED BY THE STOLEN BLOOD OF A FALLEN GOD...
...AND FOCUSED INTO THE MINDS OF HEROES.
APOCATASTASIS.
NO... WE ARE NOT READY...
NO.

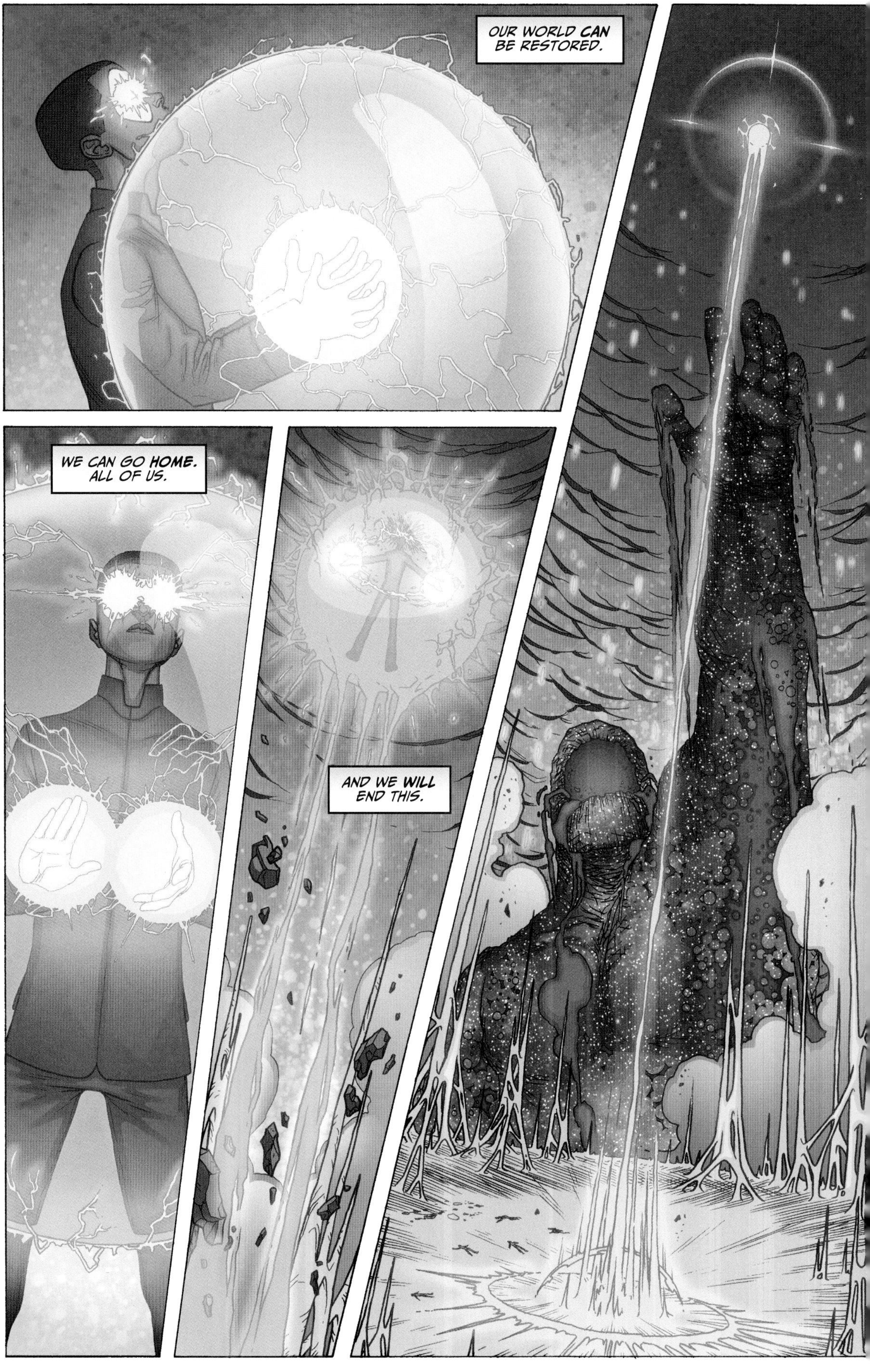
OUR WORLD CAN BE RESTORED.
WE CAN GO HOME. ALL OF US.
AND WE WILL END THIS.

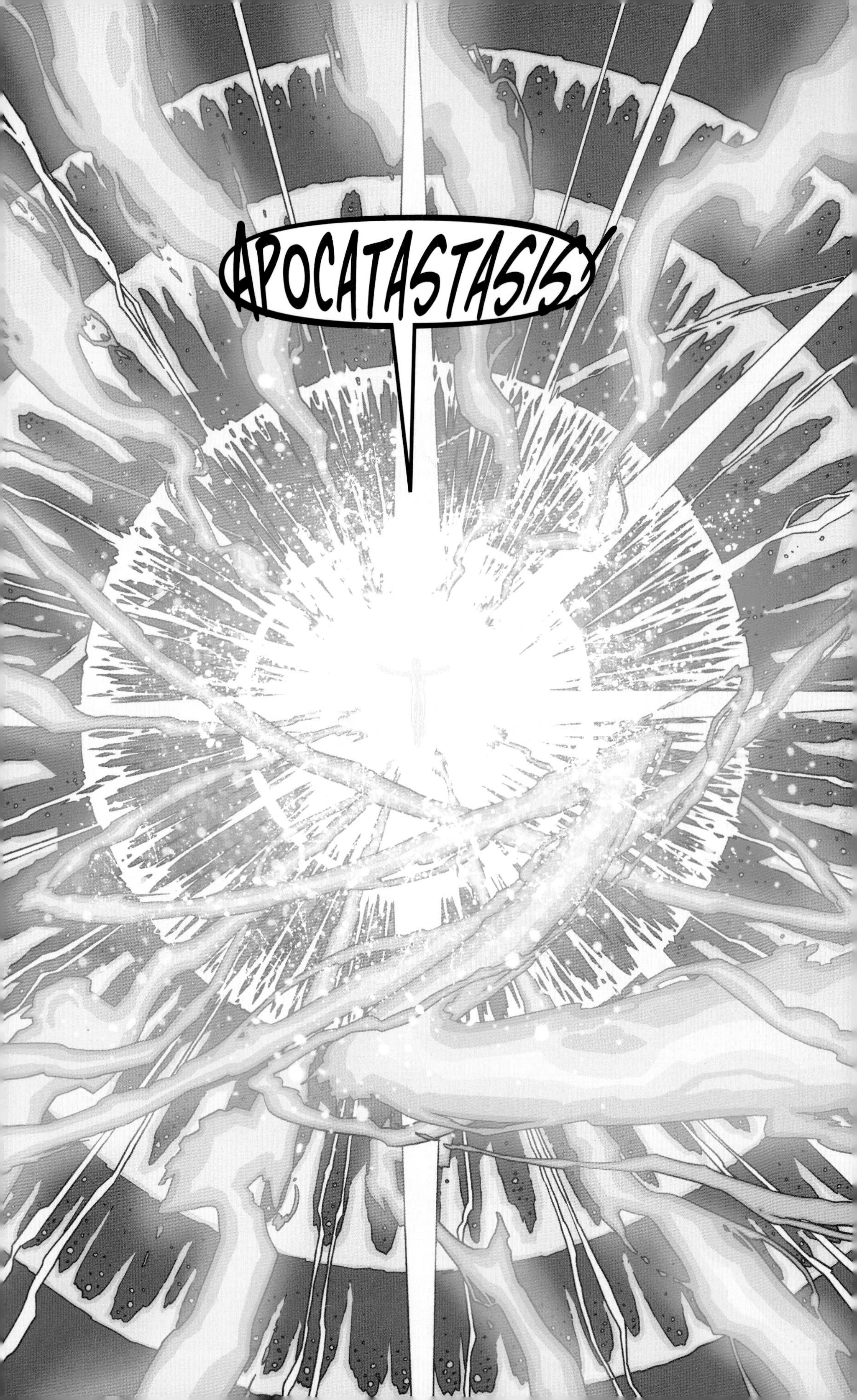
APOCATASTASIS!

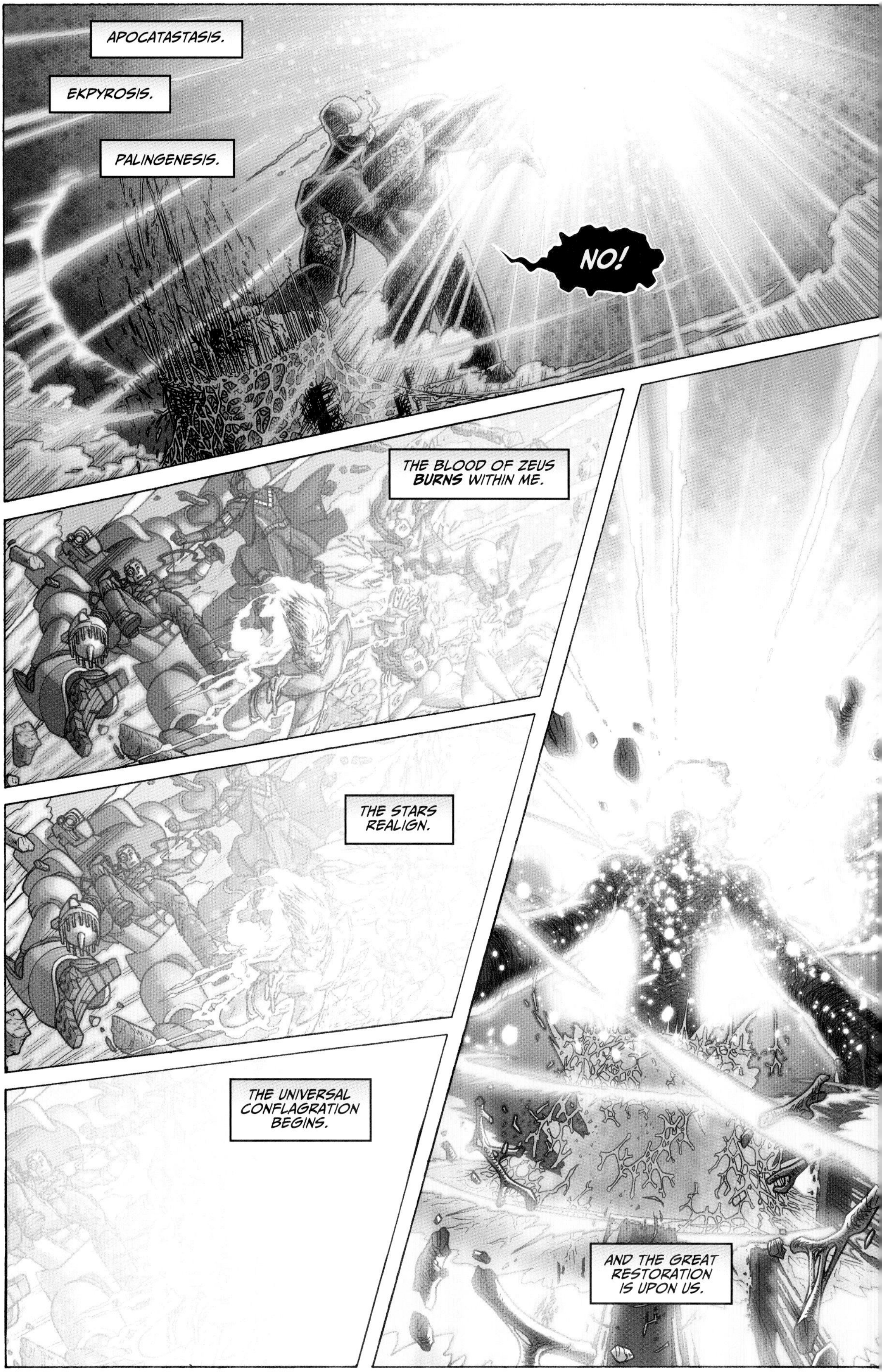
APOCATASTASIS.
EKPYROSIS.
PALINGENESIS.
NO!
THE BLOOD OF ZEUS BURNS WITHIN ME.
THE STARS REALIGN.
THE UNIVERSAL CONFLAGRATION BEGINS.
AND THE GREAT RESTORATION IS UPON US.

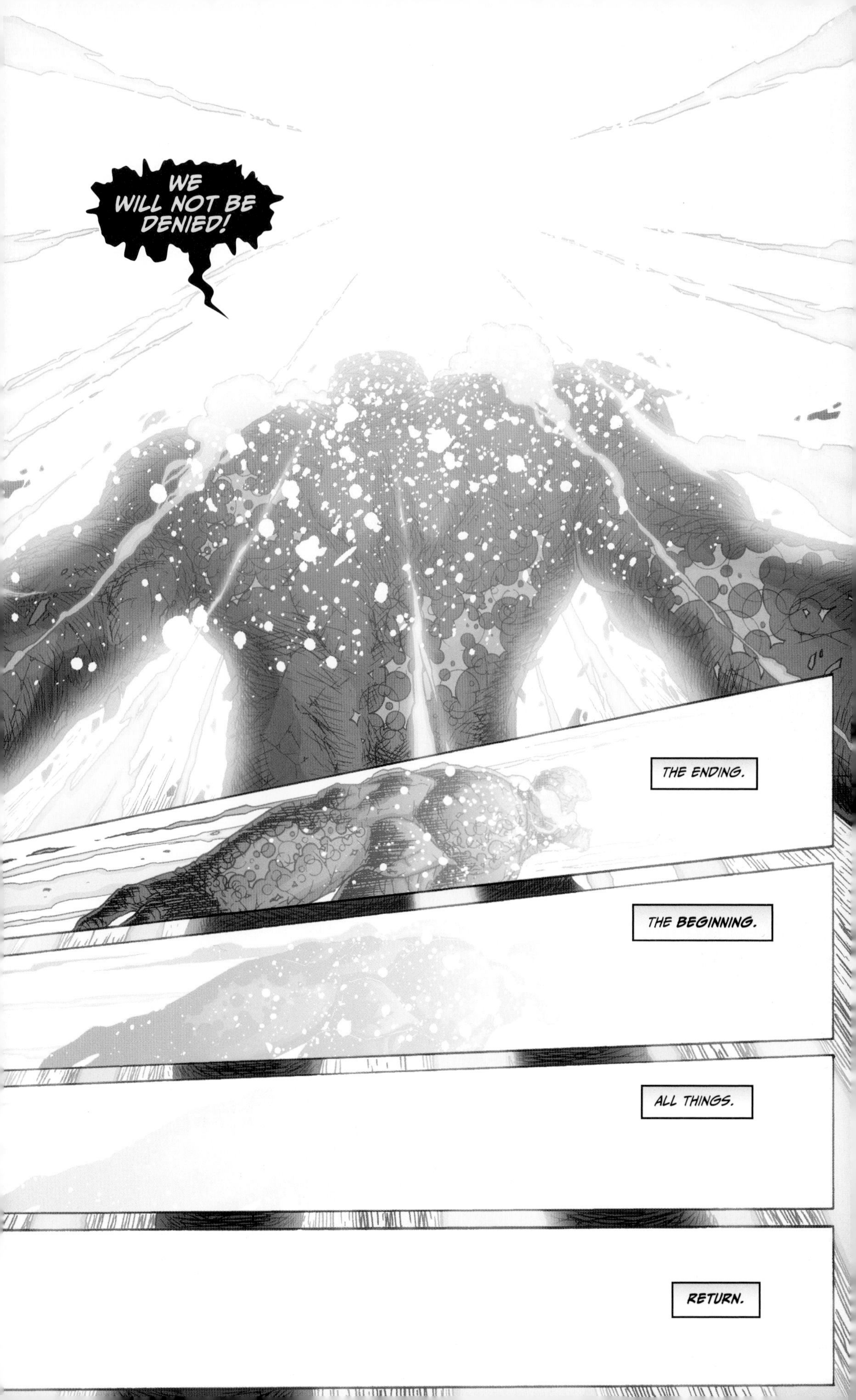
WE WILL NOT BE DENIED!
THE ENDING.
THE BEGINNING.
ALL THINGS.
RETURN.

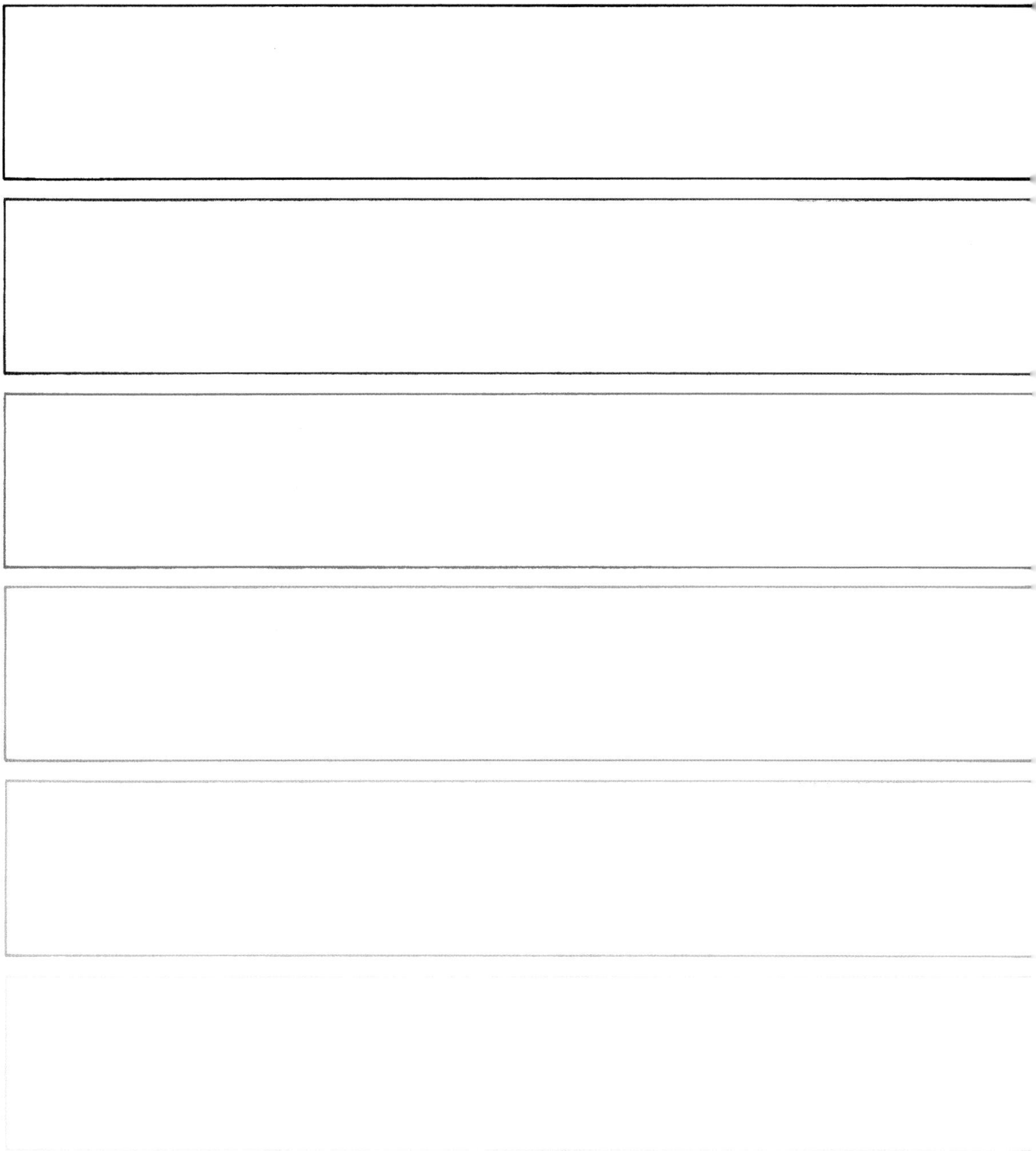

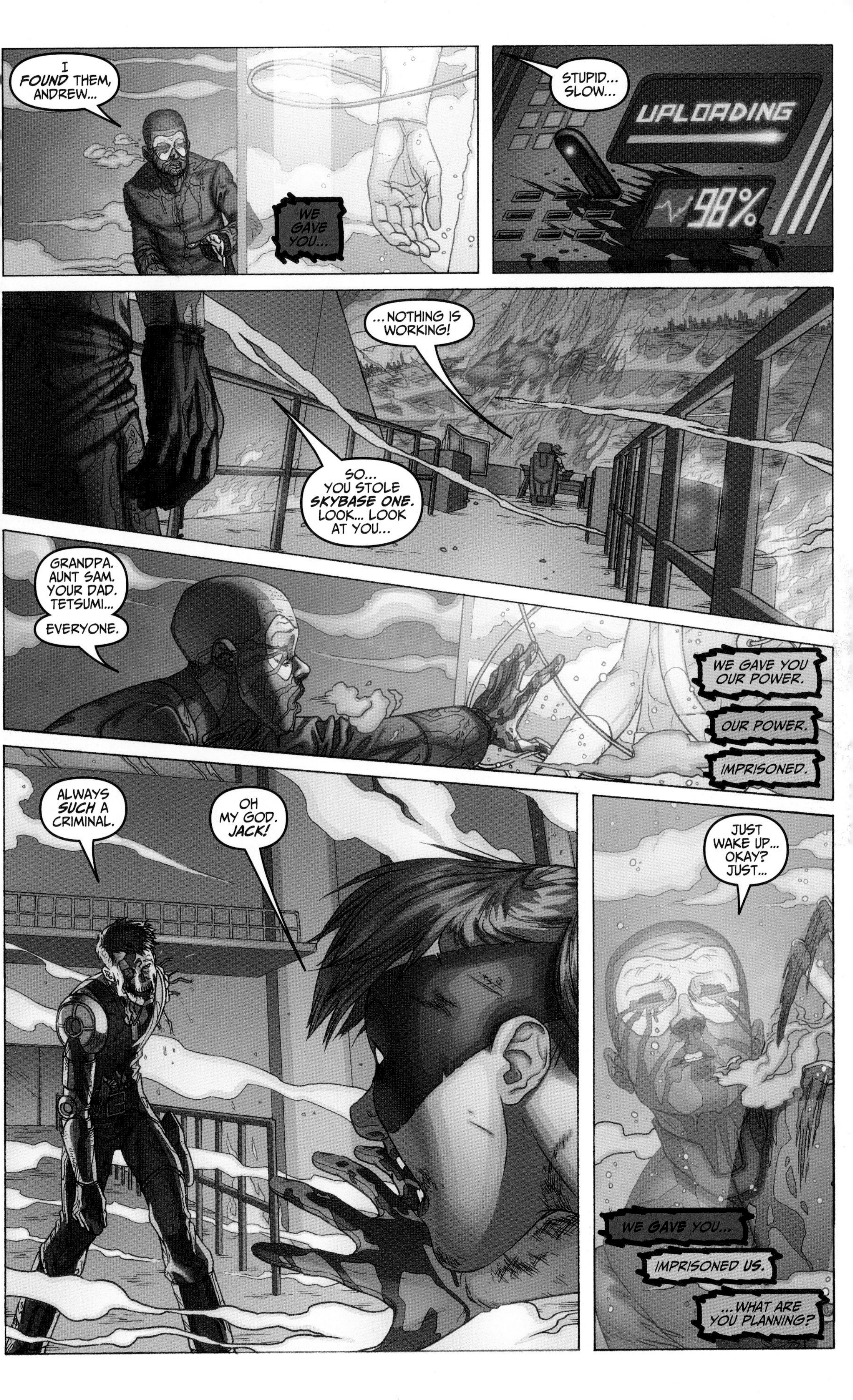

I FOUND THEM, ANDREW...
WE GAVE YOU...
STUPID... SLOW...
UPLOADING
98%
...NOTHING IS WORKING!
SO... YOU STOLE SKYBASE ONE. LOOK... LOOK AT YOU...
GRANDPA. AUNT SAM. YOUR DAD. TETSUMI...
EVERYONE.
WE GAVE YOU OUR POWER.
OUR POWER.
IMPRISONED.
ALWAYS SUCH A CRIMINAL.
OH MY GOD. JACK!
JUST WAKE UP... OKAY? JUST...
WE GAVE YOU...
IMPRISONED US.
...WHAT ARE YOU PLANNING?

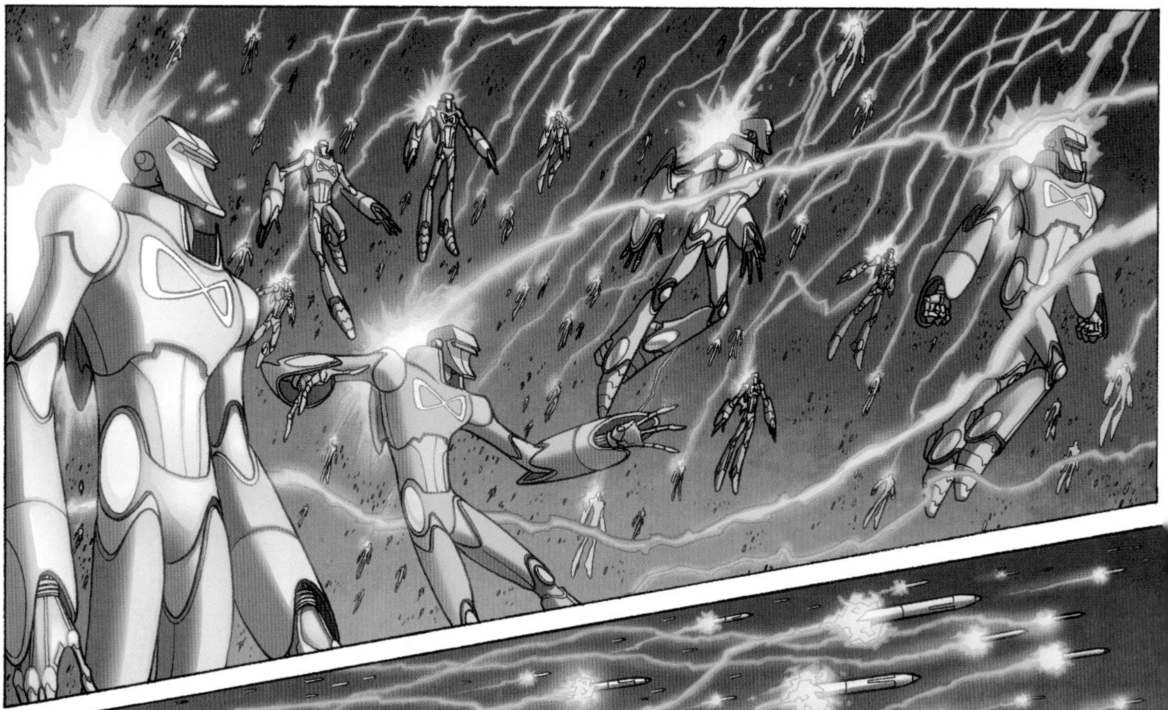
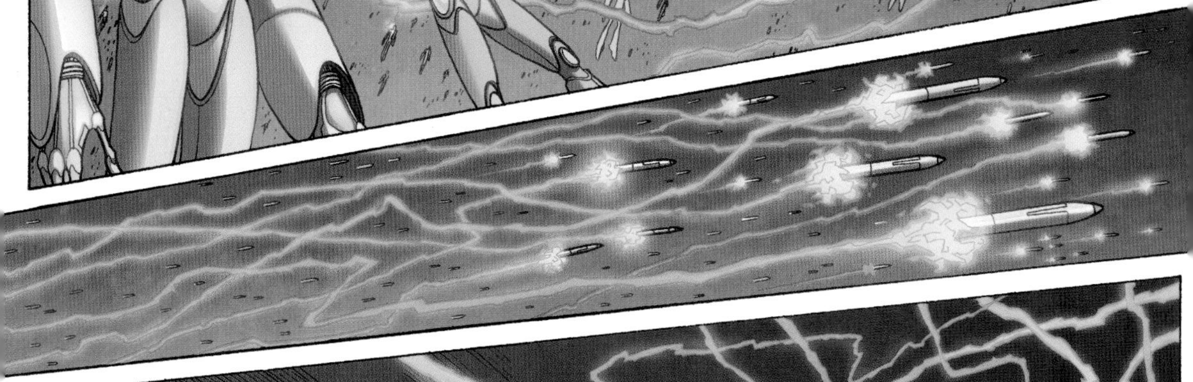
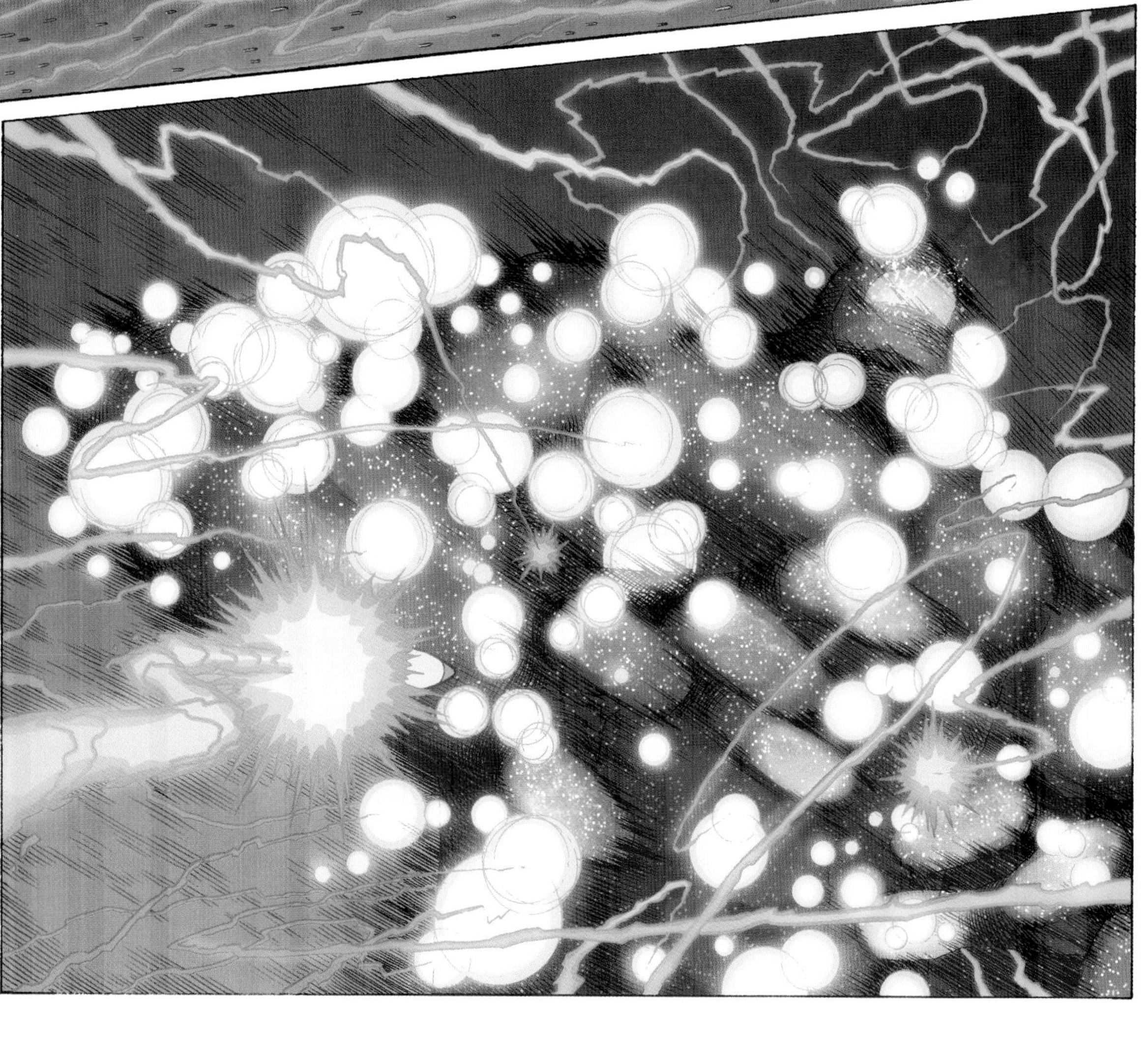

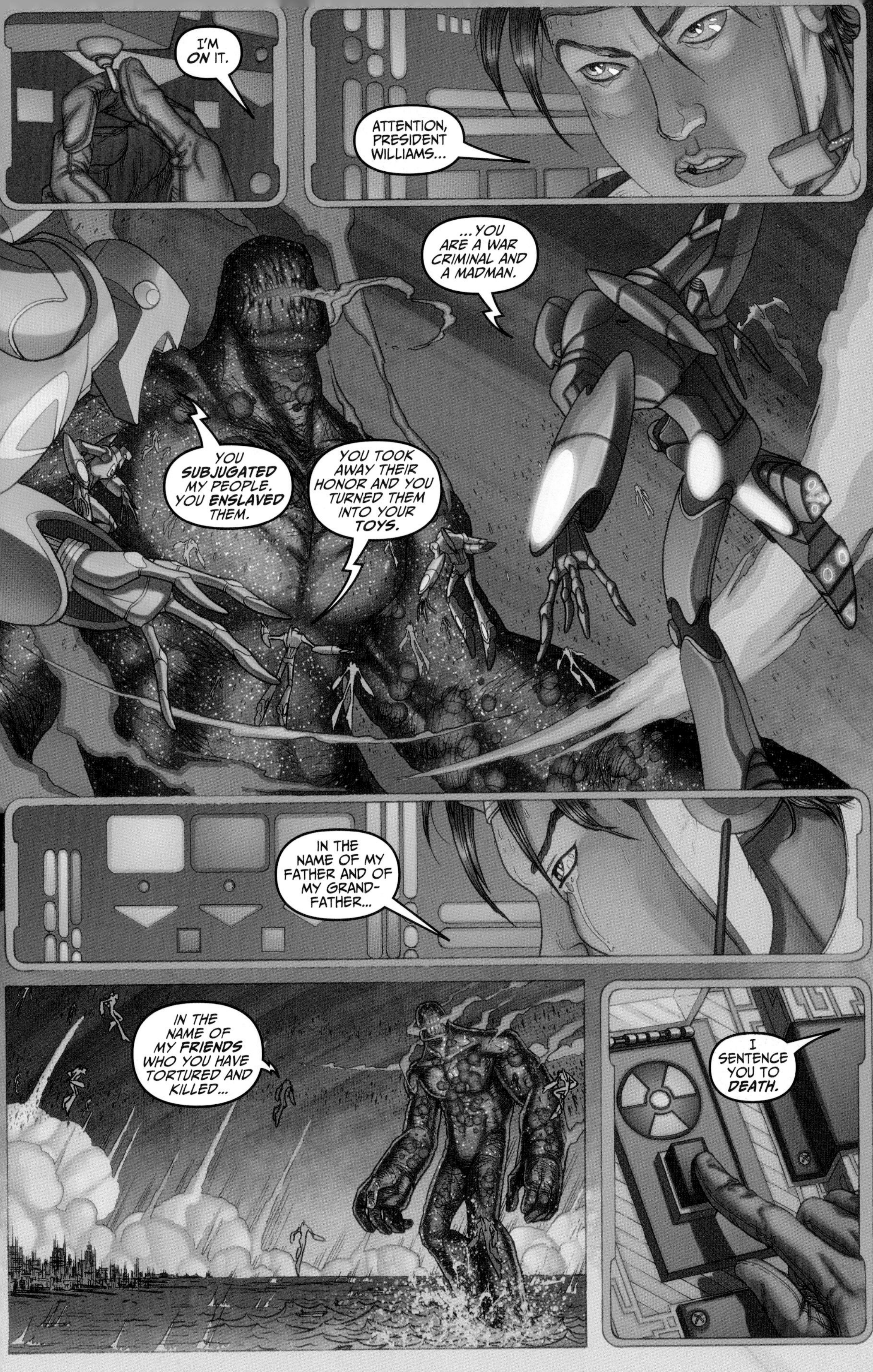
I'M ON IT.
ATTENTION, PRESIDENT WILLIAMS...
...YOU ARE A WAR CRIMINAL AND A MADMAN.
YOU SUBJUGATED MY PEOPLE. YOU ENSLAVED THEM.
YOU TOOK AWAY THEIR HONOR AND YOU TURNED THEM INTO YOUR TOYS.
IN THE NAME OF MY FATHER AND OF MY GRAND-FATHER...
IN THE NAME OF MY FRIENDS WHO YOU HAVE TORTURED AND KILLED...
I SENTENCE YOU TO DEATH.

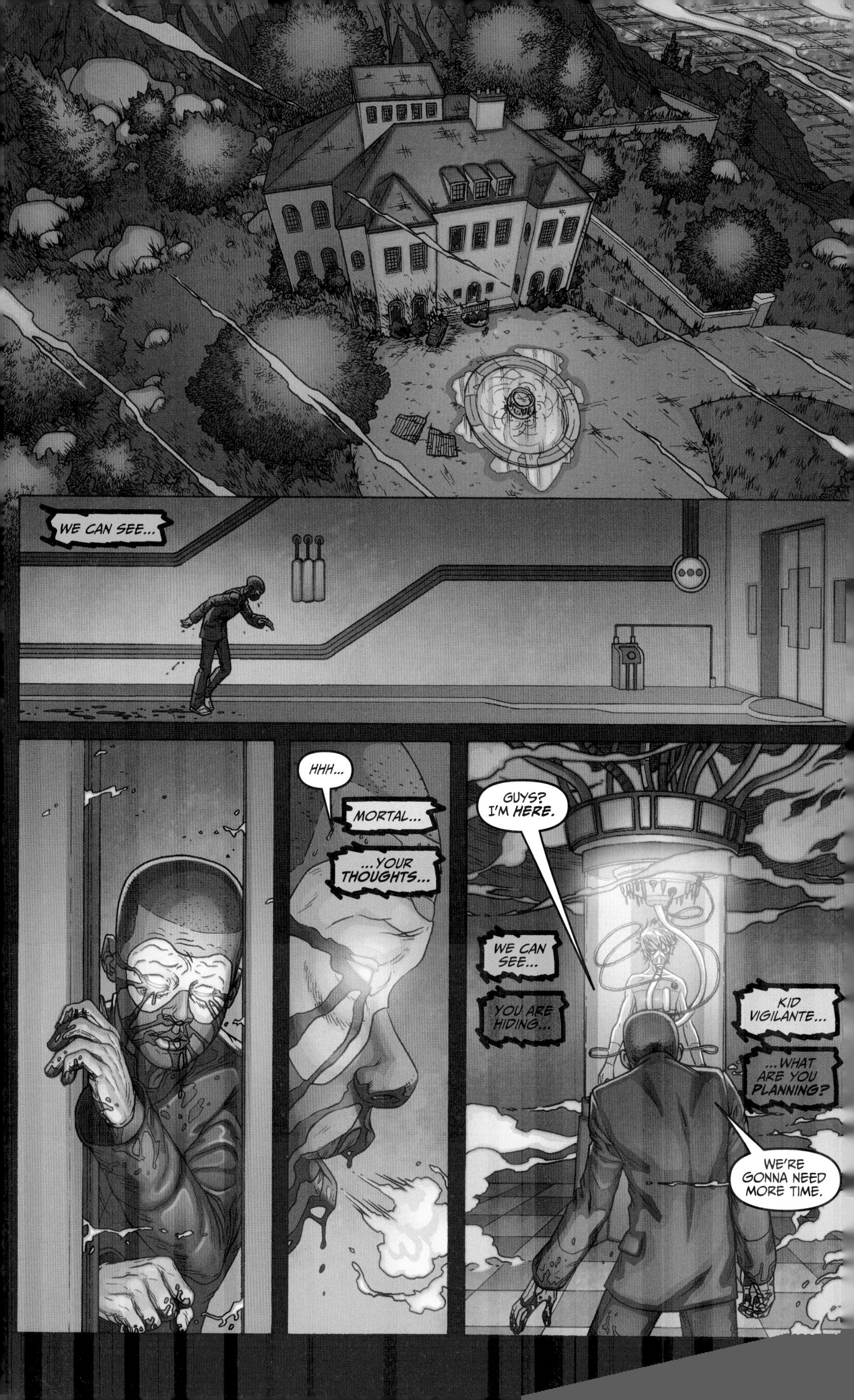
WE CAN SEE...
HHH...
MORTAL...
...YOUR THOUGHTS...
GUYS? I'M HERE.
WE CAN SEE...
YOU ARE HIDING...
KID VIGILANTE...
...WHAT ARE YOU PLANNING?
WE'RE GONNA NEED MORE TIME.

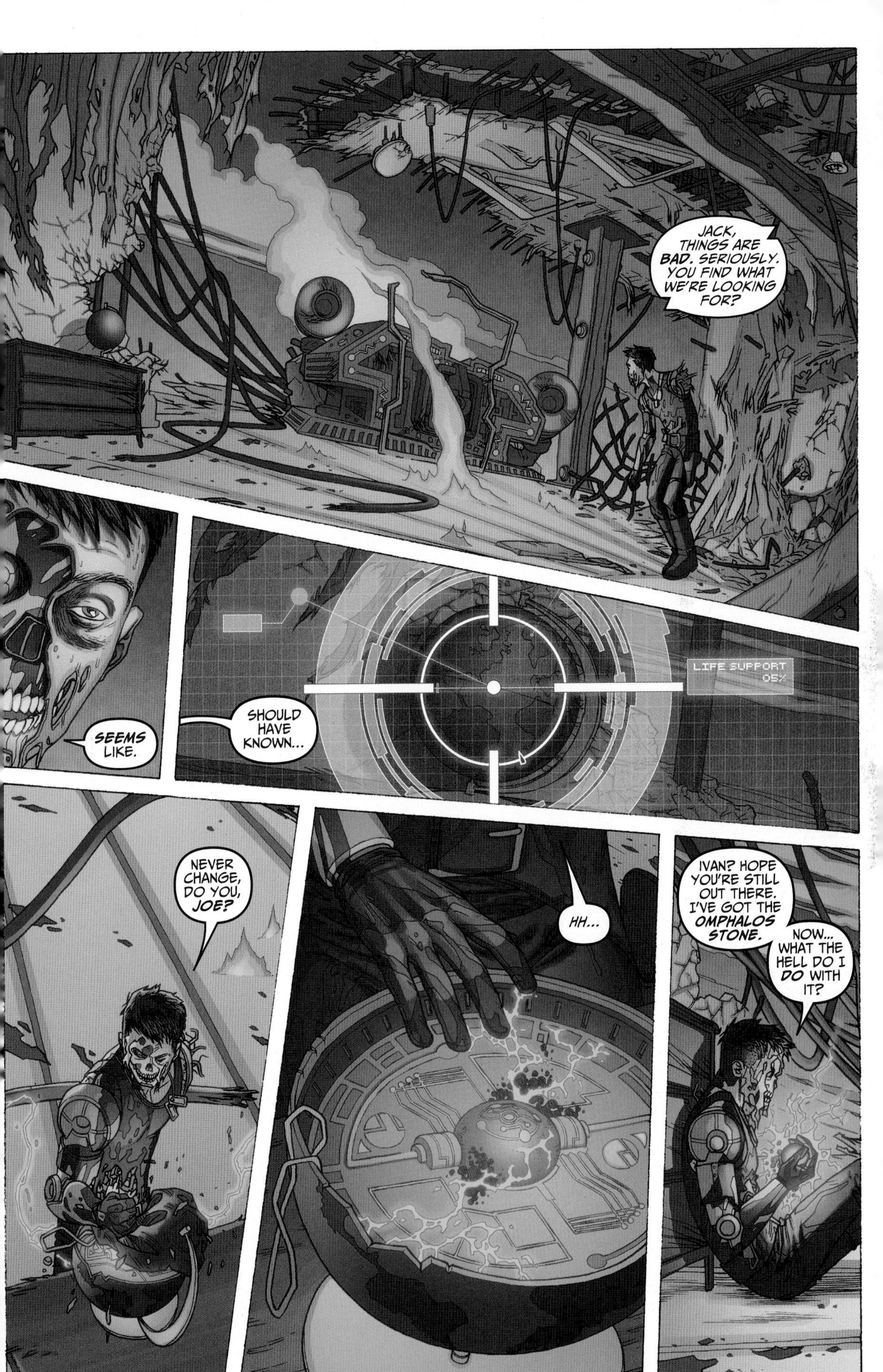
JACK, THINGS ARE BAD. SERIOUSLY. YOU FIND WHAT WE'RE LOOKING FOR?
SEEMS LIKE.
SHOULD HAVE KNOWN...
LIFE SUPPORT 05%
NEVER CHANGE, DO YOU, JOE?
HH...
IVAN? HOPE YOU'RE STILL OUT THERE. I'VE GOT THE OMPHALOS STONE.
NOW... WHAT THE HELL DO I DO WITH IT?

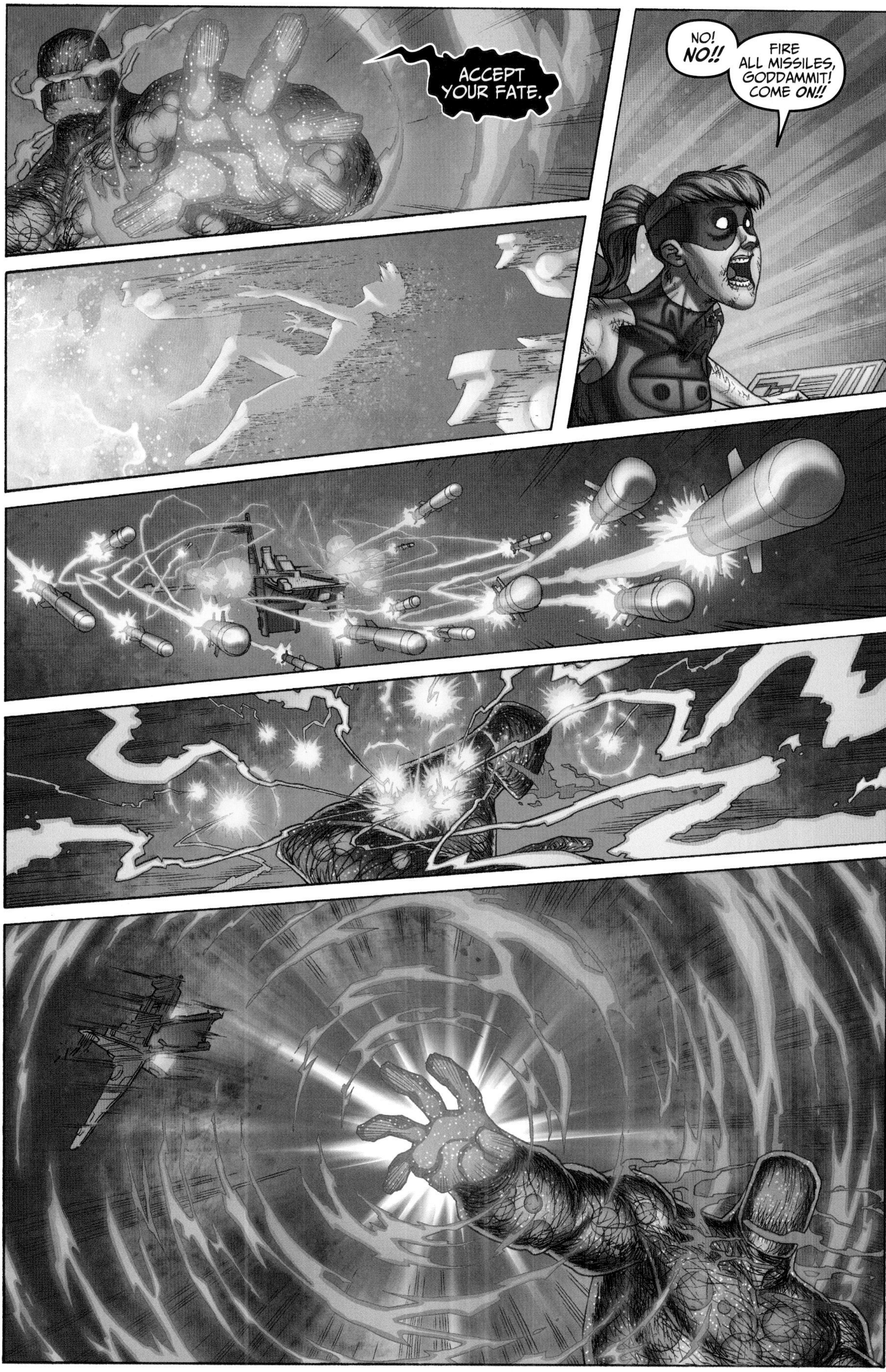
ACCEPT YOUR FATE.
NO! NO!!
FIRE ALL MISSILES, GODDAMMIT! COME ON!!

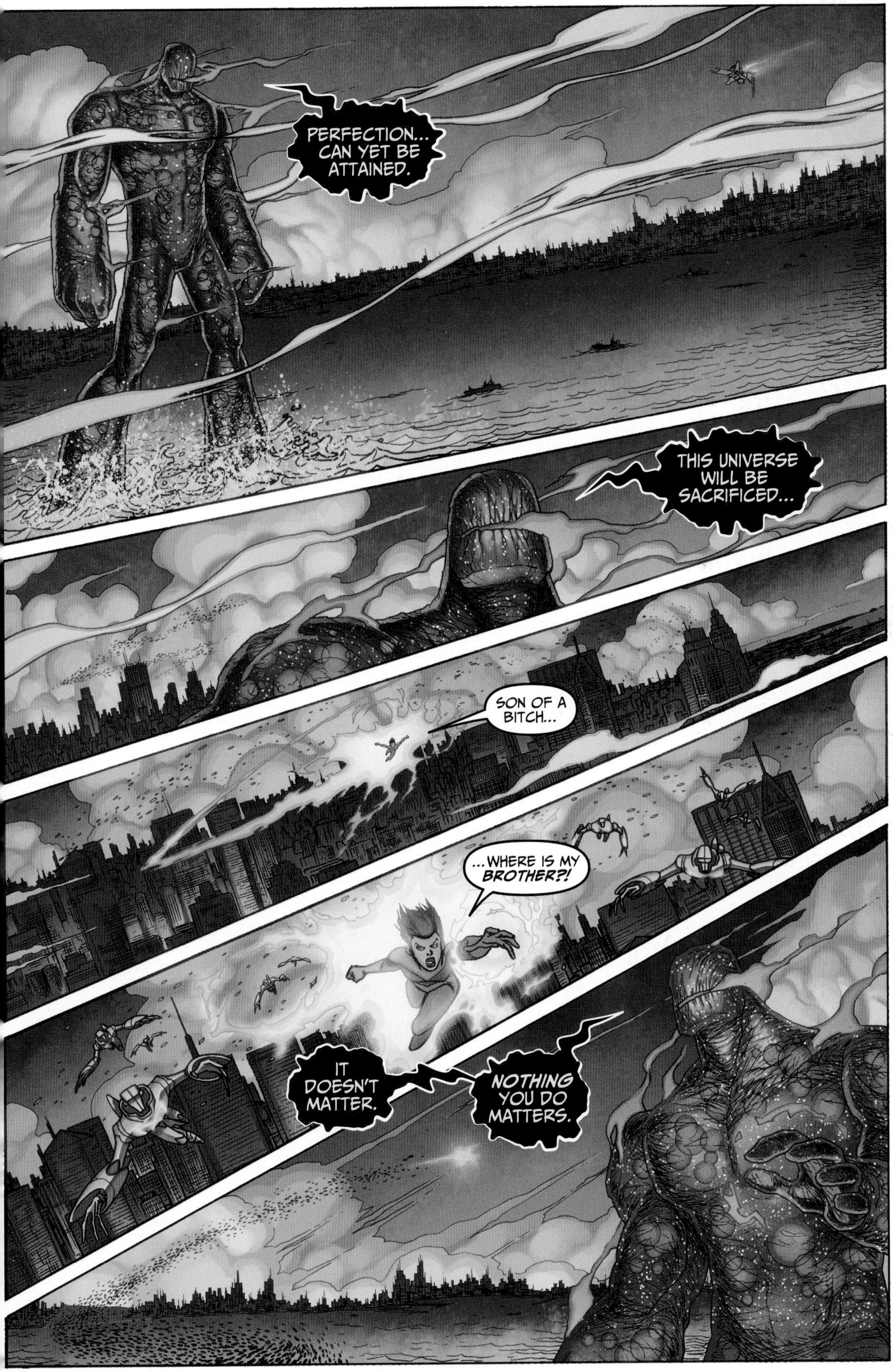
PERFECTION... CAN YET BE ATTAINED.
THIS UNIVERSE WILL BE SACRIFICED...
SON OF A BITCH...
...WHERE IS MY BROTHER?!
IT DOESN'T MATTER.
NOTHING YOU DO MATTERS.

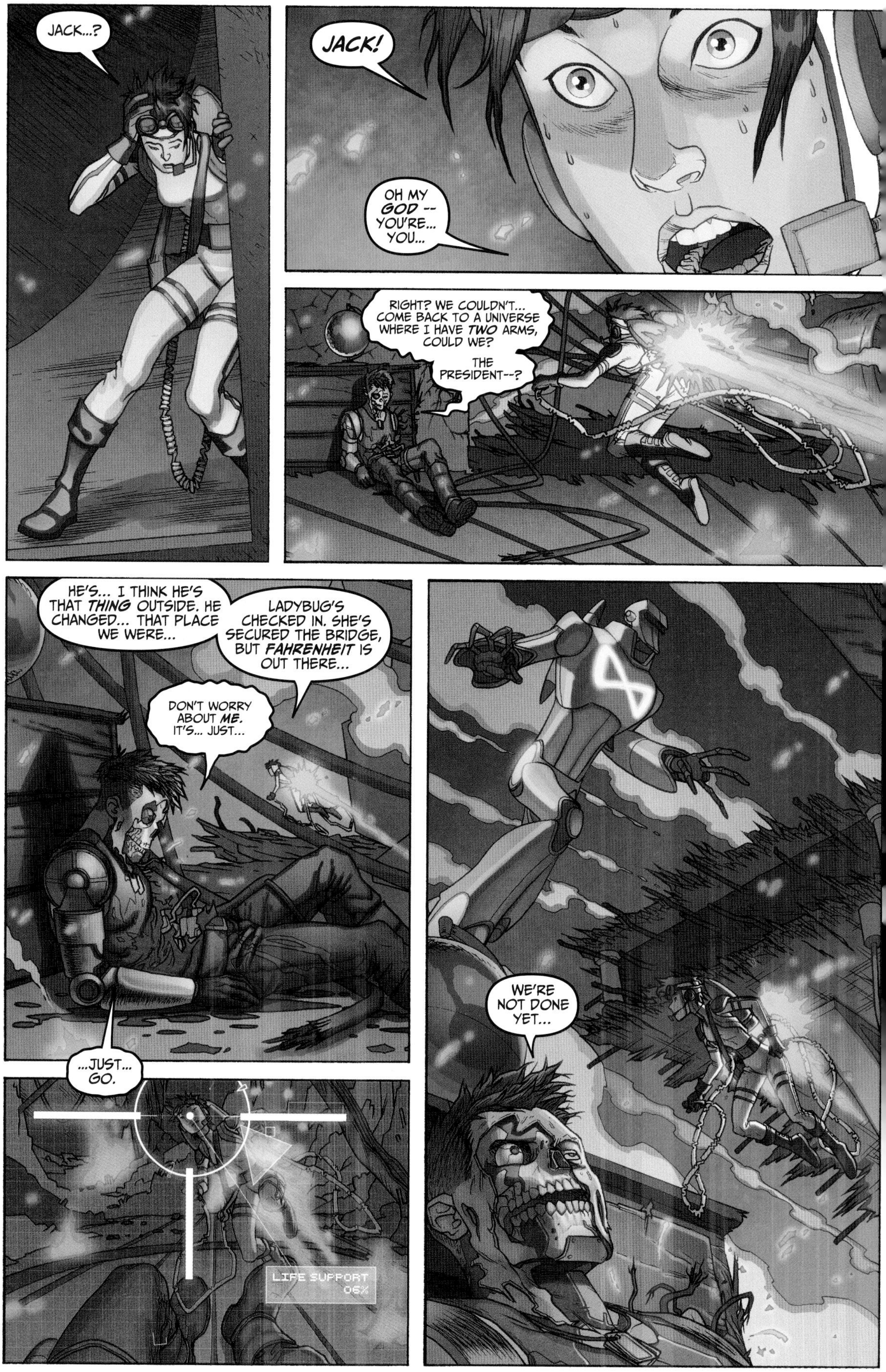
JACK...?
JACK!
OH MY GOD -- YOU'RE... YOU...
RIGHT? WE COULDN'T... COME BACK TO A UNIVERSE WHERE I HAVE TWO ARMS, COULD WE?
THE PRESIDENT--?
HE'S... I THINK HE'S THAT THING OUTSIDE. HE CHANGED... THAT PLACE WE WERE...
LADYBUG'S CHECKED IN. SHE'S SECURED THE BRIDGE, BUT FAHRENHEIT IS OUT THERE...
DON'T WORRY ABOUT ME. IT'S... JUST...
...JUST... GO.
LIFE SUPPORT 06%
WE'RE NOT DONE YET...

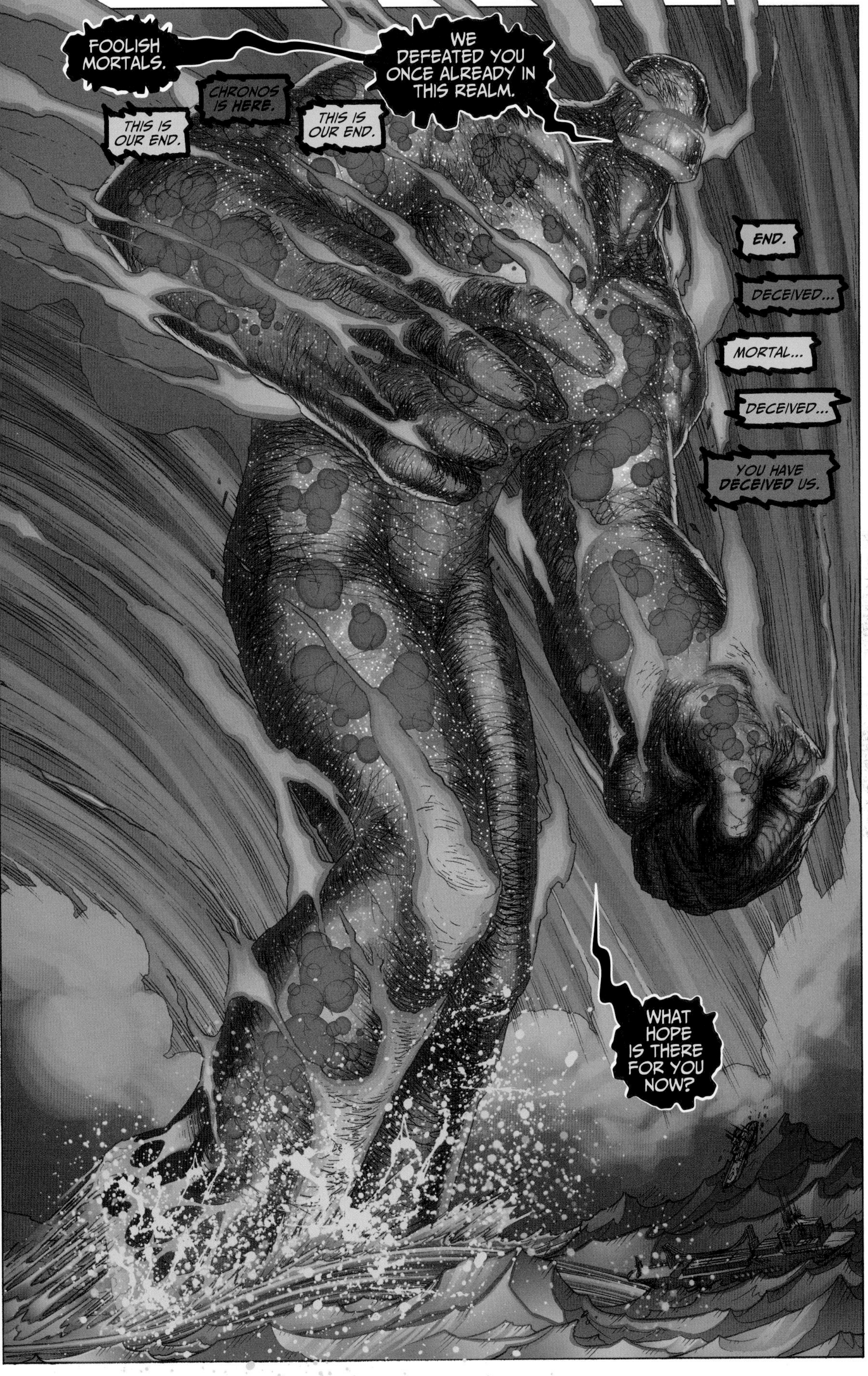
FOOLISH MORTALS.
WE DEFEATED YOU ONCE ALREADY IN THIS REALM.
THIS IS OUR END.
CHRONOS IS HERE.
THIS IS OUR END.
END.
DECEIVED...
MORTAL...
DECEIVED...
YOU HAVE DECEIVED US.
WHAT HOPE IS THERE FOR YOU NOW?

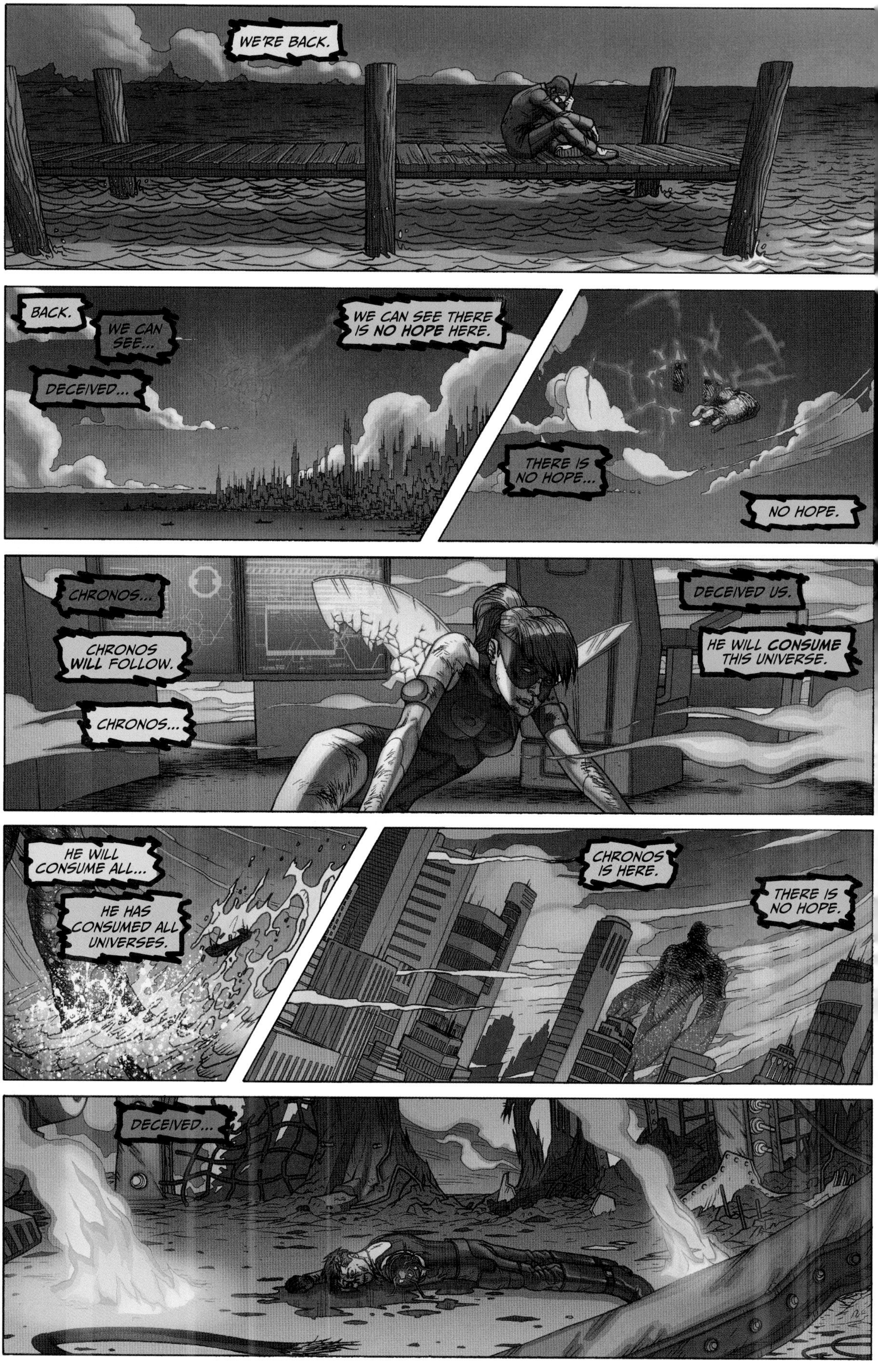
WE'RE BACK.
BACK.
WE CAN SEE...
WE CAN SEE THERE IS NO HOPE HERE.
DECEIVED...
THERE IS NO HOPE...
NO HOPE.
CHRONOS...
CHRONOS WILL FOLLOW.
CHRONOS...
DECEIVED US.
HE WILL CONSUME THIS UNIVERSE.
HE WILL CONSUME ALL...
HE HAS CONSUMED ALL UNIVERSES.
CHRONOS IS HERE.
THERE IS NO HOPE.
DECEIVED...

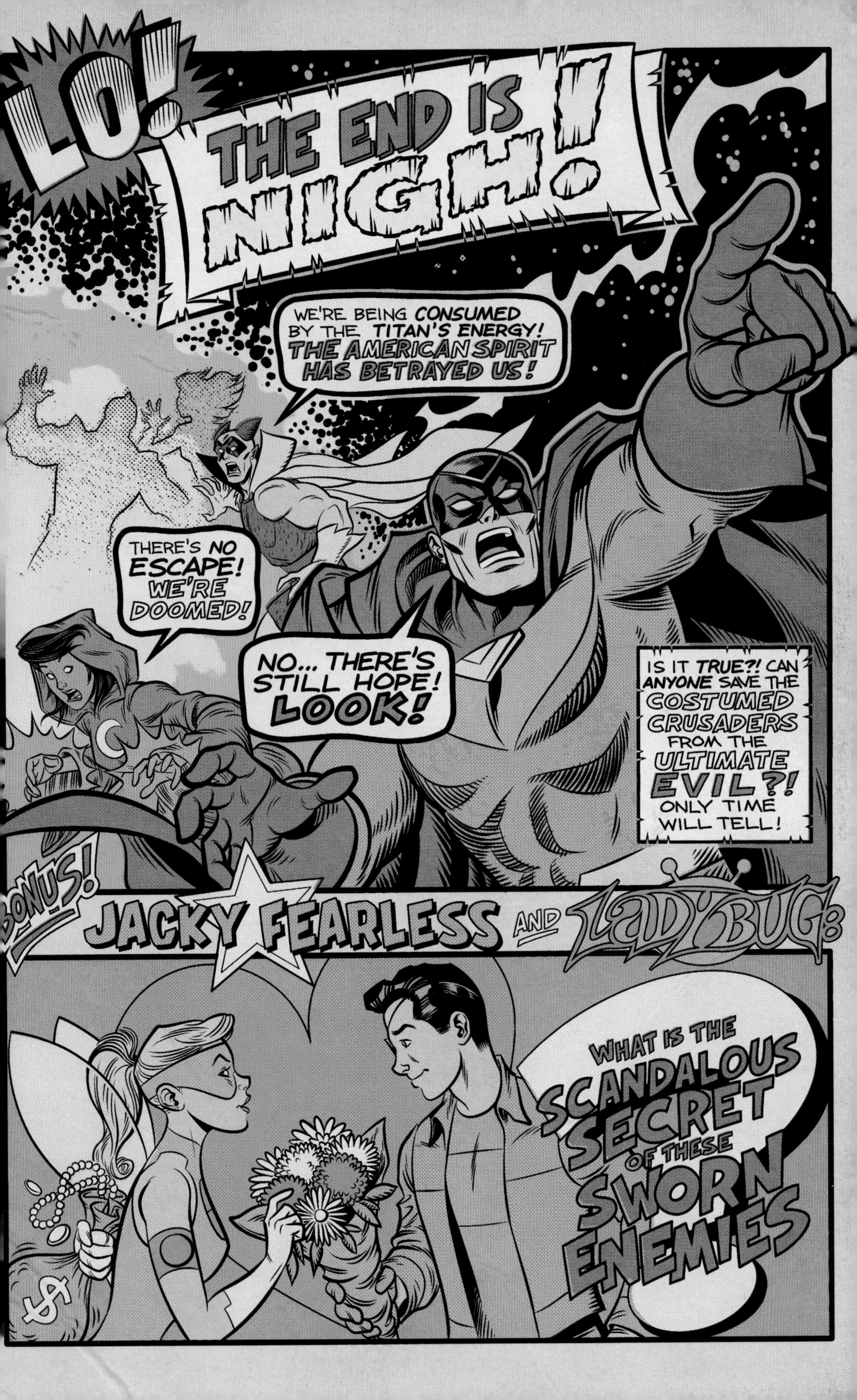
LO!
THE END IS NIGH!
WE'RE BEING CONSUMED BY THE TITAN'S ENERGY! THE AMERICAN SPIRIT HAS BETRAYED US!
THERE'S NO ESCAPE! WE'RE DOOMED!
NO... THERE'S STILL HOPE! LOOK!
IS IT TRUE?! CAN ANYONE SAVE THE COSTUMED CRUSADERS FROM THE ULTIMATE EVIL?! ONLY TIME WILL TELL!
BONUS!
JACKY FEARLESS AND LADYBUG:
WHAT IS THE SCANDALOUS SECRET OF THESE SWORN ENEMIES

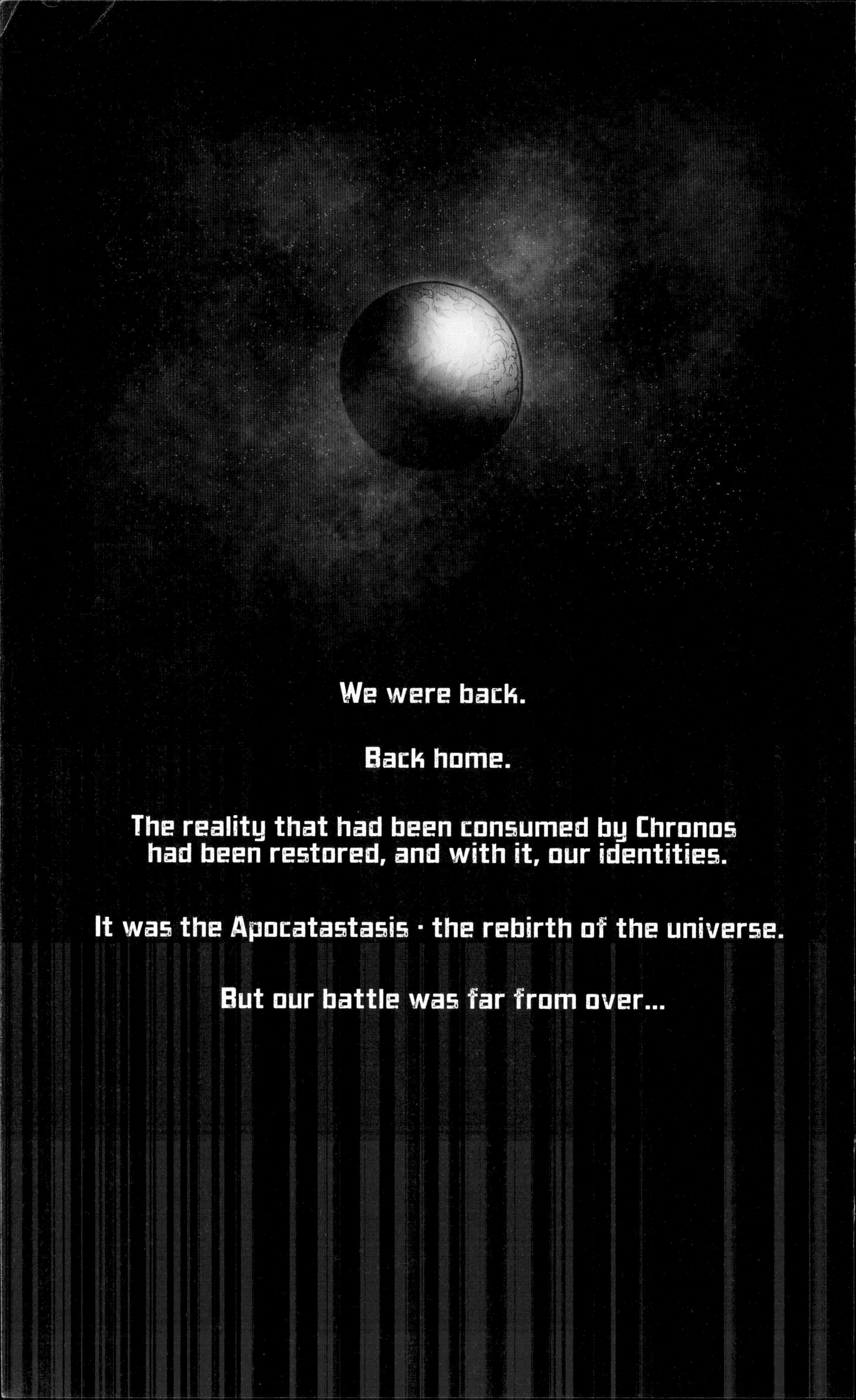
We were back.
Back home.
The reality that had been consumed by Chronos had been restored, and with it, our identities.
It was the Apocatastasis · the rebirth of the universe.
But our battle was far from over...

CHAPTER EIGHT : REBIRTH

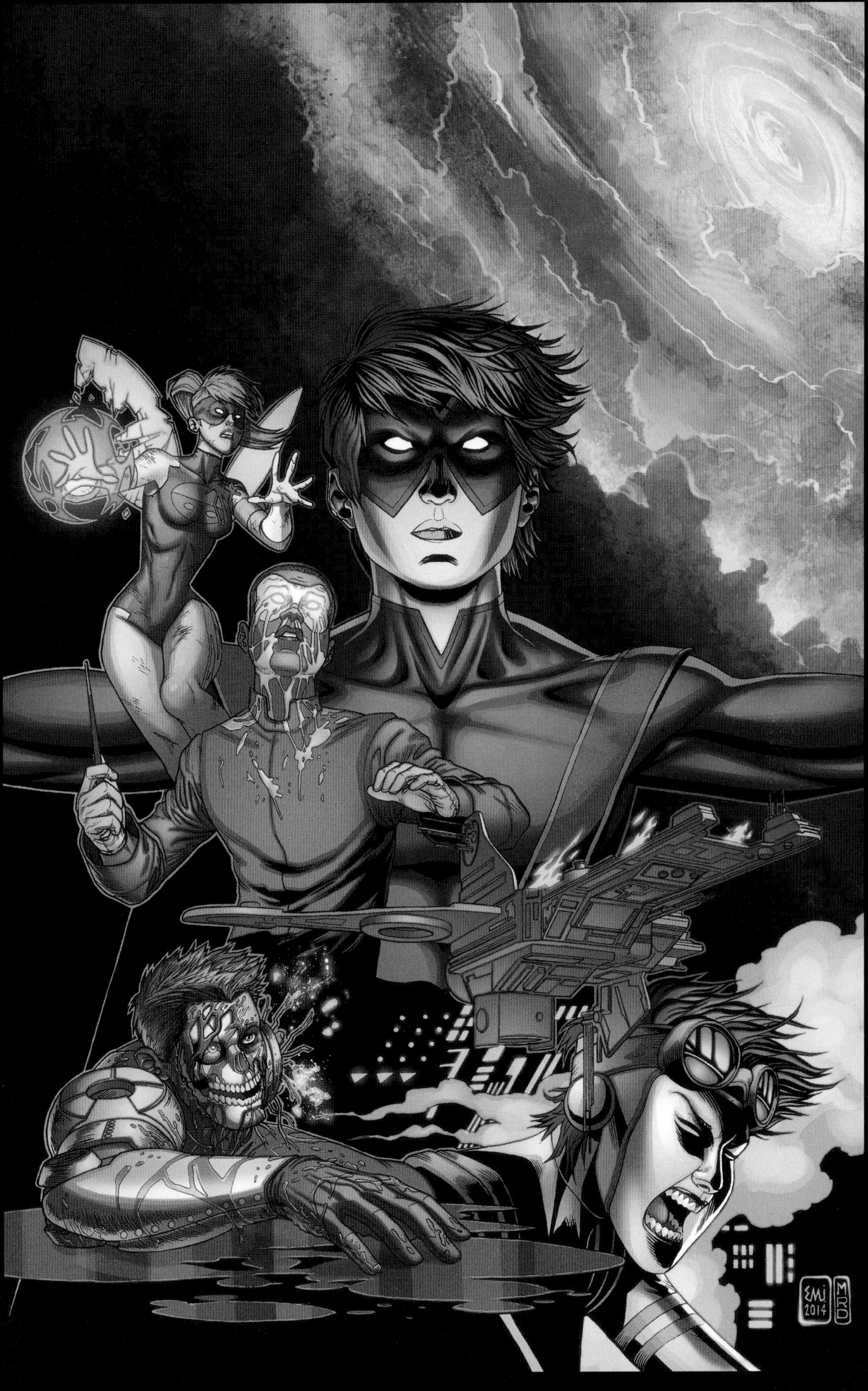

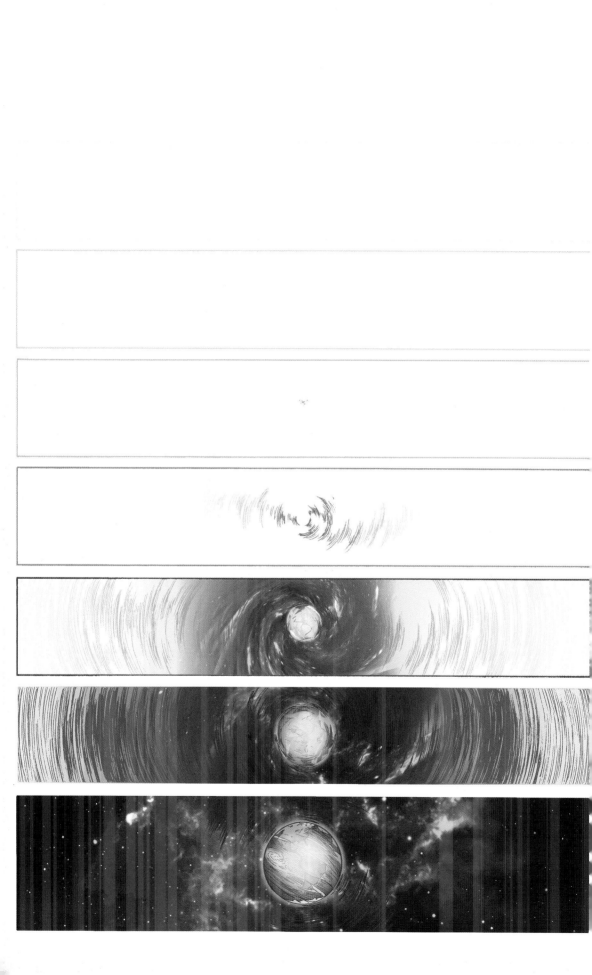

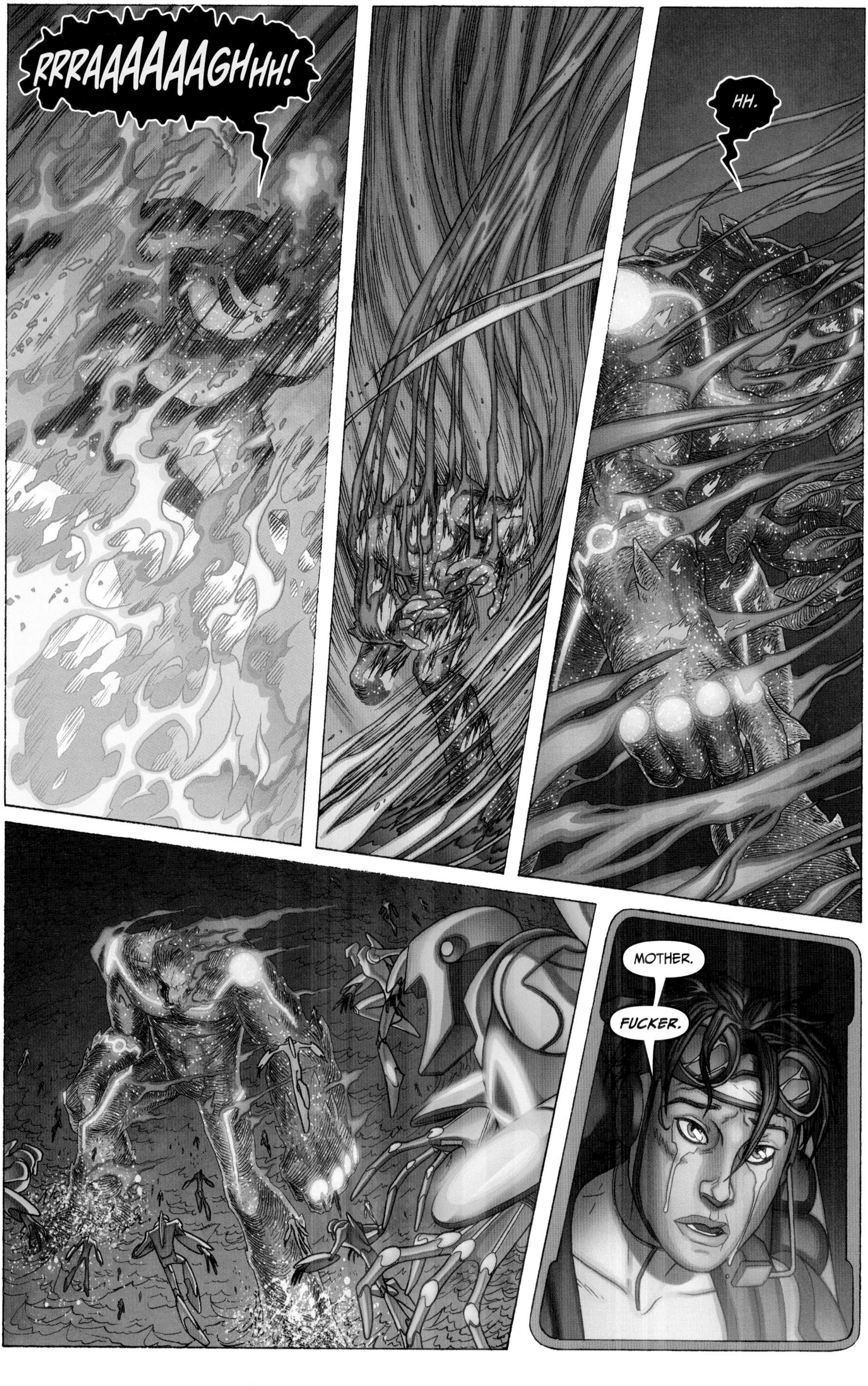
RRRAAAAAAAGHHH!
HH.
MOTHER.
FUCKER.

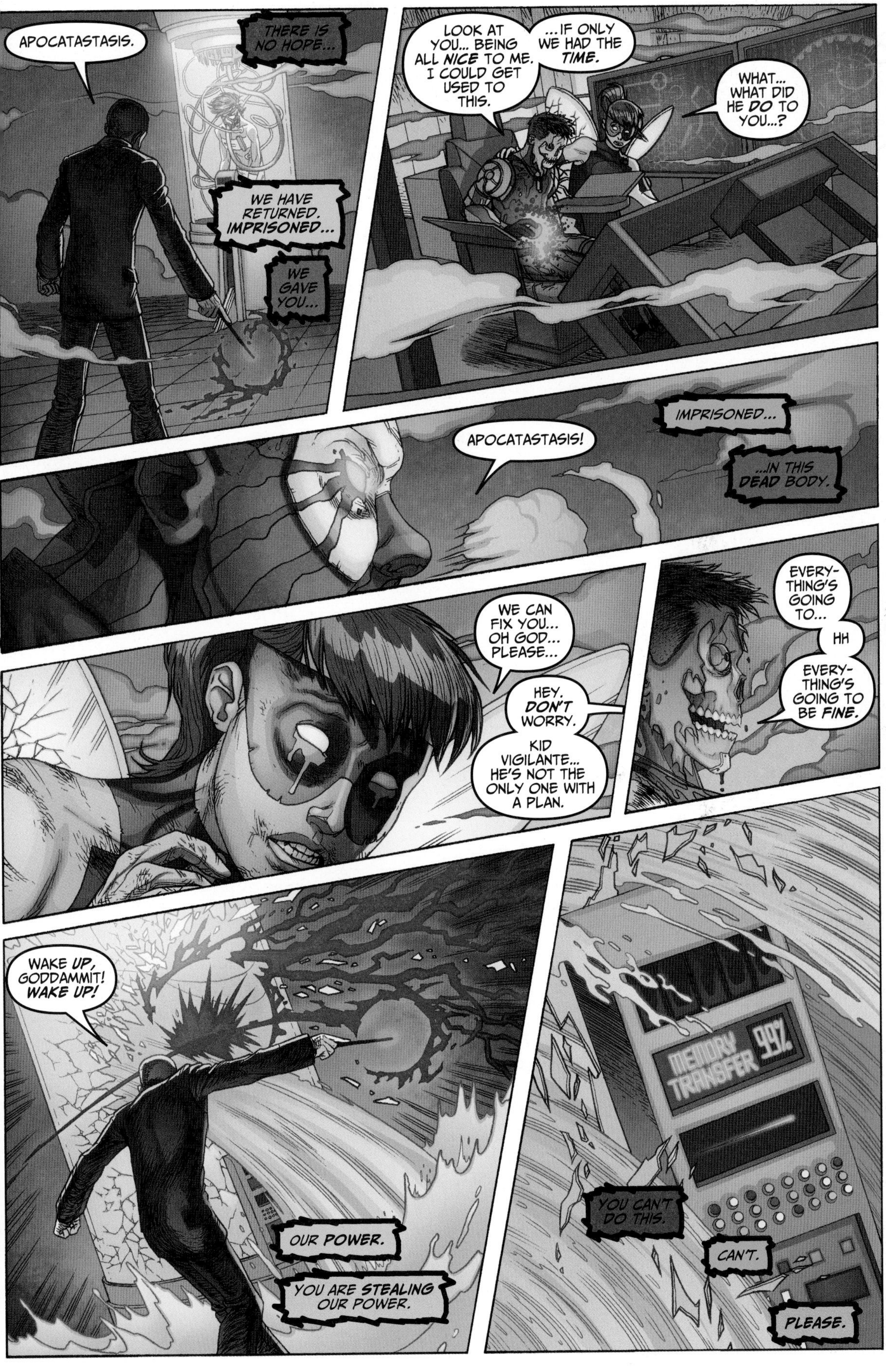
APOCATASTASIS.
THERE IS NO HOPE...
WE HAVE RETURNED. IMPRISONED...
WE GAVE YOU...
LOOK AT YOU... BEING ALL NICE TO ME. I COULD GET USED TO THIS.
...IF ONLY WE HAD THE TIME.
WHAT... WHAT DID HE DO TO YOU...?
IMPRISONED...
APOCATASTASIS!
...IN THIS DEAD BODY.
WE CAN FIX YOU... OH GOD... PLEASE...
HEY. DON'T WORRY.
KID VIGILANTE... HE'S NOT THE ONLY ONE WITH A PLAN.
EVERY-THING'S GOING TO...
HH
EVERY-THING'S GOING TO BE FINE.
WAKE UP, GODDAMMIT! WAKE UP!
OUR POWER.
YOU ARE STEALING OUR POWER.
MEMORY TRANSFER 99%
YOU CAN'T DO THIS.
CAN'T.
PLEASE.

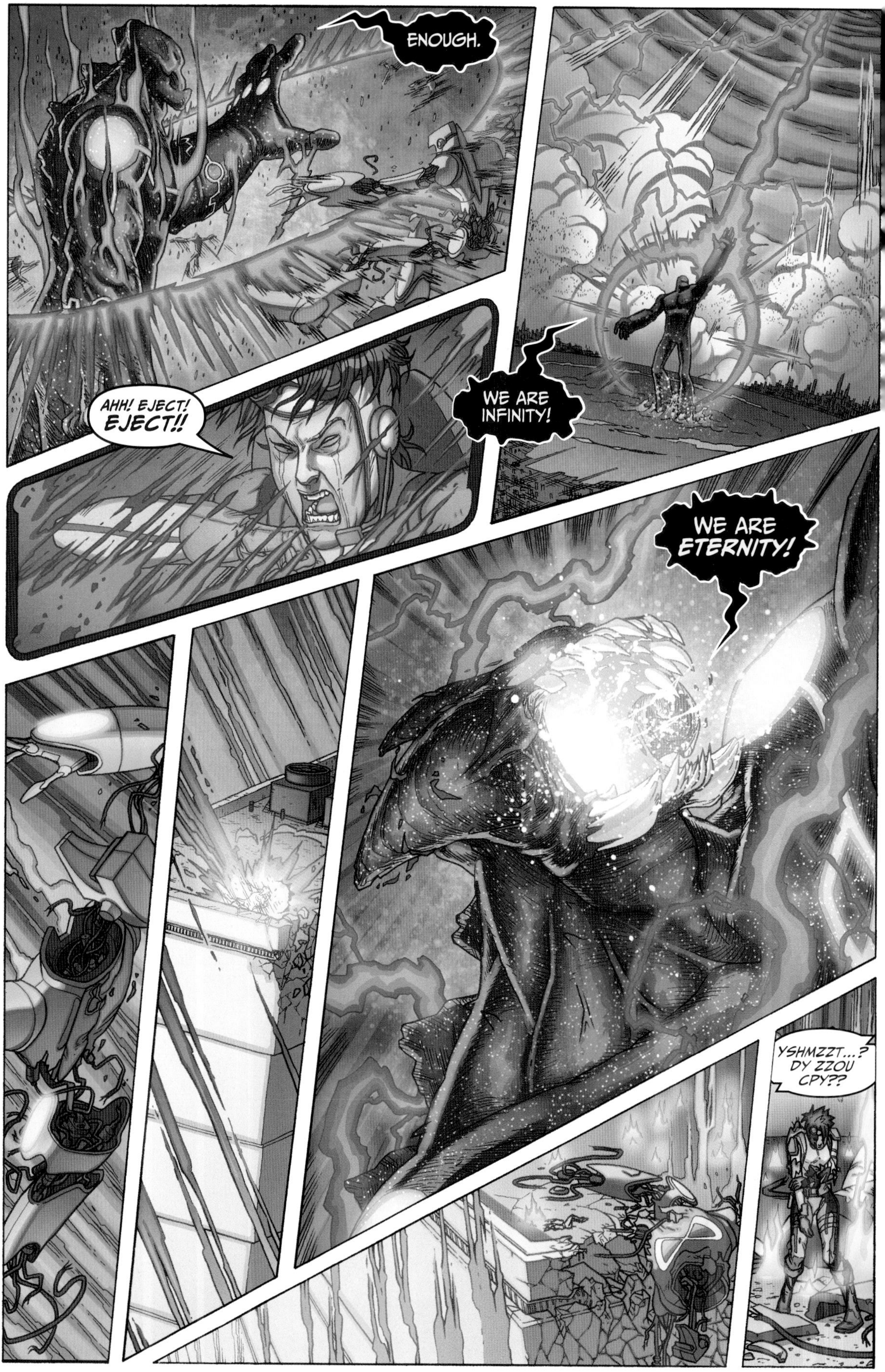
ENOUGH.
AHH! EJECT! EJECT!!
WE ARE INFINITY!
WE ARE ETERNITY!
YSHMZZT...? DY ZZOU CPY??

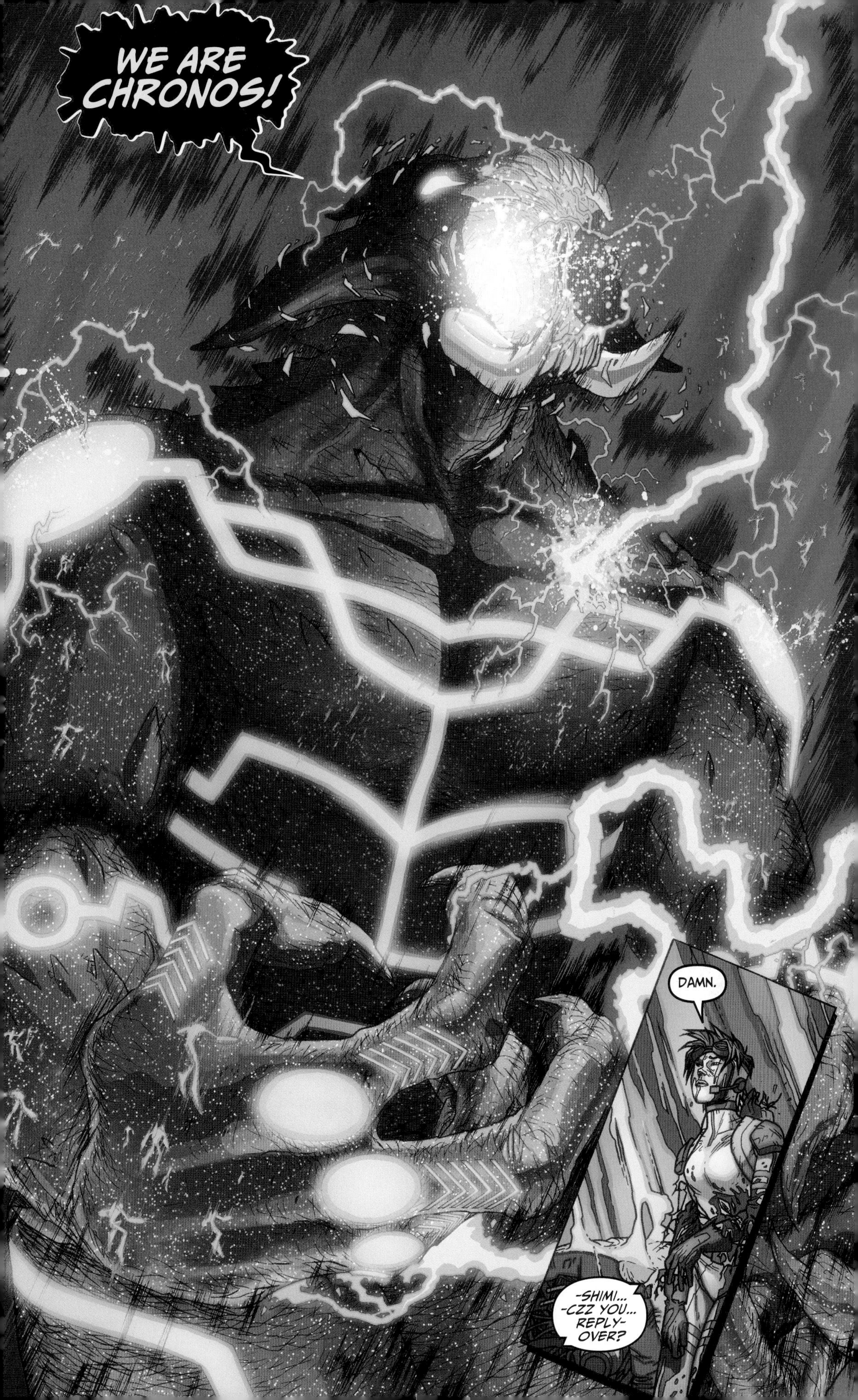
WE ARE CHRONOS!
DAMN.
-SHIMI... -CZZ YOU... REPLY- OVER?

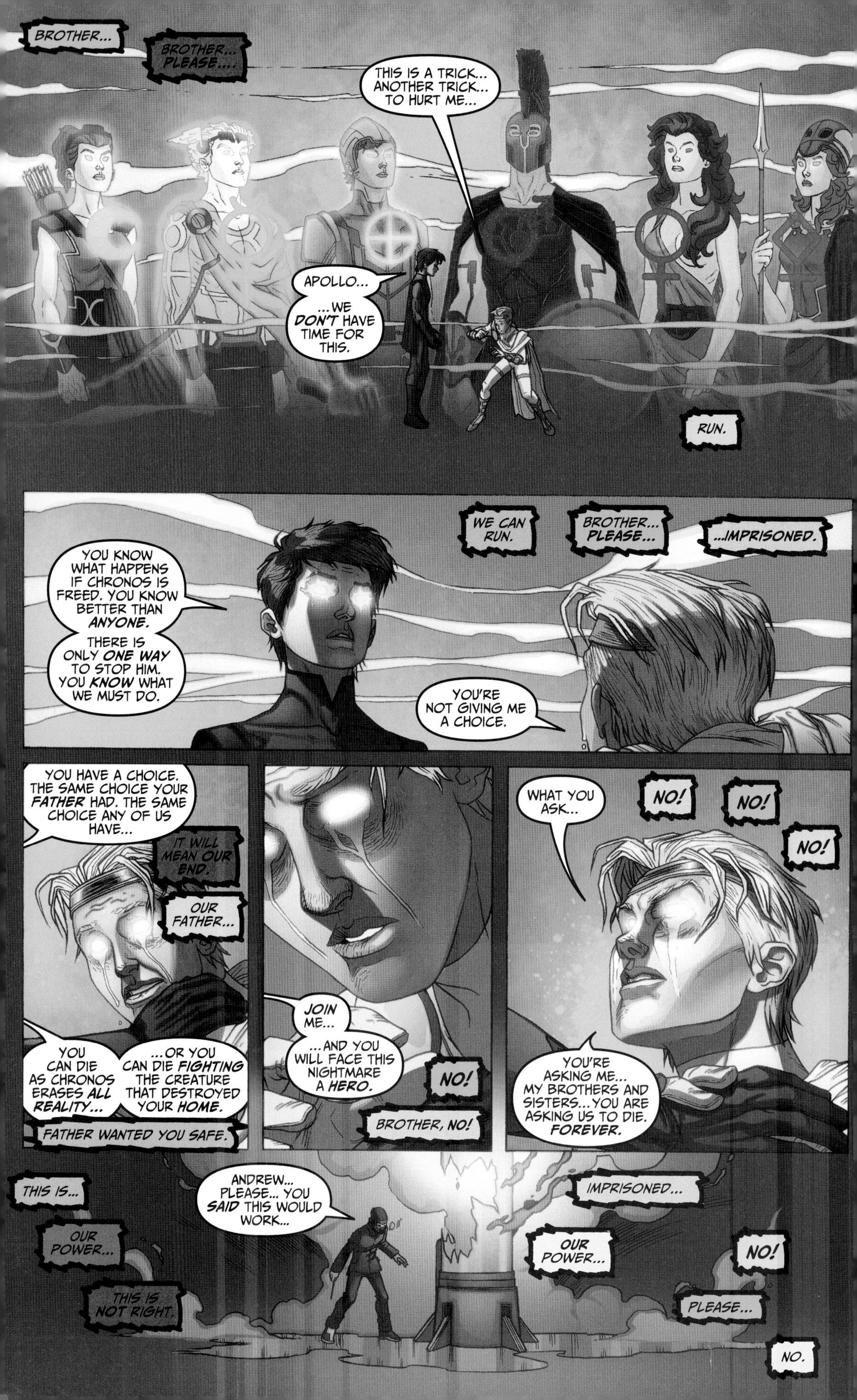
BROTHER...
BROTHER... PLEASE....
THIS IS A TRICK... ANOTHER TRICK... TO HURT ME...
APOLLO...
...WE DON'T HAVE TIME FOR THIS.
RUN.
WE CAN RUN.
BROTHER... PLEASE...
...IMPRISONED.
YOU KNOW WHAT HAPPENS IF CHRONOS IS FREED. YOU KNOW BETTER THAN ANYONE.
THERE IS ONLY ONE WAY TO STOP HIM. YOU KNOW WHAT WE MUST DO.
YOU'RE NOT GIVING ME A CHOICE.
YOU HAVE A CHOICE. THE SAME CHOICE YOUR FATHER HAD. THE SAME CHOICE ANY OF US HAVE...
IT WILL MEAN OUR END.
OUR FATHER...
YOU CAN DIE AS CHRONOS ERASES ALL REALITY...
...OR YOU CAN DIE FIGHTING THE CREATURE THAT DESTROYED YOUR HOME.
FATHER WANTED YOU SAFE.
JOIN ME...
...AND YOU WILL FACE THIS NIGHTMARE A HERO.
NO!
BROTHER, NO!
WHAT YOU ASK...
NO!
NO!
NO!
YOU'RE ASKING ME... MY BROTHERS AND SISTERS... YOU ARE ASKING US TO DIE. FOREVER.
THIS IS...
OUR POWER...
THIS IS NOT RIGHT.
ANDREW... PLEASE... YOU SAID THIS WOULD WORK...
IMPRISONED...
OUR POWER...
NO!
PLEASE...
NO.

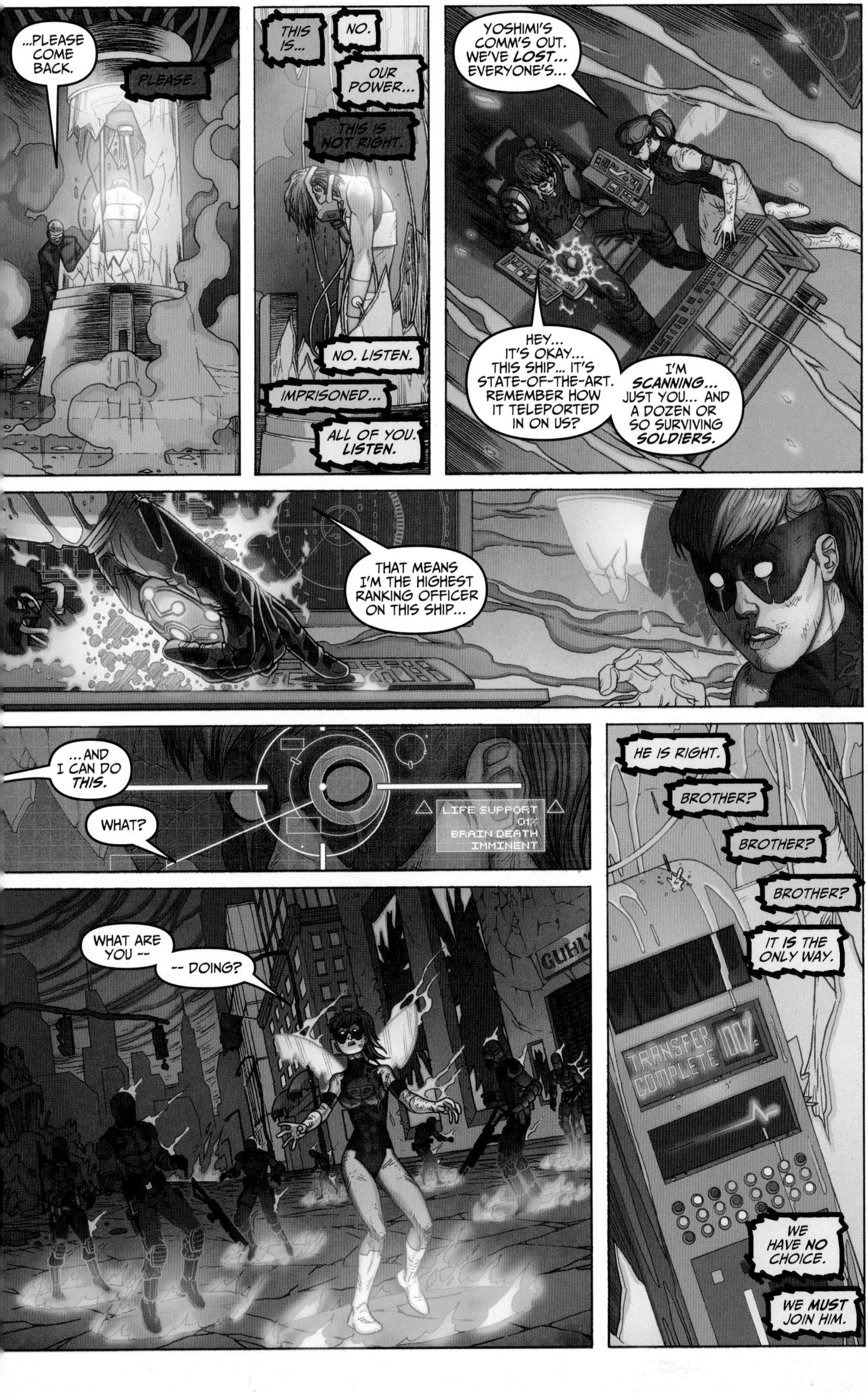
...PLEASE COME BACK.
PLEASE.
THIS IS...
NO.
OUR POWER...
THIS IS NOT RIGHT.
NO. LISTEN.
IMPRISONED...
ALL OF YOU. LISTEN.
YOSHIMI'S COMM'S OUT. WE'VE LOST... EVERYONE'S...
HEY... IT'S OKAY... THIS SHIP... IT'S STATE-OF-THE-ART. REMEMBER HOW IT TELEPORTED IN ON US?
I'M SCANNING... JUST YOU... AND A DOZEN OR SO SURVIVING SOLDIERS.
THAT MEANS I'M THE HIGHEST RANKING OFFICER ON THIS SHIP...
...AND I CAN DO THIS.
WHAT?
LIFE SUPPORT 01% BRAIN DEATH IMMINENT
WHAT ARE YOU --
-- DOING?
HE IS RIGHT.
BROTHER?
BROTHER?
BROTHER?
IT IS THE ONLY WAY.
TRANSFER COMPLETE 100%
WE HAVE NO CHOICE.
WE MUST JOIN HIM.

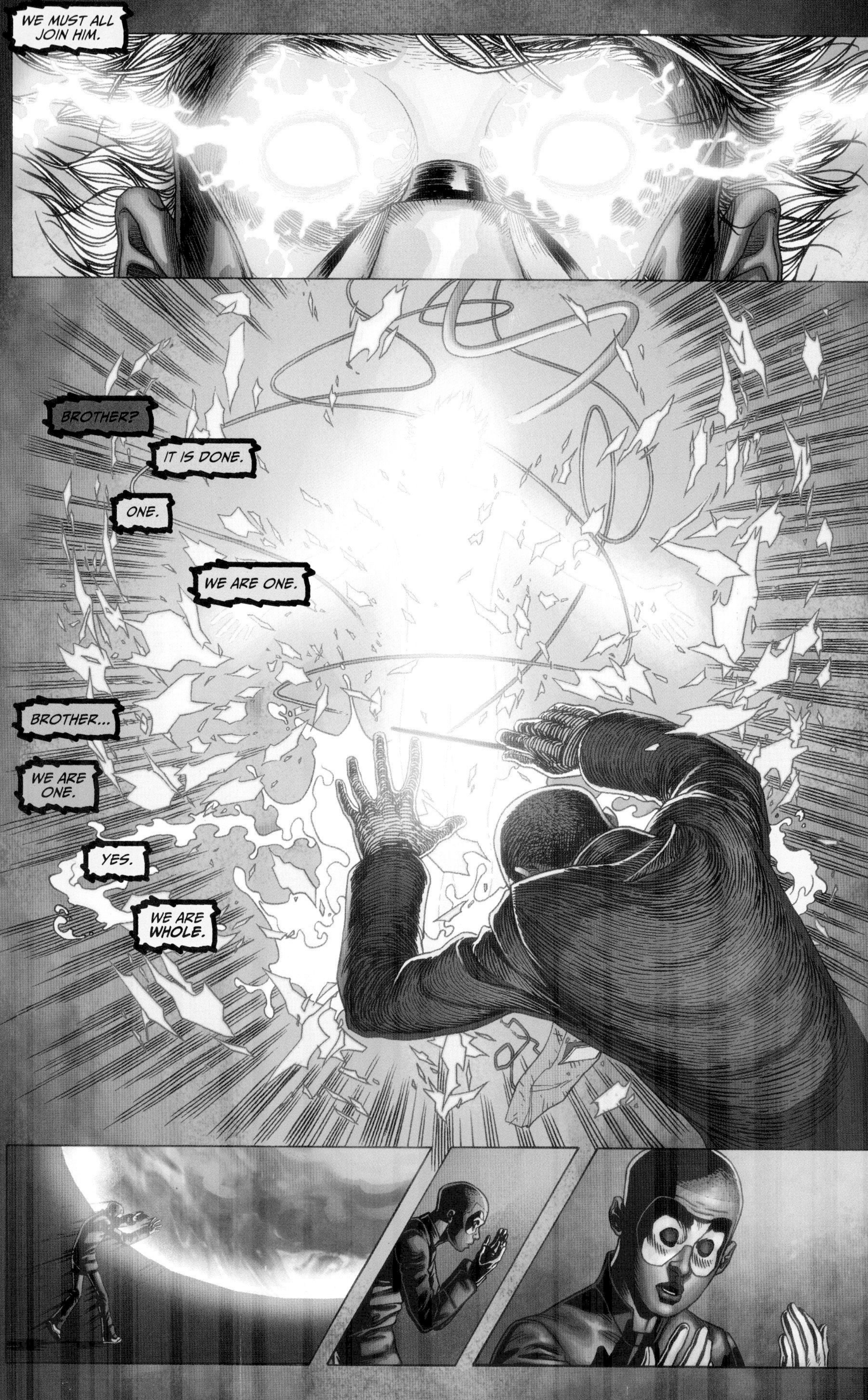
WE MUST ALL JOIN HIM.
BROTHER?
IT IS DONE.
ONE.
WE ARE ONE.
BROTHER...
WE ARE ONE.
YES.
WE ARE WHOLE.

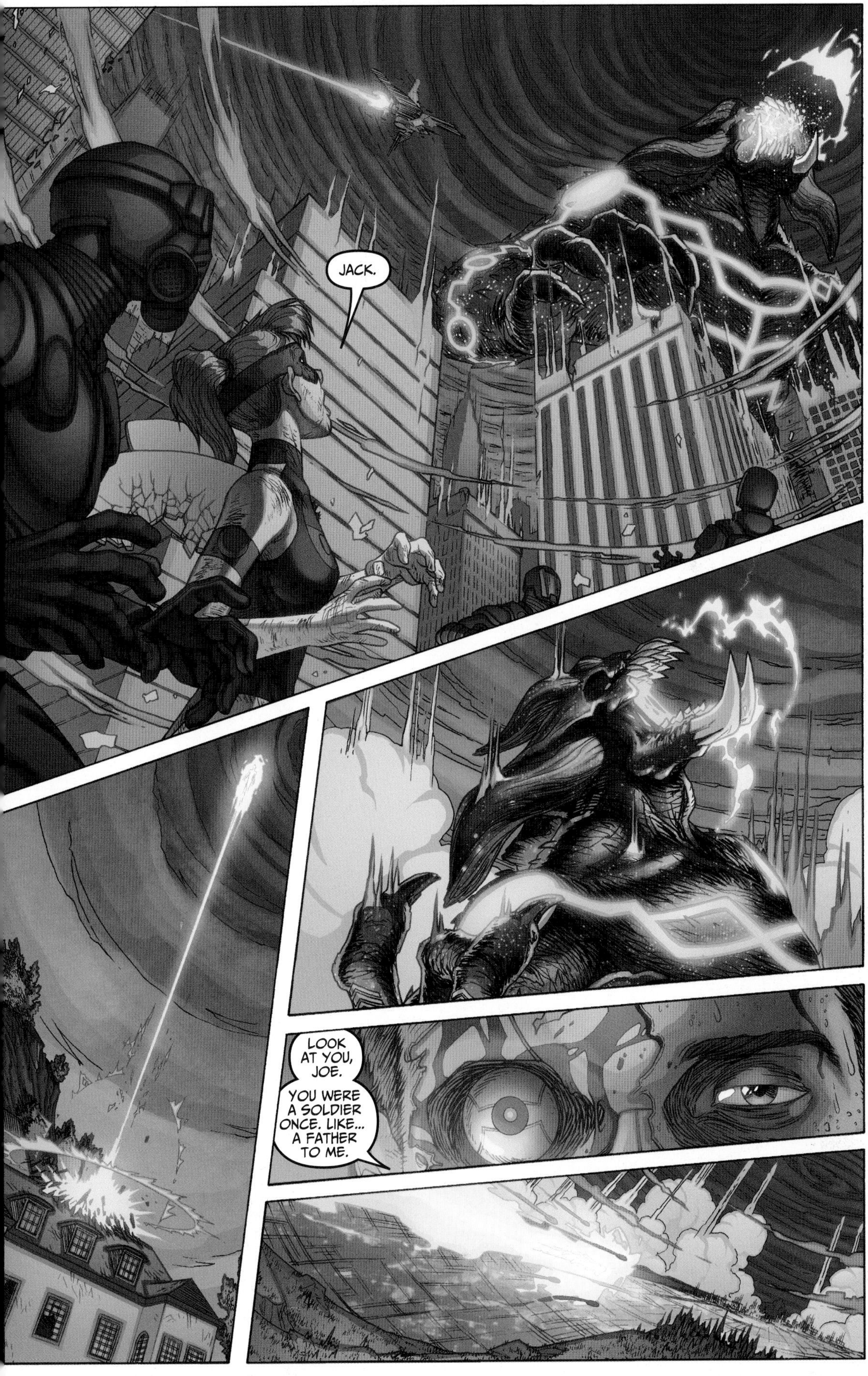
JACK.
LOOK AT YOU, JOE.
YOU WERE A SOLDIER ONCE. LIKE... A FATHER TO ME.

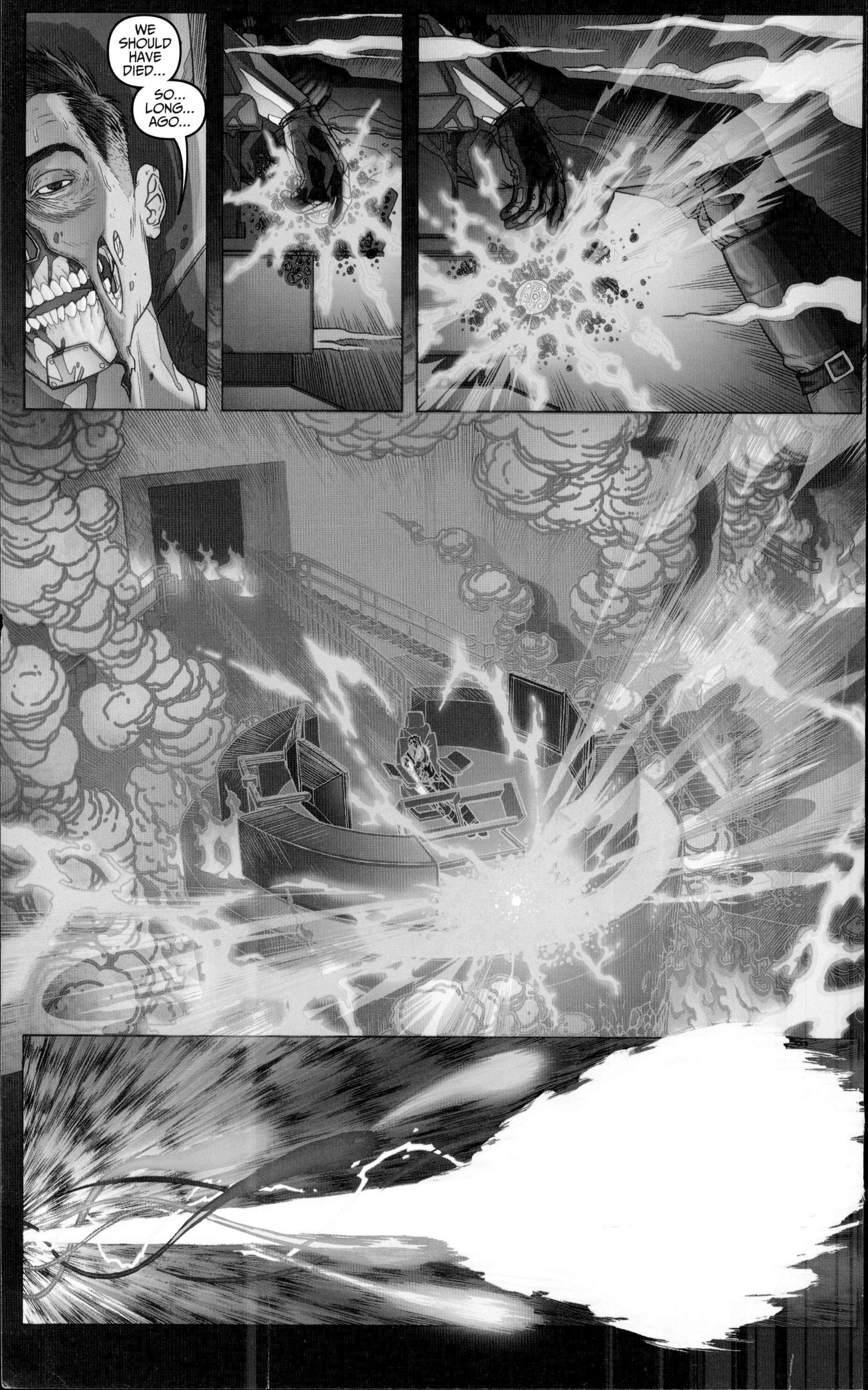
WE SHOULD HAVE DIED...
SO... LONG... AGO...

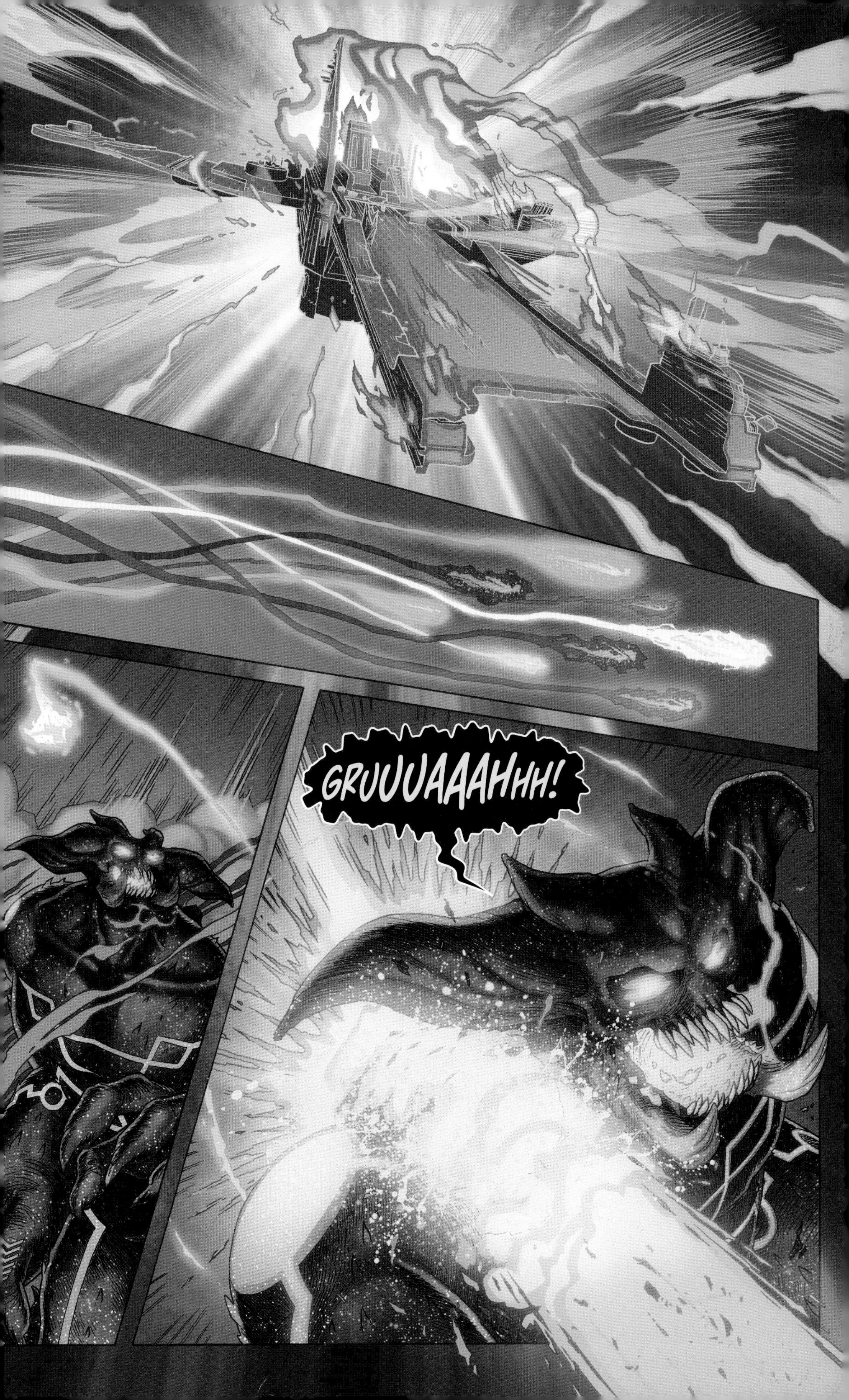
GRUUUAAAHhh!

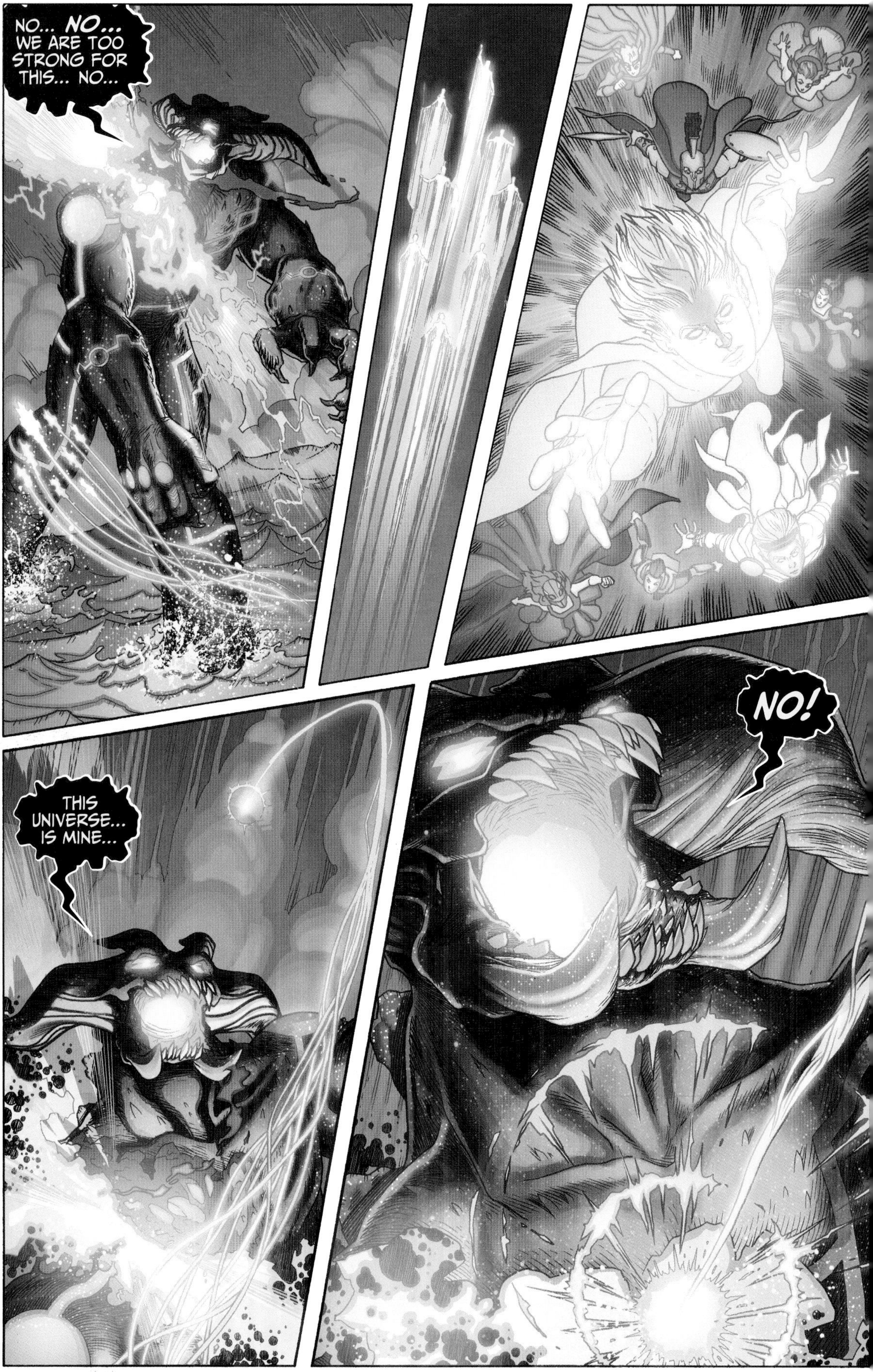
NO... NO... WE ARE TOO STRONG FOR THIS... NO...
THIS UNIVERSE... IS MINE...
NO!

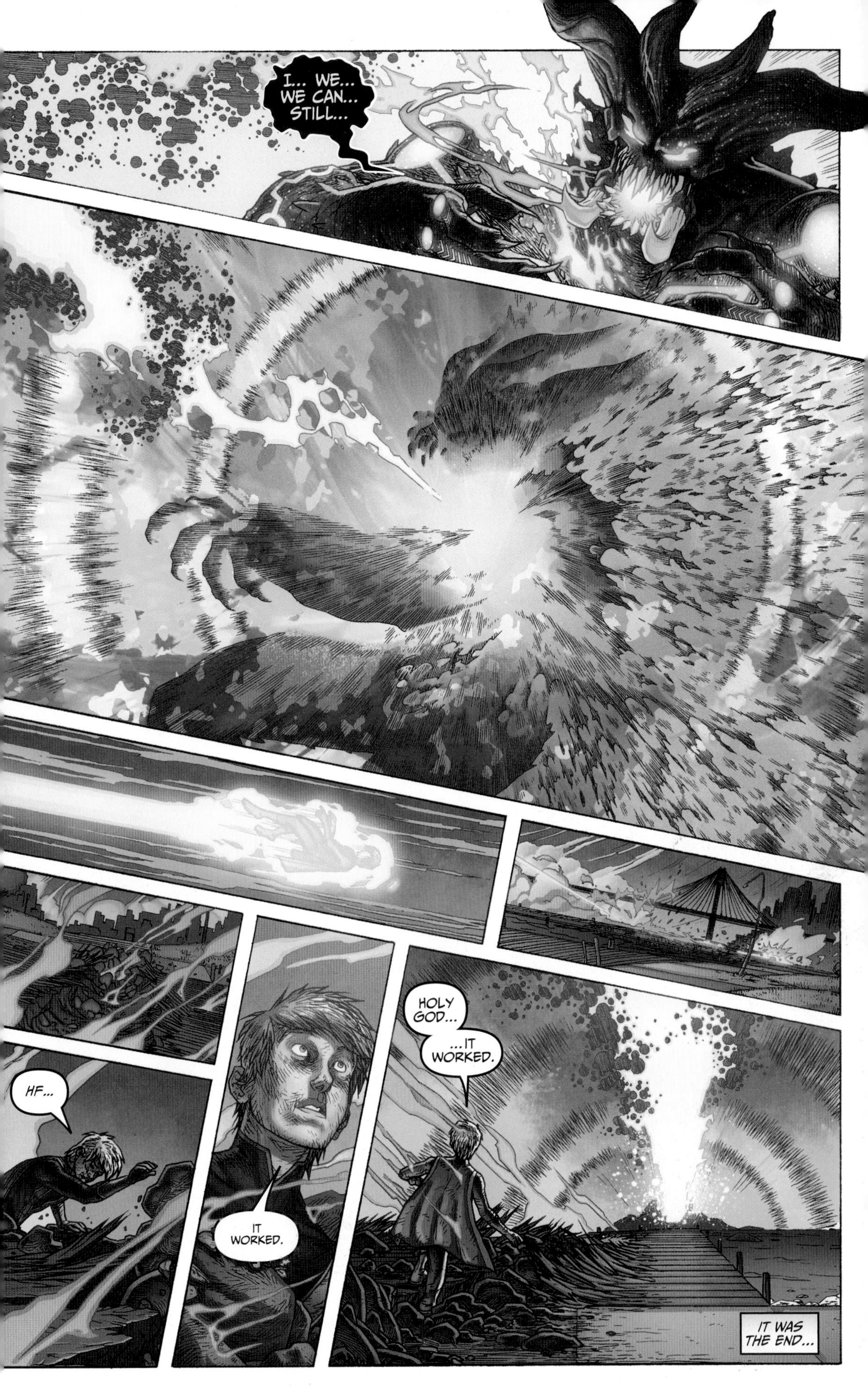
I... WE... WE CAN... STILL...
HF...
IT WORKED.
HOLY GOD...
...IT WORKED.
IT WAS THE END...

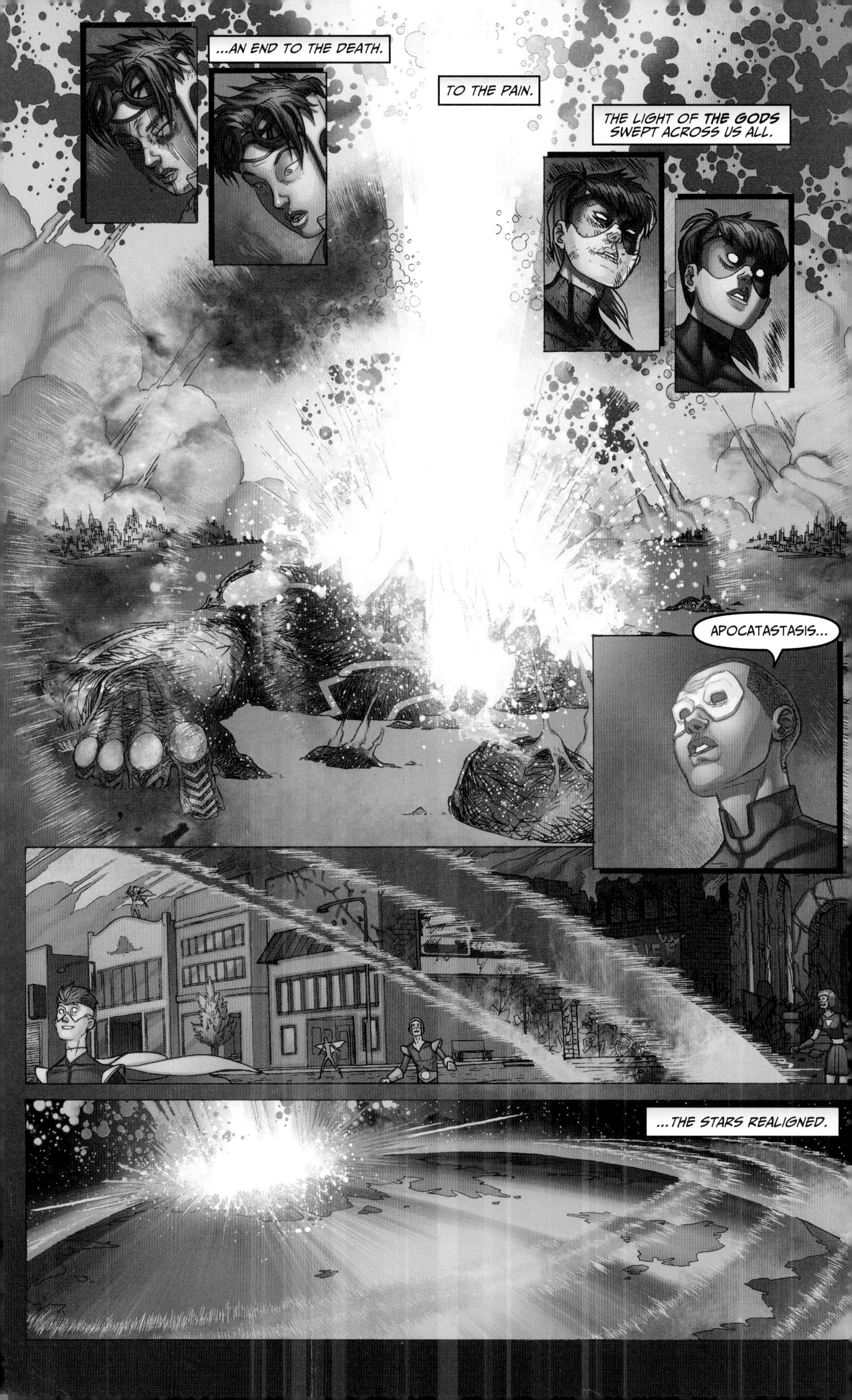
...AN END TO THE DEATH.
TO THE PAIN.
THE LIGHT OF **THE GODS** SWEPT ACROSS US ALL.
APOCATASTASIS...
...THE STARS REALIGNED.

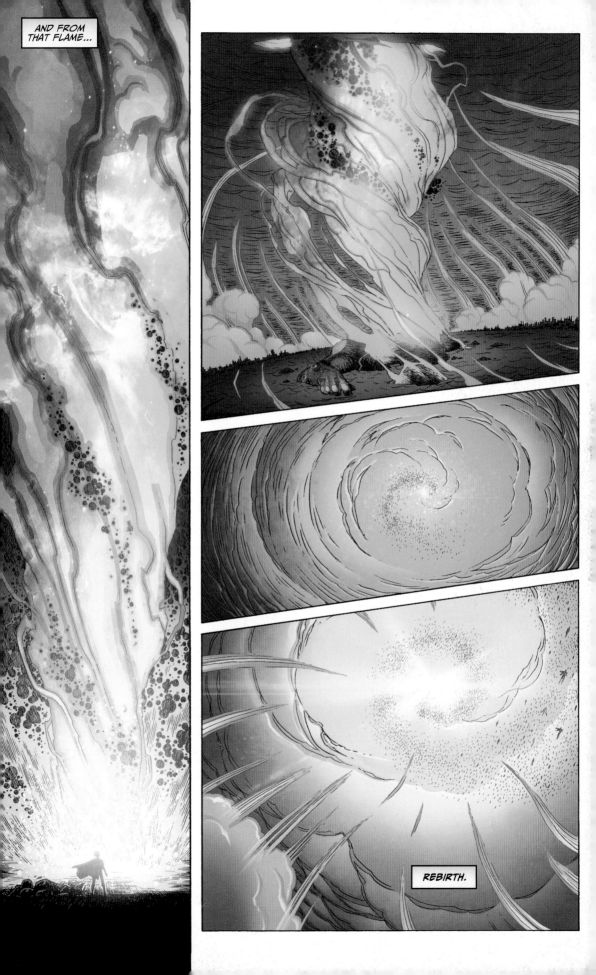

AND FROM
THAT FLAME...

REBIRTH.

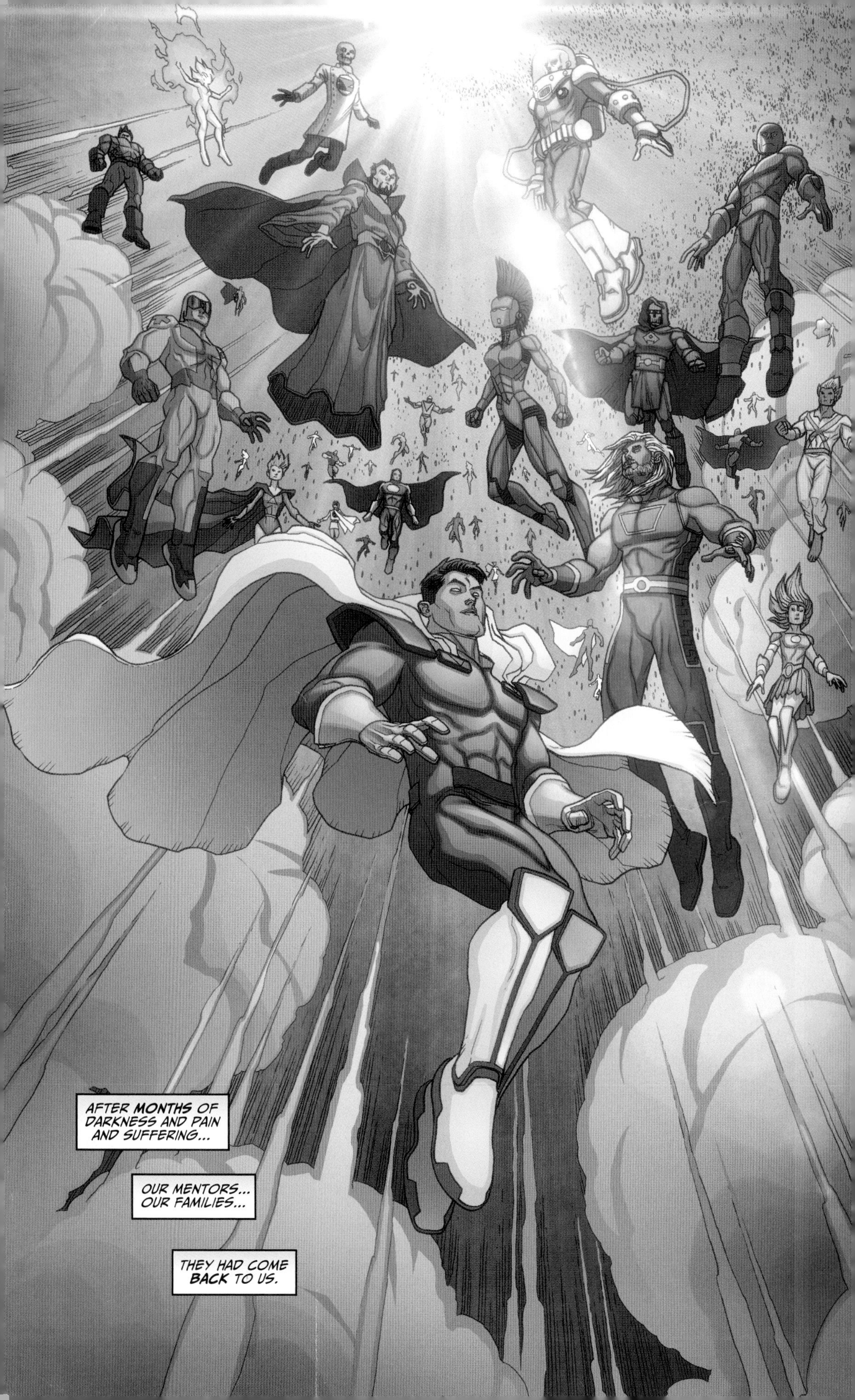
AFTER **MONTHS** OF DARKNESS AND PAIN AND SUFFERING...
OUR MENTORS... OUR FAMILIES...
THEY HAD COME **BACK** TO US.

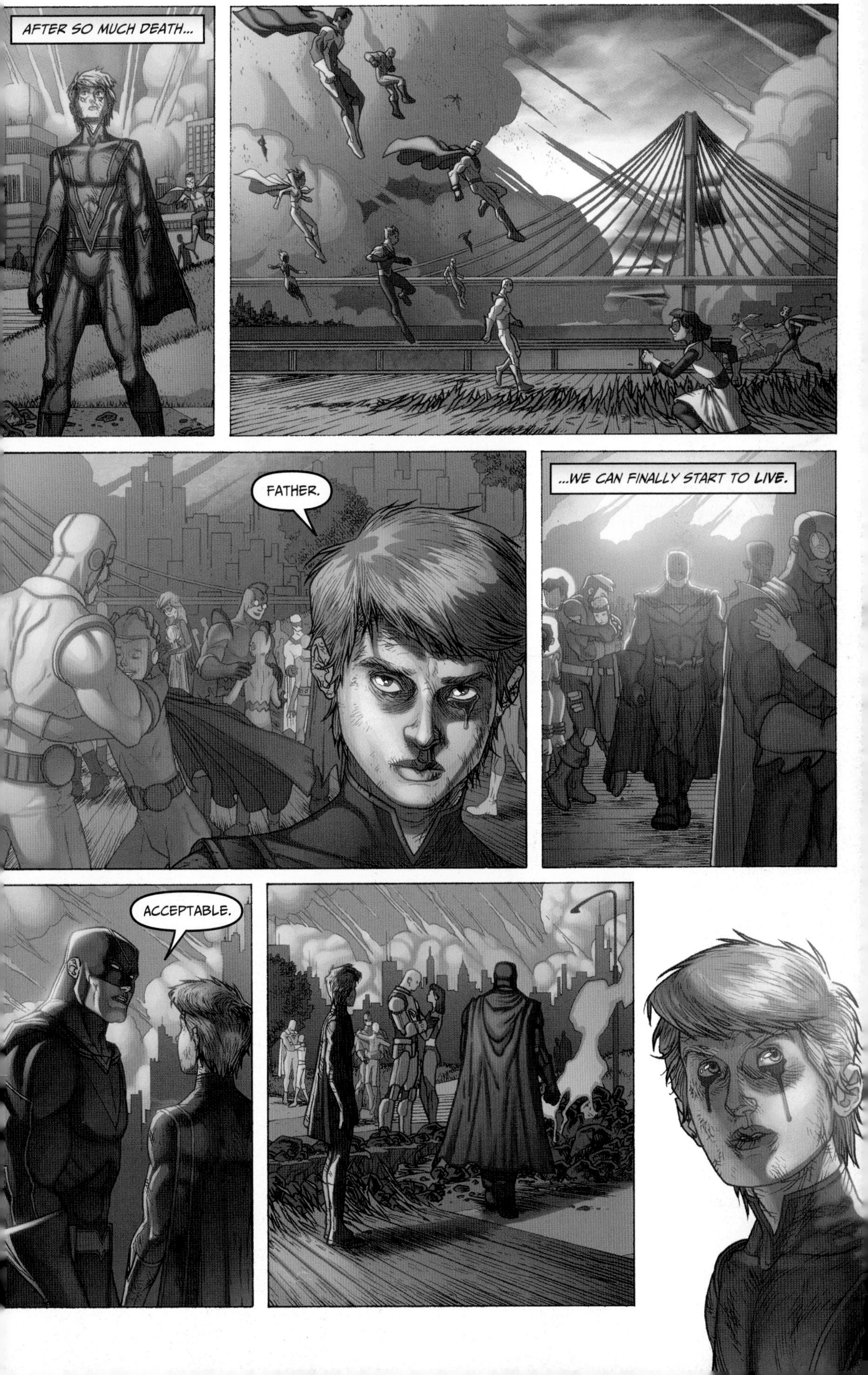
AFTER SO MUCH DEATH...
FATHER.
...WE CAN FINALLY START TO LIVE.
ACCEPTABLE.

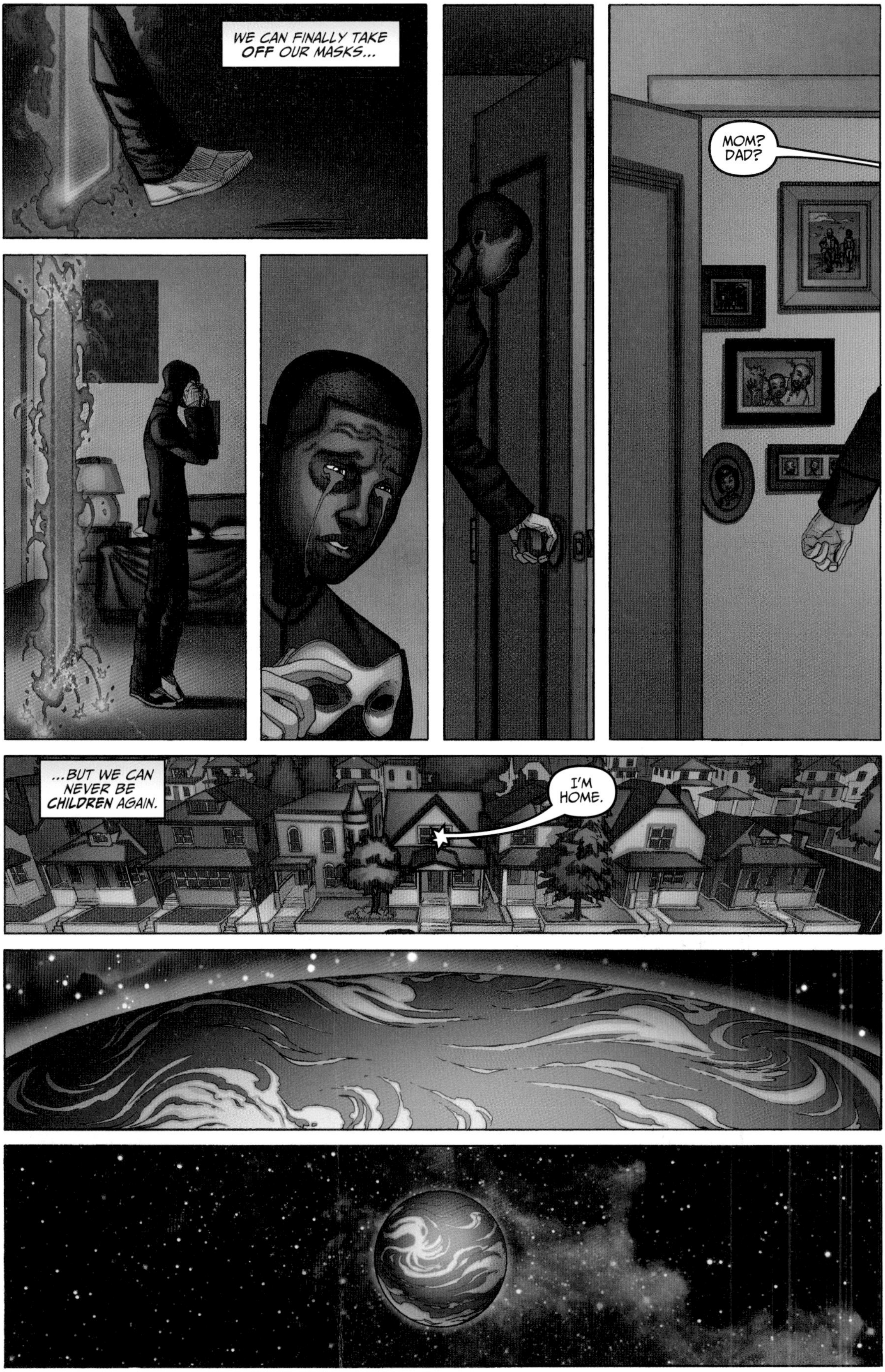
WE CAN FINALLY TAKE OFF OUR MASKS...
MOM? DAD?
...BUT WE CAN NEVER BE CHILDREN AGAIN.
I'M HOME.

THE END